UNIDENTIFIED
FUNNY
OBJECTS

Edited by

Alex Shvartsman

UFO Publishing
Brooklyn, NY

Published by:
UFO Publishing
1685 E 15th St.
Brooklyn, NY 11229
www.ufopub.com

Copyright © 2012 by UFO Publishing

Stories copyright © 2012 by the authors
Interior illustrations © Phil Selby and Mike Jacobsen
Octopus illustration © Ron and Joe (Art Parts)

Trade paperback ISBN: 978-0-9884328-0-2

Cover art: Dixon Leavitt
Typesetting & prepress production: Windhaven Press (www.windhaven.com)
Graphics design: Emerson Matsuuchi
Graphics wrangler: Joan Barger
Logo design: Martin Dare

Copy editor: Elektra Hammond
Associate editors: Cyd Athens, James Beamon, Anatoly Belilovsky, Leah Cypess, Frank Dutkiewicz, Michael Haynes, Nathaniel Lee, Fran Wilde

Visit us on the web:
www.ufopub.com

Printed in Canada

10 9 8 7 6 5 4 3 2 1

TABLE OF CONTENTS

FOREWORD

ALEX SHVARTSMAN

A GOOD HUMOR STORY IS HARD TO FIND.

Don't get me wrong—there are many outstanding humor books out there. Throughout the history of speculative fiction, humor has always played an important role within the genre. There are the clever flash fiction stories of Fredric Brown, the dry wit of Douglas Adams, the satire of Harry Harrison, the puns of Robert Asprin, and the comedy of Terry Pratchett, among countless others.

And yet, such works are but a tiny fraction of the quality genre fiction out there, especially when it comes to short stories. Top science fiction and fantasy magazines will occasionally publish a humorous story, but not in every issue. You may also find an odd humor piece relegated to the back of some anthologies as a nice way to close out those books. Yet when was the last time you held an entire collection of contemporary SF/F humor in a single volume?

When the idea to create a humor anthology first occurred to me, I researched online and was surprised to learn that no such books have been published in the last decade, at least not any that could be easily found. There were occasional humor collections with a very specific narrow theme (such as Deals with the Devil) but nothing that attempted to represent the full scope of speculative humor.

For many readers, Unidentified Funny Objects will be the first such book. The associate editors and I have labored to put together the best possible collection of humorous stories. We read well over nine hundred submissions to select the twenty-nine tales presented here.

My goal was to feature the widest possible variety of genres and styles. Within this book you'll find tales ranging from a 350 word flash piece to a 10,000-plus word novella. Stories vary from gently humorous to laugh-out-loud funny, from absurdist to zany, from family friendly to edgy and pushing beyond PG-13 limits.

We've included fiction from masters of speculative humor such as Mike Resnick and Jody Lynn Nye as well as brand-new names you will undoubtedly hear more about in coming years, such as James Beamon and Zach Shephard. There's also a translated story from Russia's most popular fantasist Sergey Lukyanenko. Although his Night Watch novels are extremely popular around the world, this is his first short story professionally published in the United States.

I hope there's enough interest in *Unidentified Funny Objects* for it to become an annual anthology. I also see it as an ongoing project, with additional free content published monthly on our web site. Please visit www.ufopub.com to read several more stories I enjoyed but couldn't fit into the book as well as bios of all the authors.

Good speculative humor may have been hard to find, but you have 320 pages of it in front of you. I hope you will enjoy the tales collected therein as much as I have.

—Alex Shvartsman

TIMBER!

SCOTT ALMES

I realized I was in trouble when my realm-appointed lawyer showed up drunk and asked for spare coins. He made a valiant effort to defend me in the courtroom, but his lack of judicial knowledge, poor grasp of language, and mispronunciation of my name proved futile against the realm's brilliant case. It didn't help that the prosecutor was an experienced medium. He used my incorporeal, perpetually disappointed mother as a character witness.

I was sentenced to death. The executioner immediately wheeled out a guillotine to a short round of applause.

"They always like this part," the executioner confided. "It's a bit dramatic, but it keeps things flowing."

"I'm glad they're having a good time," I said.

"That's why I got into this line of work." He tied up my hands and placed my head underneath the blade. "It's a people business, you know?"

I looked up. "This is a rather small guillotine."

"Travel-sized! The brochure says it has the class of a full-sized guillotine, but the portability of an axe." The executioner leaned in. "Honestly, do you think the wheels are too much? They cost extra, but I believe they were worth it."

"Completely worth it. It'd be hell to carry."

"Exactly! If I hurt my back and I'm stuck in bed, how am I supposed to live my life? I might as well be dead."

"Be careful what you wish for."

"Ha, good one!"

Then the blade came down.

It was my first beheading, but my gut told me something didn't go right.

I woke up face down on a rug. The rug was in a library, so I guessed I was there too, but I was loopy and didn't trust my logic. I sat up and waited patiently for the room to stop flipping end over end.

"You're supposed to be thanking me," said a voice.

When the world settled, I saw an old man. A shabby wizard's hat hung so crookedly on his head that his left eye peered through a hole in the brim. There was a steaming teapot sitting on the table next to him.

"Well?" he prodded.

"What?" I managed.

"The thanking."

"Oh." I paused. "Thanks for the tea."

"No, not for the tea!"

"It's not mine?" I suddenly, desperately wanted that tea.

"It is yours," he assured. "But it's essential that you thank me for saving your life. Then you will feel indebted to me and we can work together." He straightened himself. "You see, I enchanted that guillotine to summon you here when the blade came down."

He leaned forward, as if anticipating a treat.

"Thanks?" I said.

"Great! Now, to business!"

The old man jumped off his stool, circling as he spoke, each word awkwardly punctuated with a tap from his cane. He complimented my many ingenious confidence schemes. He was honored to meet the man that resold the Arduian Queen her own castle, convinced the Farwellian fishermen to drag the Desert of the Dead, and tricked the entire town of Lamden to go without pants for an entire year.

It seemed quite impressive, save for a single problem: I had no idea what he was talking about. However, he clearly went to great lengths to save my life and I didn't want to disappoint him into reversing that decision. I played along, saying "Thank you" and "Honestly, it was child's play" throughout his rant.

"My name is Pinion, grandmaster enchanter," he said at the end of his rant. "I'm sure you've heard of me."

I hadn't.

"May I call you Dunri?" he asked.

"Why would you do that?"

He blinked. "Isn't that your name?"

"Yes, of course," I lied. "I've had so many names it's hard to keep track. Dunri, Jeremiah, Copernicus, Hansel, Delilah."

Pinion led me to the window. His movements were excited and fast, like a bird walking on hot coals. I looked out the window before his excitement caused him to burst into flames.

Outside was a vast, moving forest. The giant trees swayed back and forth, snoring as they slept in the afternoon sun. A few were awake and picked at some deer carcasses.

"Treants," I said. I had heard of the mystic living trees, but had never seen them with my own eyes. "They're magnificent. Are you studying them?"

"No, nothing of the sort," Pinion replied.

"Then what?"

"Seeing as they are such magnificent creatures, I thought you'd help me round them up and cut them down. Tea?"

I DRIFTED IN AND OUT as Pinion lectured me on his craft, especially during the portion on arcane standards and regulations. Luckily he repeated the important part several times: Pinion had discovered that treant wood could hold stronger enchantments than simple glass or stone.

"Really?" I asked.

"How tall do you think you'd be if it didn't?" he replied.

I instinctively rubbed the back of my neck, remembering the wooden guillotine.

He needed a steady supply of treant wood, but was held up by activists. Their leader, Merri, had completely shut down his operation. She had forced his team of lumberjacks into a holding pattern.

"That's where you come in," he said.

"You need me to kill her?" I asked.

"No, trick her into leaving my lumberjacks alone. Why would you kill her?"

"Who said anything about killing her?"

"You just did."

"Violence is a last resort."

"There's to be no violence."

"Then why do you keep bringing it up?" I asked. "I'll accept your job, but only on the condition of nonviolence."

"Very good," he said. "Now, your fee. I have heard rumors that your special talents in deception and trickery do come at a price. Shall a thousand kovacs suffice?"

By my conservative estimates, I was worth about three kovacs.

"I accept!" I declared. "Now, let's discuss my advance."

"There will be no advance," he said. "However . . . "

He waved his hands and started to mumble. I asked him to repeat himself a few times before I realized he was casting a spell, not trying to get my attention. A wooden guillotine magically glided into the room.

"This is the twin of the guillotine you met earlier," he

explained. "If you fail, I need but repeat a simple command word and you'll be summoned underneath it. This blade is also enchanted."

"So, when the blade comes down I'll be transported back to the courtroom?"

"No, it chops your head off. The enchantment will light your corpse on fire afterwards. Now, shall we be off?"

THAT NIGHT, PINION LED ME into town to show me the inn that Merri frequented.

Along the way, I did what I believed any good conman would do, and practiced all of my fake voices. Pinion didn't seem interested and told me that most of them sounded the same. I found this a little insulting, as half of them were supposed to be women.

When we got to town, I immediately went into a store of fine gentlemen's wares and bought a fake moustache. I didn't have any money, so I traded my belt for it. I walked out wearing it proudly.

Once again, Pinion didn't seem amused.

"She's never seen you before," he said. "Why do you need a disguise?"

"A disguise is always a good idea," I said, using my wiseman voice.

"She doesn't trust people with mustaches."

"And how can you possible know that?"

Before I could explain the true correlation between mustaches and trustworthiness, he tore it off my face and suddenly I was worth only two kovacs.

JUST OUTSIDE THE INN, I employed my best confidence scheme to persuade Pinion to give me beer money. After relenting, he confided in me that he had a hard time telling the difference between trickery and shameless begging. I told him that was exactly the expertise that he'd paid for, explained there were countless tools in my arsenal, and ran into the inn before he asked any more questions.

I went straight to the bar. The bartender had some enchanting skills of her own. She poured me a beer and tapped the glass, which sent a web of frost up the sides. I was so impressed I quickly spent all of my money to see her do it again.

I was being wobbly and sad that my money was gone until I remembered that I was supposed to be looking for Merri and doing conman things. Then I realized that I had created a great cover identity, a common drunkard, and spent a moment congratulating myself.

I scanned the bar and spotted a likely candidate. Pinion had given me a detailed description, but had bookended it with two long rants, making it hard to concentrate on what he had said. I prepared to make my move, went over a few opening lines in my head, and fell off my stool.

Somebody pulled me up. I kept my bearings on where I thought I saw Merri, but was disappointed to realize that my target was actually a stuffed panther.

"That is a big cat. Not Merri," I said aloud to prevent making the same mistake again.

"I'm Merri," said the stranger holding me up.

I turned to look at her. She did, in fact, look very Merri-ish. I told her so.

"You must be a bit of a lightweight," she said.

"I haven't eaten since I was beheaded."

"Pardon?"

"I said thanks for helping me up."

She was very pretty, in a blurry sort of way. She got me a glass of water and stabilized me in a chair with armrests.

"So, what made you take a few too many pulls from the barrel?" she asked.

Even in my hazy state, I knew that was a good opening.

"I am frustrated with the cold, careless bastards that exist in our realm!" I leaned over and used my secretive voice. "Did you know there's an enchanter around here that's trying to chop down mermaids?"

"The treants, right? Not mermaids."

"Of course, treants! Mermaids? Ha! Nobody cares about mermaids."

"Actually, I've led a few marches against the wrongful fishing of mermaids."

"Naturally," I said matter-of-factly. "Everybody loves mermaids."

"But you just—"

"Said that I'm infuriated they're chopping down treants. That's what I definitely said. I remember it. I was there."

Merri paused and looked me over. "Well, if you believe what you say, perhaps you'd be interested in volunteering tomorrow?"

PINION PREPARED A BEDROOM for me at his tower. I stumbled in late and he woke me up after only a few hours of sleep. He flung open the shades and sunlight came barging through the window like a horde of barbarians.

"A conman needs his sleep," I told him sagely.

"We have to go over your plan," he said.

I thought carefully, and added, "If a conman cannot get sleep, then bacon must be provided." I then explained to him the long tradition of bacon and confidence schemes and how they were perfectly wed like the stars and the sky.

As he cooked, a fleet of enchanted brooms swept in and gave the entire room a once over. Pinion explained how he had carved each one from treant wood. I only half-listened because they would not stop chasing me around the table.

We sat down and I tried to eat, but my wooden stool kept walking away from the table. I chose to eat while standing. After I was done, I noticed that Pinion was staring at me. I leaned a few inches in either direction and his eyes followed me the entire time. He sneezed, but his eyes didn't close.

"Well?" he asked.

"Are there eggs?" I asked.

"No. I mean, there are eggs, but . . . "

I made him cook me eggs before we continued. They were a bit on the runny side. I told him so.

"Now, please," he begged. "The plan?"

I chuckled knowingly to show I was in control. It seemed like something a good conman would do. I got carried away and soon I was howling with tears in my eyes.

"Merri has invited me to march with her today to stop your lumberjacks," I said, wiping my eyes.

"How is that good news? My lumberjacks will still be stopped."

I realized that I hadn't thought the next part out. Getting to know Merri was the crucial first step. On the third step I stopped her from ruining Pinion's business. The second step was still nebulous. Since Pinion eagerly awaited an answer, I distracted him with another knowing, knee-slapping chuckle.

He seemed irritated at first. His hat quivered and gave away his mood. Then something dawned on him. His hat settled and a smile crossed his face.

"I understand," he said. "You will acquaint yourself with Merri, find a weakness, and exploit it!"

I felt instantly relaxed. Now I had a second part.

"Yes, exactly," I said. "That is my great plan! Thank the gods I'm here."

TREANTS ARE WONDROUS CREATURES, but they, too, have to eat. People have witnessed treants devour sheep like peanuts. In Buklivia, a forest of treants ate so many sheep everyone had to wear clothes made out of wheat for a decade. Nowadays, shepherds put up scarecrows with axes in their hands.

"They sleep during the day, right?" I asked as we entered the forest.

"Most of them," Merri replied.

Pinion's lumberjacks were just arriving for a day's work. Although, thanks to Merri and her team, they hadn't swung an axe in two months.

The plan was a simple man-to-man affair. I was told to find a lumberjack and stand in front of him until the sun went down. I found the least threatening lumberjack I could and ran between him and a treant. The lumberjack was instantly displeased.

"Don't stand there," the lumberjack ordered.

"That's the point," I stated. "I'm purposefully in your way."

"I know." The lumberjack rolled his eyes. "But you're not doing it right."

"What?"

"I can still sneak an axe past." He nudged his axe past my leg. "I could chop a few inches out of the trunk with you standing there. Move a little to the left and I couldn't scrape bark."

I moved where instructed.

"Good," the lumberjack said, satisfied.

"Don't you like working?"

"I love working." He leaned on his axe. "I just hate to see people doing a bad job."

AFTER A WHILE THE LUMBERJACK got bored and fell asleep, so I went looking for Merri.

I got lost instantly. I selected a few Treants as landmarks, but some of them were sleepwalking and my mental map fluttered away. Merri found me trying to build a compass out of two pinecones and a dead squirrel.

"Isn't that the lumberjack you were stopping?" Merri asked as she ran to me.

Sure enough, the lumberjack had woken up and was now mid-swing. We ran up to him just as his axe sunk into the treant's side.

The treant let loose a scream that sounded like wood being

struck by lightning. It reached down with a branch, grabbed the lumberjack, and bit off his top half. It stuck the rest of him in its sap to save for later.

Then it charged towards Merri and I.

Instinctively, I stepped in front and told her to run. The treant bit down on my arm and it was, I quickly decided, one of the most unpleasant things I ever experienced. The other activists chased the treant away as I rolled around and screamed. I didn't stop until they pointed out that the treant had, in fact, only eaten a chunk of my sleeve.

THAT NIGHT THE ACTIVISTS celebrated a successful protest. I joined them, but was not amused by their mockery of my near-death experience. Every minute or so an activist would bend down and bite the sleeve of another, who would then cry like an infant. I pretended to be too high-browed for their sense of humor.

I saw an activist came up to Merri and bite her sleeve, but she pulled her arm away. She turned to me and caught me staring, so I glanced at random objects around the room with feigned interest.

A moment later Merri sat down at my table and passed me a drink.

"I wanted to thank you for saving me," she said. "It was very brave."

Her smile made my language skills drop. She talked while I mumbled incoherently and agreed with everything she said. Naturally, her main topic was treants, but she soon turned to Pinion. She listed each of his flaws as if she was sentencing him to death, a tone I was unfortunately familiar with.

"You're not too fond of Pinion, are you?"

"I haven't been since I was a kid," she said.

"You defended treants back then?"

"No." She blinked. "He's my father."

My jaw dropped.

Merri laughed, guided my mouth closed, and kissed me lightly on the lips.

"You're cute. Maybe tomorrow night we can spend some proper time together," she suggested.

I managed a nod.

WHEN I RETURNED TO PINION'S tower, I found him enchanting a wooden pipe. It was going poorly. The pipe kept floating around, sticking itself in his ear, and lighting stray hairs on fire.

"How's the plan going?" he asked while patting out the flames.

"Why didn't you tell me that Merri was your daughter?"

"I thought it was obvious. How did you think I knew so much about her?"

"Magic," I shrugged. "Divination."

He laughed. "By the Gods! If I could use magic to understand women do you think I'd be working for a living? I'd be up to my eyebrows in gold!"

I thought about it, and conceded he had a point. "You should've told me. A confidence scheme is a delicate creature and secrets can be poison."

I smiled. That was a particularly good bit of conman wisdom. I was about to ask for a piece of paper to write it down when I realized Pinion was staring at me with very intense, fatherly eyes.

"What?" I asked.

"Are you planning on sleeping with my daughter?"

"I'm afraid it's crucial to the plan."

THE NEXT NIGHT MERRI and I met for dinner.

Gigantic, domesticated fireflies illuminated the restaurant. A musician played a thousand-string harp and her huffs and puffs only mildly interrupted her music as she ran from one end to the other. The meal was lovely, and we stayed past when the fireflies rebelled and dropped glowing excrement on some of the guests.

We talked and laughed and poured drinks into one another until we ended up in her bedroom. She gave me a wink and a smile and disappeared into her dressing room. I immediately kicked off my pants in anticipation. I decided that being a con-man was a suitable next step in my career.

As I waited, I admired the paintings and sculptures she kept in her room. I made a mental note to pretend that I knew everything about art. I noticed a glass box that had something strange locked inside of it.

"Why do you have a giant walnut?" I asked.

"That's a seedpod," she called out. "The treants plant them to start a new forest. I rescued it last year."

I stared at the seedpod for a moment and a plan formed in my head. I hated the plan, because it required me leaving a seductive Merri behind. Sure, I could wait until after Merri and I had our sensual rendezvous, but would I have a second chance? The mental image of Pinion's endless parade of cruel guillotines convinced me to act now. I was particularly attached to my head, and I knew I would dearly miss it. Also, Merri gave little indication that she was into shorter men.

With a heavy sigh, I smashed the glass, stole the seedpod, and ran.

WEEDS AND THORNS TORE at my shins as I ran through a field and I sorely regretted not putting my pants back on. I consoled myself by imagining the vault of pants I would be able to buy when I delivered the seedpod to Pinion.

Enchanted brooms assaulted me the moment I entered the tower. They swept me from the foyer to the library, down the stairs, up the stairs, into the dumbwaiter, and around the bedrooms until I slid into the study with the seedpod gripped in my arms like a child. Pinion had fallen asleep while working and awoke with a start when I slammed against his desk.

With red, wide eyes he looked at me, then at the seedpod, and then back at me.

He screamed. It was a long, feminine scream that yellowed his open books and left him winded.

"Do you know," he panted. "What that is?"

I stood up, smiled, and presented it like a trophy. "It's a seedpod. The treants plant them to start a new forest. What did you think it was?"

"I thought it was a seedpod," he said flatly. "The treants plant them to start a new forest."

We stared at each other in silence. It continued until the silence itself felt awkward and flew out the window.

"One of us is missing something," I admitted.

"Why did you bring that here?" Pinion asked. His face was growing whiter by the minute and was moments away from becoming transparent.

"We can use it to plant a hidden forest that you can harvest in secret. It's the perfect plan!"

Then I felt the tower quake.

Later, I would learn that treants are fiercely protective of their young. Once a seedpod had fallen in the Mercian river and an entire forest followed it downstream with a vengeance. The region never recovered.

"They're going to tear this place down!" Pinion screamed. "What have you done?" Books toppled off the shelves. Brooms stampeded into the room to clean up the mess.

"I'll admit that this is an unexpected turn of events."

"And how is Dunri, the genius conman, going to make this right?"

"Who?"

"You, you imbecile!"

One of the walls fell off and I could see the moving forest surrounding the tower.

"I'm not entirely who you think I am," I admitted.

"What do you mean 'not entirely'?"

"I'm a small-time thief named Francis."

Flames appeared behind his eyes. "What did you steal?"

"A lime," I said sheepishly.

"The Ystarians were going to execute you for stealing a lime?"

"The Ystarians are very particular about their limes."

I thought about explaining the complex social and religious history between limes and the Ystarian people, detailing the great scurvy epidemic, the barbaric Feud of the Lemons, and the annual Festival of the Martyred Cistruses, but since the floor was falling out from underneath us I decided to leave it at that.

The tower shook and shed another wall. A naked servant fell from the floor above and his bath followed him a moment later. The bathtub smashed Pinion's enchanted guillotine to pieces, saving me from a second beheading. A mop glided from a closet and attempted to clean up the soapy water.

Pinion grabbed the mop and swung it at me.

"This is exactly why I asked for an advance! If you're a little dissatisfied with my service . . . " I was interrupted when the mop caught me in the stomach.

I curled up into a ball. The tower rocked again and I rolled towards the stairwell. Pinion charged at me, so I just kept rolling. I ran as soon as I hit the ground floor. The treants lashed out at me with branches and roots and I was plenty bruised by the time I made it to the safety of a nearby hill.

Exhausted, I sat down and watched the chaos.

"HE'LL MAKE HIMSELF DISAPPEAR before the towers come down," Merri said, appearing beside me. She handed me something. "You forgot your pants."

I took them but didn't bother to put them back on.

"You knew about Pinion's plan, didn't you?" I asked.

She nodded. "I helped the real Dunri escape in exchange for somebody else to be sent in his place."

"How did he guarantee that?"

"He played the executioner."

"He was very talented," I said, rubbing my neck. "You knew I would take that seedpod."

"You were a little predictable. But . . . I didn't expect you to step in front of that treant."

"I didn't expect a tree to be so mean."

"You are, in all respects, a terrible conman."

"Thanks?"

"However, I could be convinced to let you buy me a drink."

"Really?"

"The treants are safe at the moment. A drink will help me find a new way to irritate my father."

"How's that?"

"Well," she smiled. "I'm certain he won't approve of you."

THE ALIEN INVASION AS SEEN IN THE TWITTER STREAM OF @DWEEBLESS

JAKE KERR

Tim Becker @dweebless
    @minnyjotg I'm getting those tweets, too.
It must be a viral ad campaign for a movie
called Alien Overlords or something. It's
everywhere.

The Aliens @alienoverlords
    People of Earth: There is no reason for

panic. Simply relocate to Canada and everything
will be fine.

Tim Becker @dweebless
    @alienoverlords Dude, how are you in my
timeline? I most definitely did NOT follow you.
Reporting you for spam.

Tim Becker @dweebless
    Just reported the idiot @alienoverlords
for spamming me. How much you wanna bet they
reappear? Money talks. :/

Henry Bloch @imissthenorthstars
    @dweebless I did the same thing. Do they
really think people will see the movie after
this kind of crap?

Jo Guinee @minnyjotg
    @imissthenorthstars @dweebless I can't get
away from it! It's all over Youtube + they're
doing some BS thing on TV where they cut into
shows

The Aliens @alienoverlords
    People of Earth: Honestly, we don't think
our instructions are that complicated. Move to
Canada.

Tim Becker @dweebless
    @alienoverlords This would be funny if it
were real. Like, dude, I'd rather be dead than
move to Canada. LOL.

The Aliens @alienoverlords
    @dweebless That can be arranged.

Tim Becker @dweebless
    Hahahaha. A viral campaign is trolling me! RT @alienoverlords @dweebless That can be arranged.

Tim Becker @dweebless
    Just saw the Youtube video. WTF. It's freakin' static and a voice telling us to relocate to Canada.

Jo Guinee @minnyjotg
    @dweebless I think it's brilliant. The @alienoverlords movie is totally the next @oldspice. The aliens are on a horse!

Tim Becker @dweebless
    @minnyjot LOL!

The Aliens @alienoverlords
    There seems to be a misunderstanding. This is a warning, not a joke. We really don't want to kill anyone.

Tim Becker @dweebless
    Do the aliens realize Nickelback and Rush are from Canada? #deathbymusic! RT @alienoverlords We really don't want to kill anyone.

The Aliens @alienoverlords
    @dweebless Hey, if you're going to retweet
our messages, can you at least not edit the
meaning? Not cool.

Henry Bloch @imissthenorthstars
    @dweebless The @alienoverlords account is
totally trolling you. And notice they didn't
defend Rush or Nickelback ;)

The Aliens @alienoverlords
    People of Earth: We have nothing against
Nickelback or Rush or anyone else. We just
need lots of space. So hightail it to Canada.
NOW.

John Scalzi @scalzi
    "Hightail it to Canada" is the name of my
next band.

Monica Becker @skifanatic89
    @alienoverlords Hey, I'm going to school in
France, do I have to move to Canada, too? ;)

Tim Becker @dweebless
    @skifanatic89 Watch it, sis. These guys
like Nickelback. I wouldn't taunt them. WHO
KNOWS THE DEPTHS OF THEIR EVIL!

The Aliens @alienoverlords
    @skifanatic89 Yes, you need to move to
Canada, too.

The Aliens @alienoverlords
    @dweebless For crying out loud. We're not

EVIL! Just misunderstood. Anyway, we just destroyed Tulsa.

The Aliens @alienoverlords
    We destroyed Tulsa since you all were not moving fast enough and not taking us seriously. Video coming to our YouTube channel shortly.

Tim Becker @dweebless
    This Alien Overlord viral campaign is like watching a car wreck. You don't want to watch, but it's so compellingly awful you can't stop.

The Aliens @alienoverlords
    We're having some transcoding problems with YouTube, so be patient. But trust us, Tulsa isn't there anymore.

Tim Becker @dweebless
    Noobs. RT @alienoverlords We're having some transcoding problems with YouTube, so be patient. But trust us, Tulsa isn't there anymore.

Monica Becker @skifanatic89
    .@alienoverlords Couldn't you have destroyed Montreal instead? I can't stand the Canadiens fans.

The Aliens @alienoverlords
    @skifanatic89 No, Montreal is in Canada. Haven't you been paying attention?

The Aliens @alienoverlords
   Video is online now. If you have the
bandwidth, you should really check it out in
HD. Totally awesome explosions.

The Aliens @alienoverlords
   We apologize. The previous tweet was in
poor taste. We're sorry for all those that
died but we can't wait forever for you to
move to Canada.

Jo Guinee @minnyjotg
   @dweebless Just saw the video. The CGI in
the movie is amazing I have to admit. Maybe
Michael Bay is directing! LOL.

Tim Becker @dweebless
   @alienoverlords I don't think anyone is
really missing Tulsa. You guys need to up your
game.

The Aliens @alienoverlords
   @dweebless Sadly, we think you're right. We
have decided to destroy France.

   Tim Becker @dweebless
   @alienoverlords Ha. I don't think anyone
will miss France either! But my sister is
there so how about destroying someplace else--
North Korea?

The Aliens @alienoverlords
   @dweebless Sorry, dude, it's too late--we
destroyed France already. We actually destroyed
North Korea first, but no one seemed to notice.

Tim Becker @dweebless
    Look out @skifanatic89! RT @alienoverlords
Sorry, dude, it's too late--we destroyed France
already.

The Aliens @alienoverlords
    You know, we didn't have high expectations,
but we did expect at least SOME effort. France
is now destroyed. Don't be next. Move to
Canada.

Henry Bloch @imissthenorthstars
    @dweebless Did you check out Reddit? The
front page is full of evidence that this
is actually real if you can believe that.
Conspiracy nuts.

Tim Becker @dweebless
    @imissthenorthstars Saw that. Waiting for @
skifanatic89 to pipe in and totally bust them
since she lives in France.

The Aliens @alienoverlords
    Really Earthlings? Missiles? We're being
all peaceful and understanding and you pull
that kind of stunt? We're not angry. Just
disappointed.

The Aliens @alienoverlords
    Oh, and for the smartypants who are asking
how we can live on the planet if we destroy
it all... Don't make us show you.

Tim Becker @dweebless
    @imissthenorthstars This couldn't be real,
could it?

The Aliens @alienoverlords
    You guys are hilarious. A spaceship
armed with nukes? I mean you get points
for chutzpah, but really, did you think we
couldn't handle that?

Tim Becker @dweebless
    Holy shit. This is real guys. The @
alienoverlords thing is a REAL invasion! Going
offline as I head to Canada.

The Aliens @alienoverlords
    @dweebless Nice try Captain Obvious, but
you and the rest of your idiot planet are too
late. We've already decided to destroy you
all.

Canada @canada
    What about us?

The Aliens @alienoverlords
    Sorry, we're destroying you, too. We finally
listened to Nickelback.

DREAMING HARRY

STEPHANIE BURGIS

Making a bad night even worse, Elizabeth Nichols woke at 3 a.m. with an unmistakable feeling of nameless, creeping dread. A cold chill brushed her cheek.

Bloody hell.

She opened her eyes with deep reluctance.

An ancient, tentacled horror as old as time was lurking in the corner of the room.

She moaned and kicked her sleeping husband. "Your turn."

"Mwha?" Dan fought his way up out of the cocoon of duvets he'd buried himself in after their last wake-up. His hair stuck out in all directions; he focused blearily on the horror across the room, then flopped onto his back, groaning. "How can it be my turn? I went last time."

"You're the one who left that Lovecraft book where he could find it." Elizabeth buried her face in her pillow and squeezed her eyes shut. "You deal with the results."

She heard the scuffle of duvets being shoved aside, and then a thump followed by a yelp—Dan's bare feet hitting the floor. *That* must have been chilled by the horror, too. Elizabeth wrapped her duvet more tightly around herself, shivering at the very thought of it. Her husband's curses filled the frigid air as he stumbled down the hallway to their son's room.

After a minute, she couldn't help herself. She rolled over and cracked her eyes open to peek.

The horror was still there, exuding a miasma of turgid hopelessness and fear. Its tentacles drooped against the floor.

"You'll be gone soon," Elizabeth told it. "I hope."

She waited a full twenty minutes before it finally disappeared, though. Dan stumbled back into the room a few moments later, yawning.

"I told him they were completely misunderstood," he said. "Lovecraft got it all wrong. They're big cuddly toys, really. Terribly shy, like bunny rabbits."

"Probably vegetarian, too," Elizabeth mumbled. "Lucky for us."

Dan slid into bed, wrapping himself back up in his cocoon. His voice was muffled by his duvets. "Dr. Margo says none of his dreams can actually hurt us."

"Easy for Dr. Margo to say," Elizabeth muttered.

But the bedroom was already warming up, and when she woke up again it was nearly seven. There was a thumping sound in the corner of the room, but that came from a gathering of bunnies, playing some elaborate hopping game with Elizabeth's shoes.

She pulled the curtains open, waited for the bunnies to disappear in the sunlight, then picked up her shoes to examine them. Apart from a few pellets in one of her Skechers, they were fine.

"Success," she said, and headed for the kitchen to make coffee.

Harry was already there, eating Weetabix with the jar of sugar sitting open beside him and a comic book lying open on the table. Elizabeth eyed the lurid illustrations with foreboding.

If any women that well-endowed showed up in their bedroom at night, she wasn't sure Dan would agree to send them away.

Still, Dr. Margo was very clear that they had to let Harry exercise his imagination, so Elizabeth didn't confiscate the comic book. She only dropped a kiss onto Harry's mussed-up brown hair and tried not to wince as he spilled a spoonful of Weetabix and milk onto the table.

"Mum!" He swivelled around, spilling more milk in an arc. "I had the coolest dreams."

"I know," Elizabeth said. Then she heard the sourness in her own voice and sighed. "Tell me about them, darling."

He did, chattering away in the background as she made her coffee and toast and peered through the window at the birdfeeder, which a squirrel was currently raiding.

Too bad they couldn't send Harry's dreams after that squirrel. See how many seeds he'd want to steal after a Cthulhoid horror came after him ... or a hooded, dark rider, the kind who'd screamed in the corner of her bedroom all night after Harry had watched *The Fellowship of the Ring* with his friend Simon last Saturday.

Simon's mum hadn't taken Bennerol during her pregnancy. She didn't have to worry about her son's dreams.

Lucky cow.

"Mum!" Harry said. "Are you even listening to me?"

"Of course I am," Elizabeth said automatically. "You were saying—"

The doorbell rang just in time, before she had to hazard a guess. "I'll just get that," she said, and scooped the sugar jar out of Harry's reach as she left.

She was still holding it when she opened the door and found Dr. Margo standing on the doorstep, next to a dark-haired man in a tailored charcoal suit, a wide-brimmed hat, sunglasses, and the kind of gentleman's gloves that Elizabeth had only ever seen in movies.

Elizabeth glanced down at her own decidedly untailored, five-year-old M&S pajamas, which had a fresh milk stain on one knee, courtesy of Harry's breakfast. "Ah . . . "

"Elizabeth!" Dr. Margo beamed as she stepped forward, forcing Elizabeth to move back. "I'm sorry to interrupt you so early, dear, but we wanted to be sure to find you at home. Elizabeth is always so busy," she added to the man behind her, as she bustled through the doorway. "Always on the go, aren't you, dear?"

"Ah . . . I suppose so?" Elizabeth thought of the state of the living room, which she'd been too tired to tidy the night before, and rallied her energy. "I'm sorry, but we're actually in the middle of having breakfast now, so perhaps—"

"Oh, don't mind us! This is what the health service is for, you know—giving you a helping hand just when you need it. And it'll be good to observe Harry in his natural habitat, so to speak. Always meeting him in the office is so impersonal, don't you think?"

Elizabeth gritted her teeth and gave in. Dr. Margo's companion had remained on the doorstep, with punctilious courtesy; she waved him in, sighing. "Would you like any coffee?" she asked.

Dr. Margo swept ahead of her down the hallway. "Tea for me, dear. Milk but no sugar. Nothing for my colleague, though."

"Are you sure?" Elizabeth asked, trailing behind them into the kitchen. "I have decaf if you'd prefer."

The dark-haired man turned and smiled at her. "Thank you," he said. He had a heavy accent, which sounded Eastern European. "But I do not drink . . . coffee. Or tea, for that matter."

"I see," said Elizabeth, and cursed the fact that Dan had already left for work. He'd taken off the first two weeks of Harry's summer holiday while she'd stayed at the office. During those weeks, no officious health workers had shown up, and as far as she could tell, they'd spent most of the time playing video games and eating cinnamon rolls from a tin. Now, of course, it was her turn.

She pasted a smile onto her face, and said, "Harry, Dr. Margo's come to see us. And she's brought . . . ?"

"My colleague," Dr. Margo said, sitting down in the chair beside Harry. "From the government. Everyone's so interested in our Bennerol babies, you know."

At the word "babies," Harry gave her an outraged look and scooted his chair away from her. Elizabeth didn't blame him. It was a different word that had caught her own attention, though. She'd been in the middle of setting down the sugar jar, but now her hand tightened instinctively around it.

"From the government?" she said. She tucked the sugar jar up against her stomach. "Which branch of the government would be interested in Harry?"

"Oh, you needn't worry about that, dear!" Dr. Margo tittered, tipping her head back. "Why, you look as if you're thinking of some terrible MI5 conspiracy—science fiction films and the like. We're nothing like that. No, indeed! Isn't that a funny idea?" she said to her colleague.

"Ha," he said. "Ha. Ha." He drew out a chair, pulled it into the shadiest corner of the room, and dusted it off carefully with one gloved hand. "Very amusing indeed," he said, and tipped his hat to cover more of his face.

Bloody hell. Definitely MI5, Elizabeth thought. Or was it MI6? Dan was the one who would know about all that. He liked to read political thrillers when he wasn't reading terrible horror stories that sent Harry's dreams haywire.

She inched toward the telephone in the corner. "Let me just give my husband a call," she said. "I'm sure he'd like to be here for our discussion."

"Dear Dan," Dr. Margo said. "Such a good father. So involved. But you needn't drag him home from work just for us. We can explain it all to him when he comes home tonight."

Elizabeth blinked. "We can?"

"Yes, yes. This is in the nature of a surprise inspection, you see. Of course we all know that you two are doing a splendid job in terribly difficult circumstances, but not everyone in the government completely understands that—or understands just how these difficult Bennerol babies could possibly be managed in a home environment."

Harry looked across at Elizabeth with big eyes. "Am I difficult, Mum?"

"Of course not, darling," Elizabeth told him, and offered up a silent novena in apology for her shameless lie.

"You see?" Dr. Margo turned to her colleague. "Didn't I tell you she's handling it all marvellously? And that's just what you'll see for yourself tonight."

Elizabeth set the sugar jar carefully down on the counter. "I'm sorry, I don't quite understand. Do you mean that you're planning to actually stay the night? Both of you?"

"You'll barely even notice we're here," Dr. Margo said. "Well, apart from having to cover up the mirrors, of course. But that's just a silly little preference of my colleague's, nothing to worry about. We won't interfere at all in your routines— we're only here to observe, you know. Think of us as being like that TV show—*Big Brother*, isn't that the one? Only without the cameras, of course."

"Of course," her colleague echoed. "Ha. Ha. Cameras. As if we would want any of those turned on."

"Ahem." Dr. Margo gave him an admonishing look and turned back to Elizabeth. "We all want to lay those silly official worries to rest, don't we?"

"But we're not really prepared—I mean, we don't have a guest bedroom, and the living room isn't—"

"Oh, don't worry about any of that," Dr. Margo said. "My colleague doesn't sleep much anyway."

"Bennerol babies are creatures of the night," her colleague said. "So we must spend the night awake to understand him, must we not?"

"Of course," Elizabeth said faintly. She reached into the sugar jar and dug out a spoonful for her coffee that would have made even Harry quake.

She was going to need it.

"WHAT THE HELL IS GOING ON?" Dan hissed, eight hours later. He'd dragged her into the kitchen, promising the others tea, and closed the door behind them. "Why is Dr. Margo making Lego towers with Harry in our living room? Who's that bloke dressed up like the Invisible Man in the corner? Why's the hallway mirror covered with a pillowcase? And damn it, why didn't you warn me about any of this before I got home? If I'd known social services was visiting, I wouldn't have been carrying a case of cider when I walked through the door. Now they probably think we're alcoholics!"

"I couldn't help it." Elizabeth pushed the kitchen door back open so that she could hear Harry's piping voice. Reassuringly (under the circumstances), he was cackling with manic glee. She heard the telltale crashes of Dr. Margo's Lego towers being bashed over by his newest inventions: giant multi-coloured Lego frogs of doom. She dreaded to think how much space one of those might take up in the bedroom at night. For once, though, sleep was the least of her concerns.

"They've been here all day," she whispered. "I thought about trying to ring you from the toilet, but Dr. Margo looked at me like I was a pervert when I said I wanted to take Harry in with me, and I didn't want to leave him alone with them while I went. I'm bursting now, though, so if you could just keep an eye on the situation for a moment "

"First, tell me." Dan clamped his hand around her arm. "Harry had an accident, didn't he? How bad was it? One of his dreams must have spilled over. Or he had one in the daytime. Or—did the neighbours see something and complain? For God's sake, when you think how many times their dogs have kept us up—"

His voice was rising. Elizabeth pressed her free hand against his mouth to stop him.

"It's not the neighbours," she hissed. "It's the government."

Dan lost his grip on her arm. "Bloody hell," he whispered against her palm.

Then they both turned, as the silence coming from the living room finally struck them. The crashes of falling towers had ended. The only sound that carried was a soft murmur—Dr. Margo's voice, speaking too quietly for them to hear. Their eyes met in a moment of perfect understanding.

Dan took off for the living room so quickly, Elizabeth was surprised not to see flames erupt underneath his boring black loafers. When she joined them five minutes later, carrying the tea tray, she found him standing behind Harry like a bodyguard, arms crossed and legs spread apart, glaring at Dr. Margo's colleague across the room. She elbowed him in the stomach as she passed.

"Be nice," she whispered. "Don't offend him."

Dan bared his teeth in a menacing smile. The other man smiled back, with a courteous nod of his head. Elizabeth blinked at the sight.

She had never seen teeth so bright white and . . . well, sharp-looking, before. Even in the fading light of early evening, in his shadowed corner of the room, they positively sparkled. And was it just a trick of the light, or were his canines a bit longer than was usual?

Dr. Margo cleared her throat loudly. Her colleague closed his mouth. Dan widened his stance by at least an inch.

"You're standing funny, Daddy," Harry said. "Do you have something wrong with your—"

"What would everyone like for supper?" Elizabeth asked brightly, speaking over Harry's final word as she handed out the cups of tea.

Dr. Margo said, "Oh, anything, dear. Except for any food with preservatives in it, of course. Or anything that's been frozen, or come from a tin. Or anything with red ingredients. You can never really trust red ingredients, can you?"

"Well . . . " Elizabeth mentally ran through their kitchen cupboards, feeling her heart sink.

"But I wouldn't want to put you to any trouble," Dr. Margo said.

"Of course not." Elizabeth smiled tightly. "And . . . ?" She started to turn to the man in the corner.

"Oh, you needn't worry about my colleague," Dr. Margo said. "He isn't hungry."

"Are you sure?" Elizabeth asked, trying not to sound hopeful.

He nodded regally. "I do not eat . . . supper. But should you not be going to bed, very soon? You need not stay awake for us, you know. Dr. Margo and I can look after your son very well without you."

Elizabeth didn't have to look at her husband to know that their thoughts were in perfect unison, possibly for the first time since their wedding ceremony.

Still, with the health service—not to mention the government—watching, there was no excuse to keep Harry up late. Elizabeth supervised his tooth-brushing under the silent, looming observation of Dr. Margo's colleague, and Dr. Margo beamed maternally from one corner of Harry's bedroom as Dan sat down to read him his bedtime chapter of *Captain Underpants*. She winced, though, at the first fart joke, and looked more and more pained as the chapter went on.

"Isn't there something a bit more traditional that Harry might like?" she whispered to Elizabeth. "One of those nice *Narnia* books, perhaps? Or—"

"Trust me," Elizabeth said. "Waking up to find the White Witch in my bedroom is not an experience I want to repeat. And Aslan may be friendly in the books, but that's not terribly reassuring at three a.m., when he's keeping us all up with his roaring."

"I'll find out what that's like myself, tonight," Dr. Margo said, regaining her cheer. "I must say, I can hardly wait! Nighttime really has become so much more interesting ever since Bennerol was invented, hasn't it?"

Elizabeth smiled weakly in return. It wasn't until five minutes later that she finally lost control.

She was leaning over Harry's bed to kiss him goodnight when he said, with sleepy consideration, "I don't think I like those pills Dr. Margo gave me, Mummy. They're making everything look a bit funny."

"What?!" Elizabeth straightened with a jerk. "Dr. Margo gave you pills? When?"

Dr. Margo rose from her seat in the corner. "Now, dear . . . "

"It was while you and Daddy were in the kitchen," Harry said. "And again just after dinner, when you were clearing away. She said it would be instead of pudding. But then you gave me pudding anyway, so that was all right."

"Let me get this straight," Dan said to Dr. Margo. "You gave Harry two different pills, without asking us? Without even telling us?"

"Oh, Harry." Dr. Margo shook her head sorrowfully. "Didn't I tell you those pills were our little secret?"

It was a long moment before Elizabeth could trust herself to speak. "You did just right to tell me, Harry. You're a good boy. Now go to sleep." She leaned over and pressed a second kiss against his tousled brown hair. "If you start feeling really ill from those pills, just call us. We'll be close enough to hear." She turned to Dr. Margo and was glad to see the other woman step back under the heat of her gaze. "We'll be in the living room, having a little chat with Dr. Margo about ethics and the law."

She stalked out of the room, her spine rigidly straight. Dan waited, pointedly, for Dr. Margo to leave before he followed.

The other man was already sitting in the living room when they arrived, flipping through one of the horror novels that Dan kept on the top shelves of the bookcases in almost every room of the house, well out of Harry's reach. He looked up questioningly as they walked in, but Dr. Margo ignored him.

"If we can all please refrain from overreacting—"

"Overreacting? You drugged our son!" Elizabeth kept her voice low for Harry's sake, but it shook with rage. "How do you think the General Medical Council is going to feel about that? When we report what you've done—"

"Oh, I really don't think you want to do that, dear."

"Why not?" Dan demanded. "If you think you can walk all over us now, just because Elizabeth let one brainless midwife talk her into taking those pills in the first place—"

"I beg your pardon?" Elizabeth stared at her husband. "You and I both agreed I should try the Bennerol! Everyone said there weren't any side-effects. They said—"

"Children!" said Dr. Margo. "Please. The pills I gave Harry are completely harmless. All they're intended to do is strengthen the results of his dreams."

Elizabeth didn't say a word. She couldn't. Distantly, she heard Dan say, "Why in the name of God would you want to do that?"

Dr. Margo sighed. With her carefully-curled grey hair, pink silk blouse, and patterned scarf, she looked the very definition of a kindly grandmother. "You see? This is why I couldn't discuss it with you ahead of time. Parents are always the same. So conservative. *So* narrow-minded."

Elizabeth said, "I'm ringing NHS Direct right now, to find out how to register a complaint. Dan—"

"Do it," he said. "And as for you two—"

"If you do," said Dr. Margo, "you will regret it. Because those pills work . . . and the Government would be very interested in discovering that."

Dr. Margo no longer looked in the slightest bit vague or harmless. For the first time since Elizabeth had started taking

Harry to his monthly sessions with her, four years earlier, she looked past the air of kindly, fluffy condescension. There was a scientist behind the candy-pink blouse, and behind Dr. Margo's old-fashioned, cat's-eye glasses, her hazel eyes shone with far more ambition than Elizabeth had ever recognized before.

"I thought *he* was from the government," Elizabeth said, gesturing to the heavily-swathed man in the corner. He had moved on from the horror novel to one of Harry's *Calvin & Hobbes* collections and was sniggering over the pictures . . . but with an alarming expression of hunger on his face.

Was that drool slipping down from one of his sharp teeth?

"It made things simpler for you to think so," said Dr. Margo. "But trust me, dear. I'm the only one standing between you and a whole host of exciting government agencies, all of whom would love to know that our Bennerol babies could turn into real weapons. Without me, Harry and all the little children like him would have been taken away from their parents years ago. You can hardly begrudge me a few experiments of my own, can you? Just for my own personal satisfaction—as a small payment, you might say, for my protection?"

She smiled gently, as Elizabeth and Dan said nothing. "No?" she said. She sat down on the couch, patting down her trousers. "I thought not. Now, I'd like some tea, please. Elizabeth?"

Elizabeth met Dan's eyes. They looked darker than usual against his pallor. He shrugged, the gesture despairing.

"Fine," Elizabeth said flatly. "Milk?"

"But no sugar," Dr. Margo said, as she opened up her notepad. "It's so unhealthy, don't you think?"

Elizabeth couldn't think of any answer that didn't involve cursing.

Luckily, Dr. Margo didn't seem to expect a reply. She was already tutting softly over an earlier page of notes. Harry's parents, it was clear, were old business.

Elizabeth didn't bother to ask Dr. Margo's colleague, this time. She already knew what the answer would be.

As she filled up the electric kettle in the kitchen, her eyes went to the darkness outside the window. It felt like a palpable force, pressing in on her chest until she could barely breathe.

She couldn't see the birdfeeder in the dark, nor the squirrel who'd driven her so wild that morning. Was it really less than twelve hours since she'd stood here idly wishing she could send Harry's dream-creatures after that pitiful little animal, to frighten him away? It already seemed like a different world. This morning had been just another day of summer holiday. Harry had been safe, warm, and protected in her kitchen, chattering about his dreams, and her biggest worry had been the comic he was reading, because she knew how it might affect them.

Cold water overflowed from the electric kettle. It splashed across Elizabeth's hand as she stood unmoving, her mouth open.

She might not be a scientist, like Dr. Margo. But she had learned something important all those years ago, after she'd let that damn midwife reassure her about the Bennerol. She'd learned to never, ever again let anyone intimidate her out of listening to her instincts, especially when it came to protecting her son.

And Harry wasn't the only one who had an imagination.

When Elizabeth stepped into the living room ten minutes later, carrying her best tea service on a tray, Dr. Margo didn't even look up. She was too busy making notes. Excitement glittered in her eyes. Ten minutes ago, that would have sent alarm flaring deep in Elizabeth's gut.

Now, Elizabeth lowered her own eyes submissively and set the tea tray down on the coffee table. It was laid out exactly as her mother-in-law had taught her one excruciating Sunday afternoon, like a souvenir from the Victorian era. Normally, it would have elicited a sarcastic comment from Dan. Tonight, though, Dan sat with his head propped on his fist, staring hopelessly into the empty fireplace. He didn't move to pick up his tea, or comment on the leaf that fell off Elizabeth's hair as she stepped back from the coffee table.

She shifted casually in place to cover the leaf with her shoe, and ran one hand over her hair to check for any other giveaways. For the first time ever, she felt deeply grateful for just how quiet Harry could be when he was sneak-reading a book in bed after lights-out . . . especially one that had always been off-limits, hidden on the tallest shelf of the bookcase in his parents' bedroom.

He had been so thrilled to finally get hold of this one, he hadn't even asked why Elizabeth was climbing in through his window to give it to him, along with her mini-torch.

When Elizabeth turned around, the man in the corner was leering at her neck. Rather than showing any embarrassment as he met her gaze, he waggled his eyebrows meaningfully, tilting his head toward the kitchen. His eyes seemed to burn with urgent invitation.

Heat swept across the room. The scent of temptation filled her senses. All she had to do was give in.

Elizabeth smiled serenely and sat down beside her husband, patting his knee affectionately. Sometimes, it was good to be a mother.

If Mina Harker or Bella Swan hadn't managed a single full night's sleep in six years, they wouldn't have had the energy to be mesmerized by a vampire's stare, either. Daniel could have warned the other man about that issue, if he'd been asked.

She picked up a magazine from the table and began to read about the season's latest fashion innovations. Across the room, she heard a mournful sigh.

"Harry's dreams always manifest in your bedroom, don't they?" Dr. Margo asked half-an-hour later, when she finally looked up from her notes.

Dan only grunted. Elizabeth looked up placidly from her magazine and said, "Yes, always."

"Well, then, I'm afraid we'll have to use that room tonight. You won't mind sleeping on the couch, will you, dears?"

Elizabeth sighed heavily. "If you insist . . . "

It was three a.m. when the first scream sounded. Dan jerked out of sleep, still sitting upright on the armchair. "Wha—? Was that—?"

"Shh," said Elizabeth, and put one hand on his arm to hold him back. "They wouldn't want us to interfere."

It was seven-thirty when she finally opened the door to her bedroom. Harry was still fast asleep, of course—he always slept in after staying up to read a particularly gripping novel.

Powerful though they might have been, his dreams had still dissipated in the morning sunlight. Harry had, after all, had only two doses of Dr. Margo's experimental pills. She could only imagine how many more doses had been used on some poor child to create Dr. Margo's "colleague" . . . or what might have happened before Dr. Margo took over his supervision.

A small pile of ashes lay on the floor next to Dr. Margo. Elizabeth made a note to clear them up as soon as she emptied out the vacuum cleaner.

Dr. Margo herself sat on the bed, glassy-eyed and staring. Her pulse was rapid, but her eyes were glazed. As Elizabeth walked into the room, she repeated, as if by rote, "I will not create vampires. I will not . . . I will not . . . "

"Shh," Elizabeth said. "Of course you won't. You won't ever do anything to any of the children again."

She patted Dr. Margo on the back. The other woman, still in a deeply hypnotized state, didn't even blink.

Good for Harry, Elizabeth thought. *And good for Dr. Van Helsing.* He had always been her favourite character in the Dracula book and movies. She was pleased she'd been able to convey her abiding love for him—and all of his varied abilities, from hypnotism to vampire-staking—in the five-minute pep talk she'd given her son last night.

"Come along," she said to Dr. Margo. "I'm making break-fast. You can drink a cup of tea while you tell me exactly how long it'll take for Harry's doses to lose their effect. Because . . . "

She smiled. Of course, Dan might have his own ideas, but surely he would agree that tonight was her turn?

" . . . I think today might be the perfect day to introduce Harry to Jane Austen. Starting with *Pride and Prejudice*—the Colin Firth edition."

FIGHT FINALE FROM THE NEAR FUTURE!

JAMES BEAMON

Agent Brody Omen doesn't walk with a little swagger. He swaggers with a little walk. Everyone stops and stares as he enters the agency's command center. Gay men want him. Straight men want to be him. Women are a finicky demographic.

Brody is all pecs and triceps and locks of fair hair. His smile goes without saying. His name is Brody as in bro. Your big bro. He is the agency's number one, their lead agent, which makes him a leading man.

He is accompanied by a femme fatale. This is obvious. The curves in the leather catsuit make her femme. Her willingness to shoot men for looking at her ass, even though it's deliciously on display in a catsuit, makes her fatale.

The general stands in the command center, overseeing all.

He is a father-mentor. Gruff is his manner. He has more decora-
tions on his chest than most Christmas trees. He leads soldiers,
which makes him a leading man.

The general spots his number one field agent. His eyes
light up. He says, "Omen! You can't bring a civilian in here."

"General," Brody says, "Katya saved my life and helped me
get that cipher. And if things go as they should, you're looking
at my future ex-girlfriend, so watch how you speak to her."

The general harrumphs. "Well, we've used the cipher to
decode M. Vella's plan. You'll never guess what that madman
has built."

"Vella is the most dastardly villain I've ever matched wits
with," Brody says. "Surely, it's a doomsday device."

"Wrong!" exclaims the giant display screen in the heart of
the command center. The image jumps to life and there, with
his sneer sharp as a knife, is M. Vella.

Satan worships Vella. He is dark eyes, dark suit, dark hair
slicked back, dark heart. M. Vella leads a legion of nameless
goons, which makes him a leading man.

"I have built a doom*verse* device," M. Vella says. "The
doomverse device is fueled by quantum computers factoring
the crushing despair of child sweatshop laborers, the bleak pes-
simism of calling customer service and discovering it's been
outsourced, the heady anguish of Cubs fans! All this, and a
small helping of contained antimatter. It will not only blow
up the Earth, but will travel to every Earth in all alternate universes and blow them up, too."

"Vella, you fiend!" cries Brody Omen. "This is by far the
most heinous plot that anyone has ever seen. Now that you
have our attention, what do you want?"

"Glad you asked, Agent Omen. I want the world's most
loved treasures: the Hope Diamond, the Mona Lisa, Michelangelo's David, the Dead Sea Scrolls, the Declaration of Inde-
pendence, Dorothy's red slippers, and a mint condition Action
Comics issue one. You have twelve hours."

The screen fades to black. Brody Omen shakes his fist at the inert monitor to utter a curse . . .

"This plot seems like overkill." This is not Brody's curse, but the words of a mysterious stranger.

The voice belongs to a man in plainclothes. He wears a baseball cap and sunglasses, and not cool Secret Service-type glasses, but hard and cheap plastic sunglasses.

"Who's this guy?" Brody asks.

"He's your observer," the general responds. "We received a lot of negative feedback about your last couple of exploits. He's going with you to make sure that doesn't happen again."

The agent and his potential future ex-girlfriend raise their eyebrows. "What do I call you?" Brody asks.

"The Observer."

This is the last thing the Observer consciously remembers before he is hiding in jungle foliage at the entrance of M. Vella's secret lair in Laos. Hungry-looking dogs guard the entrance.

"How'd we get here so fast?" the Observer whispers. "Secret government teleporter?"

"Southwest Airlines," Brody replies. "Chairs so comfortable it's like riding on air. Knocked you right out."

"How do we get past the dogs?" Katya asks.

"Like this," Brody says as he marches over to the dogs.

They surround him, barking, jowls slathering. Then they sniff. And then they run off, tails tucked.

"How'd you do that?" the Observer asks.

"I asserted myself as pack leader. All it took was my insane level of confidence and a dab of Old Spice."

"Old Spice can't do that," the Observer states.

"Oh, you'd be surprised what Old Spice can do," replies Katya, eyebrow appreciatively raised.

Brody looks at the Observer. "You know what, I hate 'ob' words. Observer, obstetrician, obfuscate, obelisk, hate them all. I'm going to find a better name for you."

"To hate them you sure know a lot of them," Katya says. "Obfuscate?"

"Dictionary.com word of the day once. But enough playful banter, let's go foil evil."

Foiling evil involves stealth in some places, stylish fight moves in others. Brody is an expert on when to apply each technique. The goons either don't know the team is there, or wish they didn't. On level three, Brody runs full speed, jumps, and extends both legs so that he is rigidly parallel to the ground when he dropkicks a guard. On level five, Katya kicks a goon and her legs spread like juicy rumors. She holds the pose and she is perfectly balanced on one leg while her other leather-clad toe almost touches the ceiling. The Observer observes.

They reach the doomverse device. They guess. It's not like any of them have ever seen a doomverse device before, but the giant metal sphere pulsing purple lightning from the seams looks ominous enough. Besides, what else do you keep on the top floor of a secret lair filled with progressively tougher obstacles to surmount? Plus the metal sphere is suspended over an abyss and accessible only by a precarious catwalk. By all accounts, doomverse device is a good guess.

"You both stand back," Brody says. He walks carefully across the catwalk. Then he hears the hammer of a gun cock back.

This is a needless gesture, as the only guns that require manually cocking to fire are Old West single-action revolvers. But he hears it, and cringes despite the fact that anyone who wanted him dead would have killed him already unless their firearm was made before 1890. Brody turns slowly to face his nemesis.

Brody sees M. Vella on the catwalk. Behind the villain, Katya is tied up. M. Vella has left the Observer alone because observing never hurt anybody. Apparently, stealth is also useful for foiling good.

"And now, Agent Omen, I will explain to you my plan's finer points," M. Vella sneers as he raises the gun. "I call them hollow points."

A shot rings out, loud, jarring. Silence follows.

M. Vella looks down. The slow spread of red from the wound in his chest stains his dark suit. He turns and discovers the source of his distress. It is the Observer, holding the smoking gun.

"Fool!" M. Vella cough-spits. "I'll never get this blood out without the stain fighting power of Oxi-clean!" He staggers and falls off the catwalk into the abyss below.

"That wasn't an optimal use of product placement," observes the Observer. "State Farm would've paid through the nose for him to plug their term life policy just then."

"You did it, Observer!" Katya exclaims.

"That makes you a hero, Observer," Brody says as he unties Katya. "And I'm not calling a hero the Observer. From now on I'm calling you the Viewer."

"Suit yourself," says the Viewer.

"What now?" Katya asks.

"It's Miller Time!" proclaims Brody.

"Now that I'm thinking about it," says the Viewer "if the M. Vella in *our* universe made a doomverse device, then it's very likely that other M. Vellas in alternate universes also made doomverse devices. If the many worlds interpretation of quantum physics is true, then all possible outcomes exist in their own alternate universe. This means that in one of those universes we fail to stop M. Vella and he destroys our world from an alternate world."

Silence grows. Brody leans over to Katya and whispers, "I didn't know the Viewer was so smart."

"That's because we haven't seen his face," Katya replies. "Take off your glasses and ball cap. Show us your face, Viewer."

The Viewer shakes his head. "My face is reserved for those who buy the Director's Cut Special Edition. Those lucky guys can upload their own faces. Then they can be the Viewer and the hero."

"But what about the ladies?" asks Katya.

No one answers, despite it being a legitimate question. They ignore it, just like they ignore pervading quantum theory, which says *this* Earth should be nothing but a crusty aftermath of charred rock fragments because Vella succeeding from an alternate universe must exist as a possible outcome. They ignore Katya's question because that will make it go away. But the answer is simple.

Women are a finicky demographic.

TEMPORAL
SHIMMIES

JENNIFER PELLAND

This was the night that Nadia was finally going to get it. She
was going to show her body who was boss.

Then the teacher said she was going to lead the class
through a "fun shimmy drill," and Nadia knew she was fucked.

Her body immediately rebelled. Her hip shimmies stut-
tered in a wild arrhythmia that set her incipient bingo wings
flapping. When the teacher had the class layer on upper-body
isolations, the shimmy escaped entirely from Nadia's hips and
traveled up to her shoulders, and for one horrifying moment,
her neck. She tried to fight it back down, but her body just
laughed at her.

The teacher came over and quietly said, "Just work on
your hip shimmies. Don't worry about adding anything to
them yet."

Nadia felt her face go flaming red and she looked down at
the floor so she couldn't catch the sidelong glances she knew

she had to be getting from her fellow students. Slow, old Nadia, too ridiculous to realize that no one could pick up dance at the ripe old age of forty-five.

"It's all right," the teacher murmured. "We all learn at different speeds."

She knew that was bullshit, if only because she'd been telling her physics students the same thing for over a decade. And even the slowest of them hadn't had to take her course more than twice before moving on. Nadia, on the other hand, had spent a full two years in the beginners class before being allowed to move up to advanced beginners just last week. She was beginning to suspect she'd only been promoted out of pity.

She shot a quick look at her friend Meghan, an adjunct professor in the mathematics department who'd started tagging along to classes with Nadia a year ago. Damn it, she looked like she was actually enjoying herself. And her bingo wings were barely twitching.

The song ended, and the instructor said, "Good job, everyone!"

Nadia called bullshit on that as well.

"I've got a treat for you next week. One of my former students, Joy March, will be teaching class while I'm on vacation."

Joy March?

But . . . Joy had been a classmate of hers the first time she took beginners. And Joy had graduated out of it at the end of her first eight-week session and had rocketed through the rest of the levels just as quickly. She'd been dancing in restaurants for nearly a year now, and had even started her own dance company with five other hot young things. She was so fucking cute and talented that Nadia could just vomit.

Meghan shot a knowing look at her, and mouthed, "Drinks."

Nadia nodded, and stuffed her sandals on over her swollen,

pink feet, vowing to herself never to come back to class again.

She followed Meghan across the street to the ice cream bar, where she ordered a cosmo and a petite hot fudge sundae, in token deference to her perpetual diet. "Joy? Seriously?"

"Fuck Joy," Meghan said. "She's a perky little bitch who probably isn't old enough to have her period."

Nadia downed her cosmo in one long gulp, then plunked the glass down on the table with a sigh. "A *talented* perky little bitch."

"She may be talented, but have you ever noticed how her smile doesn't actually reach her eyes? I think she's dead inside," Meghan said, swirling her straw through her rum-laden raspberry-lime ricky. "She's got no artistry. It's all technique."

"I'd give my left ovary for her technique."

"You'd give your left ovary for a *Kit Kat.*"

Nadia bobbed her head. "True." She caught the bartender's eye and pointed to her empty glass.

Damn it, she should have started younger. Back when touching her toes didn't result in more popping sounds than a bag of microwave popcorn. Back when she could have impressed a guy with her dance moves instead of making him think she was having a seizure. Some nights she would lie in bed, headphones on, imagining just how she wanted her body to move. But once she got up and actually tried, the illusion revealed itself as being just that.

She was an old woman. She should have known better.

"Well, it could be worse," Nadia said as her second cosmo arrived. "We could be taking burlesque with a bunch of firm-breasted sophomores."

"Bitch, please," Meghan said. "Your life is so hard. You have tenure."

"I would trade that in a hot second to be able to dance without embarrassing myself."

Meghan scoffed. "No you wouldn't."

Actually . . .

She drained her glass. "I have to go. I just remembered, I left something in the office."

Meghan waved her straw at her dismissively.

Nadia stumbled out the door and onto the subway. Time to put that grant she'd gotten to study time travel to good use.

Time travel. It was a load of hokum, but the grant money meant she didn't need to teach classes for the next three years. Half of her students were morons who had only gotten admitted due to a family legacy, most of the rest only took her classes to fulfill their science requirement, and the handful of leftovers were her future competition. She didn't need that continued reminder of her own academic mortality. Bad enough she had Joy to remind her of her body's ticking clock.

Time to play a drunken hunch.

She'd been spending all her time trying to determine how to move a physical object into the past, but what if instead she used the university's particle accelerator to shoot subatomic particles backwards through time and leave a Morse code message for her younger self? Not that she had access to it after hours. No, tonight she'd just play around with the old Van de Graaf accelerator to get a feel for the project. Mostly, she was too mad and drunk to just go home without doing *something*.

UGH. WHAT WAS SHE THINKING? This would never work. At best, once she got her hands on the actual particle accelerator, she'd create a fork in the time stream and give some other version of herself her dream life.

Well, *one* version of her might as well be happy.

Nadia waved her badge at George, the night guard, then swiped her way into the lab. "Fuck it," she told no one in particular, and started fiddling semi-randomly with the accelerator's settings, letting inspiration and alcohol guide her calculations. Sending Morse code back through time. This was so *Star Trek*. Good thing she hadn't put this crazy-ass idea on her grant proposal form, because they never would have given it to her and she'd be stuck with the undergrads. Worse, she might be stuck on a dissertation committee.

So when should she aim for? She pulled out her phone and started scrolling through the physics department's website. They had a picture of her in this lab when she was in grad school. Did it . . . ? Yes, there was the date stamp.

She went over to the whiteboard and scribbled down the math, then pushed it out into the hallway. If this literally blew up in her face, she should probably leave a warning behind of what not to do. Then she programmed in her short Morse code message and switched the generator on . . .

. . . and staggered back as a wave of new memories hit her. Her twenty-five year old self, staring in amazement as the accelerator came to life without warning and received the message: "Nadia, this is you at forty-five. Start taking belly dance now or you'll regret it."

"Holy shit," her professor had said. "You're gonna discover how to send messages back through time!"

The story had been picked up by the local news, then went national, then international. Nadia smiled gamely for the cameras as she headed to her first belly dance class at the YMCA—she hadn't liked that "or you'll regret it" part. Eventually, the hubbub died down, and she . . .

Nadia winced and tried to stop thinking. It was too much. This test wasn't supposed to have worked. It was *impossible*. But it *had*.

An impish smile creased her face as she stood up and got a steady hip shimmy going, then effortlessly layered a chest circle over it.

Awesome.

She headed out, and stopped, puzzled, at the whiteboard. What the hell? None of it made sense, even taking how drunk she'd been into account.

"I'll figure it out later," she said, and pulled her phone from her pocketbook to take pictures of it all. She emailed them to herself, then erased and spritzed down the whiteboard. No way she was going to let one of her colleagues stumble across this and take the credit.

She waved at George on her way out, headed back to the outbound subway stairs, then stopped. No, she didn't live in the suburbs anymore. She was in the city.

Even better.

As she went down the stairs to the inbound platform, she realized that her new life was coming to her more easily now. She had a brownstone downtown, with a dance studio on the top floor. And a husband, Ben. A husband! Well, she'd been right to think that belly dance done properly would be a great way to bag a man. She'd met him at a restaurant show. He'd been mesmerized by her swirling hips, she'd been mesmerized by his cheekbones, his pecs, and his deep blue eyes. Turned out he was as shallow as soap scum, but with his chiseled physique and the money he pulled in at the bank, who cared?

She took a seat on the mostly-empty subway car and pulled out her phone to see if she had any bathing suit pictures of him. Yep, there was one with him and their daughter, Sylvia.

Daughter?

She yanked up her shirt and stared in horror at the pearly stretch marks and the little pooch of saggy skin. Son of a bitch. No wonder she wore body stockings at restaurant shows.

Well, at least the kid was pretty cute, with big brown eyes and natural ringlets that would have made Shirley Temple jealous. And look, she also belly danced. She watched a short video of Sylvia and felt a warm rush of pride. Yes, this little girl would be dancing circles around Joy before she even grew breasts. What a lovely double-whammy of revenge.

She unlocked the door to her elegant brownstone and

stopped dead in her tracks at the sight of her husband having sex with Joy March on the living room sofa.

"Seriously? Her?"

Ben fumbled to pull his pants back up. "I—I thought you had a restaurant gig tonight."

"You're fucking *Joy?*"

Joy put her finger to her lips. "You're going to wake Sylvia."

"She's my daughter, and I'll damned well wake her up to tell her that her daddy is a two-timing man-whore if I want to."

"I'm so sorry—"

Nadia pointed a well-manicured finger and said, "You, bitch. Get out of my house."

Joy slipped into her dress, picked up her sandals, and dashed out the door.

How the hell had Joy gotten into her life in this timeline? Oh, she was on Joy's dissertation committee, and she had introduced her to Ben at the physics department Christmas party. Well, wasn't that just spiffy.

Ben buried his face in his hands. "I'll move out."

"That's it? You're not going to beg forgiveness? Not going to try to win me back?"

He looked up at Nadia with hangdog eyes and asked, "Would it work?"

She searched her new memories to see if she wanted to bother.

Oh hell, she barely knew him, so no great loss.

"You stay, I'll go," she said. "Keep the kid. Now, if you'll excuse me."

Time for the good stuff.

She went up to the third floor, to her home studio, and opened the closet.

"Oh ... my ... god ..."

It was stuffed to bursting. She had professional restaurant costumes, Ren Faire garb, fun fusion wear, even some American Tribal Style outfits. She knew ATS?

She pulled on a cherry red 25-yard skirt and started busting out classic Fat Chance combos in front of the mirror.

Yes, apparently she knew ATS. Awesome. She'd always meant to learn that style, but she'd always figured she should conquer basic shimmies first. It was amazing how much easier it was to have skipped past all the years of lessons and jumped straight into being a professional dancer with a well-trained body and a well-stocked wardrobe. Now *there* was a great way to monetize time travel! Maybe instead of publishing this in an academic journal, she should sell it to Google.

She heard footfalls on the stairs, and turned to see Ben standing in the doorway. "This is why it happened," he said. "You spend too much time dancing, and not enough with me."

"Oh, and Joy doesn't?"

"What are you talking about? Joy doesn't dance."

"Joy doesn't . . ." It took a second for the sentence to sink in. But once it did, she smiled so hard she could feel it all the way to her ears. "Holy crap, I've won!" Nadia didn't care if the daughter she'd never met was sleeping right below her—this called for some ceremonial jumping up and down.

Which led to her sitting on the floor, cradling her aching knees, as shocked tears leaked down her face.

"What are you doing?" Ben said. "You know you're not supposed to do that after the surgery."

Nadia pulled her skirt and pants up and looked at the angry scars over both knees. "Well, fuck," she grumbled, and swiped the tears away with the hem of her skirt.

"The fact that you're still doing restaurant gigs is bad enough," Ben said. "But you told me you were sticking to American Cabaret and not doing any of that Turkish hopping crap."

"What is wrong with this timeline? I cannot believe I married a man that would call it 'Turkish hopping crap'."

"Nadia, what's gotten into you?"

She shot him a level look. "Seriously? I walk in on you having sex in the living room while our daughter is asleep upstairs and you're giving *me* shit? Fuck this, I need to fix things." She pulled off the skirt, leaving it in an unceremonious heap in the middle of the studio floor, and headed back for the stairs. Her knees screamed at her the entire way down, but tough shit. She had to make things right.

"Where are you going?"

Work. That was where she was going. Time to send another message. She clearly hadn't been specific enough last time.

As she sat on the subway, she stared in puzzlement at the photos on her phone. The math seemed correct, but she wasn't quite sure why it had worked. Then again, in this version of her life, she hadn't spent nearly as much time on research as she had originally, so that made a certain sense. Hell, she didn't even have tenure. But who had time for that with a dancing career and a kid? At least she could understand the part of the math that targeted the accelerator to a specific moment in history.

So, should she just send a second message to arrive right after that first one, or should she try to intercept herself at an earlier time in her life?

Wait . . . hadn't she visited that lab when she was a prospective undergrad? If she could send a message to her past self then, that would mean eight more years of belly dance experience. And maybe that would leave her too busy to disfigure her abdomen with a pregnancy.

She flipped through the calendar on her phone and yes, there it was. The campus visit. Date and time.

Score!

When she got back to the university, George shot her a puzzled look. "I don't think I've ever seen you here after hours. Going for tenure after all?"

"Thinking about it," she said.

"Well, good luck. After all, you're the woman who's gonna discover time travel."

That she was. Hell, with her shitty grad school grades and lack of any meaningful publication credits, it was probably the only thing that kept her employed here. The university president would probably hang himself if he fired Nadia and she went and discovered time travel somewhere else.

She went back into the lab, set everything up again, programmed in the date and time, then set up the new message.

"Nadia, this is your future self. Start belly dancing, but take care of your knees or else."

The new wave of memories sent her crumpling to the ground.

She remembered the professor asking which one of them was Nadia and saying, "Holy shit, you discover how to send messages through time!" He immediately tried to set her up with a full scholarship, but she rebuffed him, and instead got into a local school with a sports biology program. She hadn't liked that ominous warning from the future about her knees. And while she was at it, she started taking belly dance lessons at the local YMCA, then moved on to intensive private lessons. Soon, she was gigging all over the state, then in neighboring states, and eventually got a coveted invitation to audition for the Bellydance Superstars and got in on her first try. With them, she toured the world, becoming famous for her killer shimmies, which she could keep going for hours straight. They'd even built an entire act around them—Shimmies Through Time! Because, after all, she was the woman who was going to discover time travel, even if she hadn't studied a lick of physics since high school. And tomorrow, she was going to attempt to set the Guinness World Record for the longest sustained hip shimmy.

"What are you doing here?"

Nadia picked herself up off of the ground and waved at the security guard. "Hi, George. I'm just leaving."

"How do you know my name?"

She waved vaguely at his badge, which not even

Superman could have read from this distance. "I've got crazy eyesight. Anyhow, I think I'm lost. I was looking for a bathroom—"

She was unceremoniously escorted out of the building.

But that was fine with her. She was Nadia, Queen of the Shimmy. She set her hips going, and laughed at how effortless it was. No wonder she could do this for hours!

She pulled her shirt up and took a quick peek at her stomach. Chiseled, taut, and totally unmarked. Excellent. Between that and the shimmies, no wonder she had such an extensive collection of lovers.

Oh wow. Now *that* was an unexpected bonus.

She hiked her purse over her shoulder and started to head back to the subway, shimmying all the way. A cute undergrad sized her up as he whizzed by on his bike. Perhaps she'd add him to her collection. But first, she needed to get a little rest at the hotel before tomorrow's big day . . .

She was stopped by the unmistakable sensation of a gun barrel being pressed into her ribs.

"Freeze," someone whispered.

Nadia felt the entire contents of her large intestine liquefy and she clenched for all she was worth. "You—you can have all my cash—"

"I don't want your money." Her assailant grabbed her by the arm and pulled her off of the sidewalk and into the shadows.

"Then what—?"

"I want to thank you for ruining my life."

The woman stepped forward into a sliver of light. She looked familiar. Was she one of her aunts? She hadn't seen them in years, but maybe in this alternate universe—

"I'm you, dumbass, twenty years from how."

Nadia looked again.

Oh.

Oh dear.

As soon as this was over, she was going to make a beeline for the nearest drug store and stock up on the strongest anti-wrinkle cream she could find. Jowls were not a good look on her.

Old Nadia narrowed her eyes and said, "I was supposed to be the person who discovered time travel, and you went and fucked that all up with your stupid belly dance shit."

"Stupid belly dance shit? I'm in the Bellydance Superstars!"

"Oh, yes, the Bellydance Superstars. Do you really think history will remember you for that?"

"Who cares? I'm happy. Besides, if I set that world record—"

Older Nadia waved the gun. "Blah blah, you followed your heart, blah blah, art is just as important as science. Trust me, I had all of these arguments with myself too. Fuck you, and fuck the stupid world record you were going to set tomorrow. I could have been someone important rather than a just footnote in a trivia book, and it's all your fault."

"Wait a minute, but I *do* discover time travel. I've done it twice now. And I've built an entire act around it."

"Look at the math on your phone."

"But—"

Older Nadia pressed the gun to Nadia's temple. "Look at it. Tell me you can make sense of it."

With shaking hands, she pulled her phone from her purse and called up the first picture.

It was gibberish to her in this timeline.

"You set up an auction to sell the photos to the highest bidder tomorrow. Someone from M.I.T. hacks your phone and posts the photos to the web. Scientists all over the world try and fail to reproduce your results. Someone in the physics department eventually figures out that it's because their Van de Graaf accelerator is borked. That person figures out how to *really* send messages through time, and eventually objects, then people. You're discredited and kicked out of the history books."

"But . . . all those lovers . . ."

"Abandon you once you grow these damned jowls. But do you know the worst part?"

Nadia shook her head.

"Do you know who it was that figured out how time travel *really* worked?" Older Nadia snorted. "It was Joy."

"Well, fuck."

With that, Older Nadia shot her in the kneecaps and vanished.

Nadia cried out and collapsed to the pavement, bleeding profusely from both knees. George ran out of the building, frantically calling 911 on his earpiece. She felt the world fading in and out around her with each heartbeat, and grabbed George by the shirt collar before it faded out completely. She was not going to let Old Her win, even if it might mean that she'd be erased from existence as Current Her died. Or would she? Ugh, maybe she should have studied some physics in this timeline. If she recovered from this, she'd try to send another message.

If she could just figure out the math. And get back into the building. And use the borked accelerator. And come up with a message that was Joy-proof.

Shit.

"You'll be all right, Lady. Help is on the way."

No, no she wouldn't. There would be no world record tomorrow, or ever. Not with these ruined legs. Her career was over. Maybe she could try to pick up physics again? No, she could hear the university admissions board now. Dumb, old Nadia, too ridiculous to realize that no one could pick up experimental physics at the ripe old age of forty-five.

George gave her a little shake. "Did you see who did this to you?"

If she told him that, they'd stick her in a padded room, even if for now she *was* still the woman who was going to discover how to send messages through time.

Then again . . .

Maybe she could salvage this day, if only a little bit.

And really, it wasn't a lie, if you just looked at it the right way.

With her last bit of strength, she murmured, "Joy March."

She heard the wail of the ambulance, and passed out.

THE DAY THEY REPOSSESSED MY ZOMBIES

K.G. JEWELL

T he day they repossessed my zombies was the day Andrea broke up with me. She said she knew where our relationship was going, and it wasn't someplace she wanted to visit.

I, on the other hand, knew where our relationship had been, so I wasn't surprised by her goodbye. I'd have preferred the breakup wasn't written in blood on my workshop door, but you learn to expect certain things from a witch, and I had to admit the message had flair. Her words made clear that if I ever called her again, I'd be turned into a frog.

The zombies were another matter. I'd just landed a job to scrap three dozen school buses, and that metal wasn't going to eat itself. I'd underbid three trolls and the Pixie Syndicate for the job, counting on my undead labor to get it done. Without the zombies, I was in a bit of a pickle.

I went to my usual source of emergency finance for a quickie loan, but Joe reminded me I still owed him for fronting last month's rent. I got out of his office with only two broken fingers rather than the usual three. "A discount for a frequent borrower," he said. "Come back soon."

I looked through my inventory for something to pawn, but the pickings were slim—scrap metal isn't great collateral. I considered pawning Hank, my shop gargoyle, but he threatened to bite off my unbroken fingers if I tried. I gave him a pass.

Unfortunately, I could see only one path to the funds I needed to get my zombies back. Well, two, but I wasn't about to sell my soul, even as tattered as it was.

Andrea's mother Katherine had once offered to buy my middle name. "It has a nice sound," she said. "Fadai—I could pick up some extra votes with a name like that." Katherine sat on the city council and was always working an angle on the next election.

For my part, I wouldn't miss the name. It came from the dark recesses of my father's side of the family, and I hadn't talked to them in years. I didn't know the whole story, but my mother only used the name when I was in trouble: *Theodore Fadai Schinkel, you get back here this instant!*

So I left Hank watching the shop and went uptown to visit Katherine. An a cappella group huddled in front of city hall singing an off-key rendition of "When the Saints Go Marching In." A sign said they were *The Undead Abolitionists*. I guess it was a protest.

One singer, a woman in a neon-orange sundress, approached me with a clipboard. She was alive—that is, not-dead the first time around—and kind of cute.

"Can the undead even *be* saints?" I asked her, waving off her petition, "I mean, isn't that whole eternal damnation thing how they got stuck here in the first place?"

She winked at me and kept singing. I went inside.

Katherine was having open constituent hours, so I put my name on the list and parked myself in the lobby. The faint strains of the abolitionists' rendition of "The Internationale" drifted in every time the lobby door opened. I sat next to a gentleman who was very upset about the fluoride conspiracy.

"The undead don't drink tap water," he said, "and they don't go to the dentist. Coincidence? I think not." He shook a toothbrush at me.

I nodded and then avoided eye contact until my name was finally called.

"Ted! How are you holding up?" Katherine said, giving me a long hug that meant she'd talked to Andrea.

"I've been better," I said truthfully, gingerly touching my broken fingers. I settled into the chair across from her desk. "But I was wondering if you could help me."

"Oh, Ted," Katherine said, "You're one of my favorite people in the world, but Andrea's a grown girl. She made me promise not to get involved in her romantic affairs after that unfortunate Samhain . . . incident." She shook her head. "Although, really, I think that was the right hook-up for her at the time."

"No, no, this isn't about Andrea. I just have a cash flow problem and you'd mentioned you were interested upgrading your appellation."

Katherine folded her hands on her desk and looked up at the ceiling. "That's right. Fadai. I do like that name."

"Do you like it to the tune of $1500?" That would catch me up, even get me a month ahead, on my zombie lease.

The door blew open with a billow of smoke, cutting off her response. The lights dimmed, thunder crackled, and a dark figure swept through the door.

"Hi, Andrea," I said. She was the queen of dramatic entrances.

"Hi, Ted. Did you get my note?" The smoke whirled

around Andrea and disappeared into her waist-length, jet-black hair; the lights returned to their generic fluorescence. She wore her copper bodice, which really was my favorite item in her witchy wardrobe. Little sparks still arced across the wire ties, electrostatic remnants of her entrance.

"I did. Sorry to hear that." And really, I was. Andrea had her strong points; we just didn't belong together—my drama and her drama exceeded a relationship's critical mass. "What brings you here? Trying to supplicate for a second chance?" Her eyes glowed red in punctuation.

"No, no. I understand where you're coming from. You're right—it's really for the best if we go our separate ways." I shrugged. She was looking for a battle, but this was one I could only lose.

"Oh." Andrea frowned. I think she really wanted to turn me into a frog.

"I had a business proposition for your mother. BrainCo repossessed my zombies, and I'm a little short on cash."

"Zombies!" Katherine said. "You didn't say anything about zombies."

"Oh, no. The zombies aren't your problem, they're my problem."

Katherine opened her window. The dissonant singing of The Undead Abolitionists flowed into the room, "How many roads must a man shamble down before you call him a man?" She shut the window.

"They've been out there for three days straight. They've made the zombies my problem. If it gets out that I bought your name and you used the money to rent zombies, that'll look bad. I can see the attack ads now—Katherine Wret: funding enslavement of the previously alive."

I checked my moral compass. It was missing, but that didn't surprise me. I hadn't used it since high school and I'd gathered a lot of ambiguous moral clutter since then.

"Wait a minute—have you met a zombie? They aren't

enslaved, they just have a one-track mind, and "More Brains" is the track on repeat. My hamster has more free will than a zombie," I said.

Andrea snorted. "You don't have a hamster. You're just saying that because you need zombie labor at the shop."

I stuck out my tongue. I knew that drove her nuts. "The hamster might be hypothetical, but that doesn't mean the argument isn't real." I turned to Katherine. "Do you know how I get my zombies to scrap a vehicle? I smear a dab of brains on the transmission, and they take apart the entire vehicle for the chance to lick it.

"I don't even lock them in at night. I put a Teletubbies DVD on repeat in the breakroom, and when I come back, even if I've gone on vacation for a week, they are still sitting there, watching the sun giggle."

Katherine shook her head. "It still doesn't look good. I mean, BrainCo owns them, and you pay BrainCo for their use. Sounds like slavery to me."

"I give them everything they want in undeath—brains and brain-dead television. What would change if they were free?"

"The world would be a little more just," Katherine said. I'm pretty sure she recycled that from the council debate on instituting a no-kill policy at the town animal shelter.

"And more in balance, free from the chains of capitalism," said Andrea, tracing a glowing yin-yang circle in the air.

That was the moment I realized the true injustice of zombie slavery. If zombies were free, they would still work for brains and television but I wouldn't owe BrainCo a monthly payment. If zombies were free, they'd be free.

I was a convert.

I threw my hands up in the air. "Ok, you guys are right. What can I do to support the abolition of zombie oppression?"

Andrea furrowed her eyebrows and cast a suspicious glare. "Just like that?"

"Just like that." I smiled brightly.

Katherine took my turn in stride. I imagine she'd seen some flip-flopping politicians in her day. "Well, for starters, you can stop paying BrainCo."

"Done. But what can I do for the zombies that work at my shop? I can't stand the thought of them being enslaved like that."

"Can you buy them free?"

I wanted to say *If I could buy them, I would have bought them a long time ago and we wouldn't be having this conversation.* Instead I said, "I have a buyout clause in my lease, but I can't afford to swing that." I lifted my hands helplessly. "Unless you like Fadai $150,000 worth? Freeing the oppressed could make a great ad!"

Katherine grimaced. "Let me talk to some people. We might have some cultural affairs funds in the city budget we can squeeze into this."

"Oh, this is a cultural affair alright," I said. "Zombie culture is the next big thing. It's going to make the neo-pagans look like community theatre."

Andrea glared at me, smoke leaking out of her hair.

MY ACCOUNT MANAGER at BrainCo was the only person I'd ever met in person that actually used pomade. You could smell the stuff the second you entered his office, and his slicked-back hair resembled a speed skater's helmet, only more aerodynamic. His snakeskin tie was slick too, but not in an aerodynamic way.

His name was Jeff. You knew this because he referred to himself in the third person, as in "Don't worry, Jeff is on your side," or "Jeff wants you to be happy with your undead purchase decision."

Today Jeff was a little negative.

"Thanks for paying up your account, but Jeff can't let you exercise your buyout clause."

"Why not?" I asked, waving a ridiculous wad of cash under

Jeff's nose. Jeff was clearly not used to turning down money. I think those were tears in the corner of his eyes.

"Jeff wonders if you would be interested in some house zombies? They make great trash disposals."

Katherine had come up with the cash, in part donated by one of her campaign supporters and in part covered by the cultural affairs budget. The zombies were going to have to do a dance routine symbolizing freedom when this was all done. I was thinking a "Thriller" cover.

Andrea had declared the entire procedure some type of scam and stomped off. She wasn't as good at dramatic exits as entrances. But here I was trying to buy out my zombies, and BrainCo was having nothing to do with it.

"Why won't you take my money for the buyout?" I repeated. I counted the money in front of him one more time.

"Jeff wishes he could tell you."

I set a grand down on the desk. "Can Jeff tell me for this?"

I'm sure a bribe wasn't an approved use of the city's cultural budget, but Katherine had made the mistake of giving the money to me because town legal said they couldn't execute the buyout clause of my lease directly themselves. That meant I had some flexibility. If I had to, I'd do the "Thriller" cover myself.

Jeff picked up the wad and counted it. He looked like he wanted more, but I put the rest of the funds back in my knapsack.

"Jeff was told that the pixies pushed for the repossession. You were only a couple of months behind—BrainCo would have let it slide a little further to maximize the late fees. But pixies bought your zombies— BrainCo didn't want to sell, but it was an offer they couldn't refuse. The zombies are excavating for the new syndicate headquarters under the bridge."

The Pixie Syndicate. They must be pissed I underbid them for the bus contract. Now they were playing dirty.

They weren't the only ones in this town that could play dirty.

Game on.

THE UNDEAD ABOLITIONISTS were easily swayed when I presented them with a plan of action. They were tired of the city hall scene; I think it was the perpetual smell of the hot dog vendor next to their protest site.

"Free zombies!" they chanted as we marched on Pixie Bridge.

I chatted with Lisa, the cute abolitionist in the orange sundress. She reminded me a little of Andrea, sans the hellfire and brimstone.

"Will you pay a living wage?" she asked, after I explained my plan to offer employment to the free undead.

"Oh, I'll pay an undead wage. I think they'll be happy with that, especially the brain bonus. I've got a great recipe for grey matter au gratin."

Lisa smiled, but it was an unsure smile. I think she hadn't thought through the whole zombie diet thing.

A crowd drifted along with the procession, growing block by block. By the time we reached the excavation site, we had a couple of hundred sympathizers, oglers, and hecklers, although they were surprisingly hard to tell apart.

A pixie, if you've never met one, is about the size of a pencil eraser. They are easily overlooked individually, but what they lacked in physical mass they made up in magical heft. One was trouble enough, but when dozens of the most powerful ones had swarmed together to form the Pixie Syndicate, they'd taken trouble to a new level.

That trouble had fermented into a diversified portfolio of drugs, protection rackets, and contractor fraud, and now the Pixie Syndicate was using their ill-gotten gains to build a gleaming new headquarters under their namesake bridge.

At this stage of construction, the building was a hole in

the ground; a hole filled with zombies pawing in the mud with their bare hands. Poor guys.

A construction trailer sat at the edge of the work pit. The protestors and assorted hangers-on surrounded the trailer. Lisa started the singers on a rousing rendition of "We Shall Overcome."

The trailer door opened. A pixie swarm flowed out and reconstituted in the shape of an angry old man. "Quiet! We've got a meeting in progress!"

The singers continued, "We are not afraid!"

"Well, you should be!" stamped the swarm. "I've half a mind to melt all of you like peeps in a microwave!"

"The truth shall set them free!" sang the crowd. Lisa waved an *End Zombie Slavery Today* sign in front of the swarm.

"Who's in charge here?" said the swarm.

Lisa looked at me. I suppose I had gotten folks into this. I stepped forward.

"We believe you are unfairly oppressing the undead."

"We oppress everyone. There's nothing unfair about it," said the swarm. The crisp edges of the swarm blurred momentarily as its members laughed at their own joke.

"Set my zombies free," I said. Hopefully my plagiarism was fair use.

"No." The swarm turned to go back into the trailer.

"Yes," I said. "Or we're not going anywhere."

Lisa started the singers on "If I Had a Hammer." They were amazingly off-key. The dissonance sent shivers up my spine.

The swarm froze, then turned back to the crowd. "Ok, ok. The syndicate has a traditional method for resolving problems like this. We'll pick a champion, you'll pick a champion, they'll have a duel. If we win, the rest of you go home."

"And if we win, you set the zombies free?" I said.

"Yeah, yeah, whatever." The swarm blurred again. "Who's your sacrifice?"

I scanned the crowd, looking for the meanest, most

magically powerful, abolitionist. There wasn't a whole lot to choose from.

Then I saw Lisa was looking at me with adoring puppy eyes. Damn it.

I raised my hand. "I'll represent the abolitionists. I'm going into the trailer. Send your best pixie in after me."

Lisa gave me a kiss, while the crowd sang, "You'll never walk alone."

I walked alone anyways.

The trailer was small, hot, and stuffy. A single desk and chair sat at one end, a couple of shovels leaned against the other wall. Not much to work with. I grabbed one of the shovels and crouched behind the desk.

How had I gotten myself into this, again? Oh, yeah, Lisa's kiss. A very fine smooch—hopefully, not our last.

Assuming I didn't die in the next five minutes.

The door opened, then shut. The light flickered, and a small bolt of lightning flashed across the room at my feet, making me jump. I lunged across the trailer, swinging my shovel at the source of the lightning.

I hit nothing.

This was going to be difficult. I backed up against the desk, then caught a flicker of movement out of the corner of my eye; I swung my shovel again. Nothing.

My shovel turned into taffy. Grape taffy. It drooped to the ground in the warmth of the trailer.

The pixie was playing with me.

I was never going to catch it. I couldn't even see it. Even if I glimpsed it, hand-eye coordination wasn't my strong point—I'd once spent three hours trying to catch a fly in my kitchen, and failed to even wing it.

A fly. That was the answer.

I hit speed-dial number one on my cell phone. "Andrea, I'm sorry you got so irrationally mad at me. Let's make up."

My phone glowed, and my perspective shifted—the room

grew, and my field of vision wrapped practically behind me. My legs felt thick and powerful, my tongue long and sticky.

Being a frog was kinda neat.

A tiny pixie hovered in the corner, etching into the air what looked to be runes of total annihilation.

I jumped, flicking my tongue across the room.

He was tasty.

THE ZOMBIES CAME HOME with me. In exchange for Andrea unfrogging me, I returned most of the cash to her mom, but decided the possibility of a zombie dance troupe was a real opportunity. I replaced the Teletubbies DVD with Michael Jackson and asked Hank to work up some choreography. I think it will come together nicely.

Lisa and I had a date. We went bowling, and it went pretty well. Turns out she is a fortuneteller and already knows where our relationship is going.

And she's ok with that.

MOON LANDING

LAVIE TIDHAR

1

Neil and Buzz are in the lunar module, heading down. The Eagle smells of farts and sweat and metal and oil. Mostly, it smells of each other. Neil and Buzz are tossing a coin. Buzz says, "Heads," and watches the coin tumbling through the canned air of the Eagle until Neil slams it on his wrist. Neil raises his hand, carefully, so the coin won't float away.

"Tails," he says, with quiet satisfaction.

THE EAGLE TOUCHES the lifeless surface of the moon. Neil is the first to step out. His feet touch the lunar surface and he takes his first steps on the alien soil. "That's one small step for man," he says, as Buzz watches from within the Eagle and millions of viewers watch back on Earth, "one giant leap for mankind."

Moments later Buzz follows him to the surface of the moon.

2

Neil and Buzz are in the lunar module, tossing a coin. If Buzz were religious, which he's not, he would have said that, at the exact moment the coin goes tumbling through the canned air, he felt a tremor.

He watches Neil, but if Neil had felt it he says nothing. Still, Buzz is feeling a little odd. As if space-time had suddenly curved around them, and tiny, quantum fluctuations went this way and that, making tiny changes . . .

"Heads," he calls. Neil raises his hand, carefully, and for a brief second a look of disappointment and disbelief flashes across his face.

"Heads," he says, and his voice is flat.

THE EAGLE TOUCHES the lifeless surface of the moon. Buzz is the first to step out. His feet touch the lunar surface and he whoops and jumps high into the air, tumbling like a coin, and lands again. "I never thought we'd make it this far," he says, to Neil back in the Eagle, to the millions of viewers back on Earth. He takes a deep breath and looks around, at the moon and up, at the rising Earth, a tiny blue-white marble in the distance.

"It's beautiful," he says.

3

Neil and Buzz are in the lunar module. "Did you feel that?" Neil says.

"Feel what?" Buzz says.

"Nothing," Neil says.

They toss a coin. "Heads," Buzz says. But the coin comes down tails.

"Let's toss again," Neil says.

"What for?" Buzz says.

"Something else," Neil says.

They toss the coin. It comes up tails again.

The Eagle touches the lifeless surface of the moon. Neil is the first to step out. His feet touch the lunar surface and he takes his first steps on the alien soil. "Good luck, Mr. Gorsky!" Neil says.

Buzz shakes his head.

Mission Control: "What was that?"

Neil: "Nothin'. One small step for man . . . "

BACK ON EARTH, Mr. Gorsky turns to his wife. They are sitting in the living-room on the old couch, watching the lunar landing on TV. "Remember when you said the only way you'd give me a blowjob is if the boy next door walked on the moon?" he says.

"Fair's fair," Mrs. Gorsky says, moving closer.

4

Neil and Buzz are in the lunar module, tossing a coin.

"I definitely felt *something*," Buzz says. Neil just shrugs.

NEIL AND BUZZ STAND on the surface of the moon. It's green.

Their feet sink into the lunar surface.

"It looks like cheese," Neil says, dubiously.

Mission Control: "What was that?"

Neil: "Nothin'."

Buzz takes off his helmet. He peels off his glove. He dips a finger into the lunar surface and it comes up with a globule of green goo. Buzz puts it in his mouth, tastes it, finally swallows.

"Tastes all right," he says.

5

Neil and Buzz are in the lunar module, tossing a coin.

"I have the strangest feeling . . . " Buzz says.

NEIL AND BUZZ STAND on the surface of the moon.

"Houston," Neil says, "we have a problem."

Thousands of insectoid creatures surround Buzz and Neil.

"They're selenites," Buzz says.

"What's that?" Neil says.

"Moon creatures," Buzz says. "After the goddess of the moon, Selene."

"They look just like ants, if you ask me," Neil says.

The selenites watch the two astronauts.

"What shall we do?" Buzz says.

"Let's squash them," Neil says.

NEIL AND BUZZ ARE JUMPING around on the lunar surface. Every time they land they crash a selenite. When they do, the selenite explodes. Neil and Buzz are jumping all over the surface of the moon. There are a lot of selenites.

6

Neil and Buzz are in the lunar module, tossing a coin.

"I don't like this," Neil says.

"What?" Buzz says.

Neil has a strange look in his eye. Buzz thinks it makes him look constipated.

"I don't know," Neil says. "But I don't like it."

NEIL AND BUZZ STAND on the surface of the moon.

"Is that a moth?" Buzz says.

They turn and look at the giant moth. It comes gliding over the moon's surface.

"It's a lunar moth," Neil says.

There are a lot of plants on the lunar surface. Neil and Buzz take off their helmets. The voices of Mission Control remain inside the helmets. Their voices are tinny. Neil and Buzz drop the helmets on the ground.

"Welcome to the moon," the plants say.

"Hey, look," Buzz says. "Talking plants."

"Well, how do you like that," Neil says.

The giant moth is resting on the ground ahead of them.

"Maybe we could get a ride back to Earth on it," Buzz says.

"Race you!" Neil says.

NEIL AND BUZZ RUN across the surface of the moon, laughing.

7

Neil and Buzz are in the lunar module, tossing a coin.

"I'm sure I felt something," Buzz says uneasily.

"It's the beans you've been eating," Neil says.

"Heads," Buzz says. They watch the coin tumble through the air.

"Neil?"

"Yes, Buzz?"

"Whose face is that on the coin?"

"It looks like . . . " Neil hesitates. "That's strange," he says.

NEIL AND BUZZ STAND on the surface of the moon.

"Houston? We have a problem . . . "

"Ja," a new voice says. The new voice has patched into their comm. units. The new voice comes from the leader of the men facing the Eagle. There are a dozen of them. They all wear spacesuits. They are all armed. On each suit there is a patch, and on the patch is a swastika.

"Ja,'" the voice says. It has a German accent. "You have a problem."

The German raises his hand in a salute. "Heil Hitler!" he says.

"That's who it was on the coin!" Neil says.

"Fire!"

NEIL AND BUZZ ARE LYING on the surface of the moon. They aren't moving.

"Damn Nazis," Buzz says, with what's left of his air. One of his lungs is punctured.

8

Neil and Buzz are in the lunar module, tossing a coin.
"It looks kind of Chinesy," Buzz says. They watch the coin.

"HOUSTON? HOUSTON, wǒmen yǒu yīgè wèntí," Neil says.
There's a big city on the moon, under a dome. There are banners in red with Hanzi characters. Neil and Buzz approach the domed city. They enter through an airlock and take off their helmets. There's some sort of a party going on, with a dragon dancing in the street and lots of firecrackers.
A short man with dark hair pushing a cart comes towards them. "Would you like a moon cake?" he says.
They each take one.
"Xièxiè!" Neil says.
"It tastes real good," Buzz says, politely.

9

Neil and Buzz are in the lunar module, tossing a coin.
"Did you see that?" Buzz says.
"See what?" Neil says.
"I thought I saw something flash past outside," Buzz says.
"Like what?" Neil says.
"I don't know," Buzz says. "It was nothing."

NEIL AND BUZZ STAND on the surface of the moon.
"There it goes again!" Buzz says.
"Looks like a flying saucer," Neil says.
"Yeah. I didn't want to say anything before," Buzz says.
"There's another one!"
"Houston—oh, forget it," Neil says.
The sky above the moon is filled with flying saucers. More saucers rise up from the surface of the moon.

"There's a whole fleet of them," Buzz says.

They watch the flying saucers.

"They look like they're heading for Earth," Neil says.

"Well, there's something you don't see every day," Buzz says.

10

"Did you feel that?" Buzz says.

"No," Neil says.

"Me neither," Buzz says. They toss a coin. "Heads," Buzz says.

Neil shakes his head. "Wrong again," he says.

THE LAST DRAGON SLAYER

CHUCK ROTHMAN

"**I**t looks like the king's dropping by," said Runge.

Hal didn't look up from the boot he was stitching. It was just like the old man. Runge was just short of mad, always talking about some ridiculous project or other. Hal had learned to ignore half of what he said. The king didn't visit a cobbler's shop.

So when the herald played the fanfare in the doorway to the shop, Hal was so startled he jabbed his thumb with the needle.

King Grimwood IV, wearing gold and jewels and a ratty ermine collar, stood in the doorway of the shop. "We need a dragon slayer," he said.

Hal sucked his sore thumb. "A dragon slayer? There aren't any dragons."

"Of course there are," said King Grimwood. "Don't you

listen to the town crier? Our kingdom is infested with dragons—well, with one anyway—and we need a dragon slayer."

Hal stood up, holding up his work. "You see this? This is a boot." He gestured. "That is a cobbler's bench." He pointed at the walls. "Those are shoes. Most people might get the impression I was a cobbler."

Grimwood looked distressed. "Isn't this the home of the Dragon Slayers Guild?"

"No," said Hal. "And—"

Runge cleared his throat. "Well, strictly speaking, it is."

Hal stared. "What?"

"Well, not *just* dragon slayers. A lot of the old guilds had trouble getting members. We had to merge. Then people kept getting behind in their dues and . . . well, I'm the only one left. I opened the cobbler's shop until things picked up."

"So this *is* the Dragon Slayers' Guild?" the king asked.

"Well, technically, it the Guild of Thieves, Assassins, Dragon Slayers, Greengrocers, and . . . " He pointed to a square wooden box in the corner, large enough to fit a small duck. "Computer Repairmen," he added significantly.

"What's a computer?" the king asked.

"I have no idea," said Runge. "But a seer told me they were the wave of the future, so I figured it wouldn't hurt to start early." He pointed at the box. "I do wish the seer had been more specific. I first thought that a computer had something to do with counting, you see. The problem was, all I could do was make a machine to count ones and zeros, and what good is that?"

The king turned to Hal. "You will come to our castle and rid us of this dragon."

"Me? Why not him?"

"Then I realized it didn't matter," said Runge. "All I had to do was invent something, call it a computer, and my fortune was made."

"Do you really have to ask?" said the king.

"All right," said Hal. He long ago learned not to argue with a madman. "Suppose I agree to slay this dragon. What do I get out of it?"

"You will be amply rewarded," said Grimwood. "With the hand of our son in marriage."

"Don't you mean your daughter?"

"We don't have a daughter."

"Doesn't sound like much of a reward to me."

"You'll also get half the dragon's treasure."

Hal knew the most important part of having a treasure was staying alive to spend it. "What if I refuse?"

"It is important that you perform your civic duty."

"In other words, I get beheaded."

The king nodded. "With an especially dull axe." He headed for the door. "Now, off to the castle."

"Why don't you go on ahead?" Hal said, thinking of where he had put his bags. "I'll meet you there tomorrow."

The king stopped briefly. "Very well," he said. "Of course, we will be leaving several of our soldiers surrounding the house. If they catch you sneaking away, the only difference between you and a pig on a spit is that you won't have an apple in your mouth."

"Oh, I have an apple," said Runge.

"We trust you understand," said the king.

"Perfectly," said Hal. "You've hired yourself a dragon slayer."

"HERE IS IT," said Runge with an air of reverence. "The armory of the Dragon Slayer's Guild."

The armory was what most people would call an attic, home to bats and spiders and little else. As for the weapons . . .

"Why do they all look singed?" Hal asked.

"Not all of them. Most of the metal ones are melted. Now, this," said Runge, holding up a crossbow, "is the Arbalest of Doom. It can shoot a bolt three hundred paces into dragon scales five inches thick."

Hal tried to lift it, but it weighed as much as a small cow. "Why is it called the Arbalest of Doom?"

"Turns out, a dragon's scales are *nine* inches thick. Ethelred the Unlucky was *very* surprised to find that out."

"Oh, I bet," Hal said. "Have any of these weapons ever killed a dragon?"

Runge gestured toward one side of the attic. "Here is the wall of swords."

"Wall of swords? I see only one."

"I sold the others. Cobbling isn't the most lucrative of trades."

At least the sword looks impressive, Hal thought. It was encrusted with rubies and emeralds and an occasional diamond to keep them company, the appearance only marred by an equally thick encrustation of bat guano.

"But this is all you'll really need," said Runge. He held one of his wooden boxes. It was fitted with two straps.

"One of those computer things of yours?" Hal asked.

Runge ran behind Hal and strapped the thing to his back. "It will come in handy."

"Handy? How?"

"To kill the dragon, of course. Once people learn it can do that, our fortune is made."

"*Can* it kill dragons?"

"It's foolproof."

"As foolproof as the Arbalest of Doom?"

"Exactly," said Runge.

"THAT'S WHERE THE DRAGON has its lair," said Prince Edwin, pointing helpfully to a large cave surrounded by scorched earth and a few toasted corpses of the king's guards. A dozen "Beware of Dragon" signs were posted around the cave.

"I never would have guessed," Hal said.

"Oh, it is," said Prince Edwin. "Unless we took a wrong turn somewhere."

"All right, Dragon Slayer!" the King shouted. He stood at the far back of the group of knights and guards, with plenty of expendable bodies between himself and any danger. "Now you must fight the beast if you're going to have our son's hand."

Edwin looked shocked. "You're going to cut off my hand?"

Hal sighed. "He means I'm going to marry you."

The prince's relief was palpable. "Oh. That's not nearly as bad."

"Edwin, you don't want to marry me, do you?"

"Oh, no. I'd prefer a beautiful princess, but I never expected to have any say in who I'd marry. It's all politics. You're not too ugly, at least."

"Hurry it up!" the king shouted.

Hal drew his sword from his scabbard. Once it was cleaned up, it looked mighty impressive. However, it also weighed a ton, and was about as sharp as Prince Edwin. At least the computer on his back was light enough to ignore.

"Go ahead," said Prince Edwin. "I'll be waiting for you." He handed Hal a handkerchief. "I think this is supposed to inspire you," he said.

"A clean one would inspire me more," said Hal.

"Get moving!" the king shouted.

Hal walked forward slowly; the last moments of your life were not something you needed to rush. "Here, dragon," he called. "Here, dragon, dragon."

Slowly, the dragon poked his head out of the cave.

It was as big as a castle, but moved with a catlike grace. Its yellowed teeth were bared in a fierce grin and its dark green scales glistened in the sunlight.

"Hello," Hal said.

The dragon regarded him warily.

Hal really only had one course of action: he would have to reason with the beast. "I mean you no harm. And I have a proposition for you."

The dragon paused, watching him.

"I'm certain we can work something out," said Hal, stepping forward and hoping for the best.

IF YOU IGNORED THE STENCH, the hot moisture, the murky light, and the digestive juices eating away at your boots, Hal decided, the inside of a dragon was merely horrible.

"Well, well," came a voice like a ratchet. "Looks like someone got a little too close."

Hal peered into the darkness. Except for lumps of things he'd rather not think about, he could see no one.

"You're damn lucky dragons don't chew their food."

"So are you," Hal said. He managed to locate the direction of the voice, but nothing more.

"I'm a lot smaller."

Then Hal spotted a movement. It *was* a lot smaller.

"Well," said the toad. "Aren't you going to introduce yourself?"

"I'm Hal. I'm a dragon slayer."

"Not a very good one, are you?"

There was no disputing that. "Are you an enchanted toad?"

"Exactly how many talking toads do you know?"

"None," Hal admitted.

"That's one clue."

"Can you tell me the way out of here?"

"Oh, sure," said the toad. "But I'm not in here because I like the view. If I help you out, I get something in return. You have to grant me one wish."

"Grant a wish? That's a wizard's job. What do you think I am?"

"Dragon food."

Hal sighed. "All right. I'll grant you your wish—if I can. Now, how do we get out?"

"Haven't a clue."

"You said you know a way."

"Sure. But I didn't say it was a *good* way. I don't think you're going to want to come out as dragon dung."

A cry came from further into the creature's gullet. "Help!"

"How many people are inside this dragon?" Hal asked.

"All that got in range."

"Help me!" It was a woman's voice.

"It sounds like someone's in distress."

"Someone in distress? In here? Who'd imagine *that*?"

"God damn it," screeched the woman. "Get over here!"

Hal couldn't ignore the cry. "Coming!" he shouted, making his way around a bend in the dragon.

He spotted her. Even in the dim light, he knew this was the most beautiful woman he'd ever seen. Her long blonde hair framed the face of an angel. Her eyes were the exact shade of blue a robin's egg is at sunset, her nose perfection itself. Hal was in love the instant he saw her.

"Where the hell have you been, you half-wit?" she said. "Get me *out* of here!"

Snapping out of it, Hal realized her arms and legs were bound. "Certainly," he said, jumping into action.

"Well, it's about time," she said as he freed her. "Do you know how *long* I've been waiting for you?"

"How long?"

"How the hell should I know? You think I can tell time down here?"

"No. No, of course not, Milady." Hal bowed. "I am Hal ... " His name suddenly seemed much too plain. He needed a nickname. "Hal the Merciless!"

The toad giggled.

She gave him an icy stare. "Are you a prince?"

"I'm a dragon slayer."

"Not a prince." She sighed. "I never have any luck at all, do I?"

"I want to rescue you, Milady."

She shook her head. "My sister Eileen got rescued by a

prince. My cousin Joan got rescued by a prince. At least, he said he was, and once she tracks him down she's gonna make damn sure the baby gets a piece of his throne. So if you're not a prince, I've wasted my time in here. Do you know what trouble it was to arrange to be tied?"

"You *wanted* to be eaten?" Hal asked.

"Well, no. But a girl's got to do *something* to find a prince these days. My aunt got herself locked in a tower and had to have him climb up her *hair* for God's sake. So, after all this trouble, if you're *not* a prince . . . . "

Hal thought for a very brief moment. "I *am* a prince, Milady."

The woman brightened at once. "Really?"

"Really."

"I'm *so* happy to make your acquaintance," she said in a voice like fresh honey. "I'm the Lady Catherine."

Hal stared into her deep blue eyes. "Pleased to meet you." He could deal with his imposture later.

"Excuse me," the toad said. "I know the course of true love never runs smooth, especially in a dragon's gut, but aren't you forgetting something important?"

The words broke the spell that held Hal enthralled. "What? Oh, right. How do we get out?"

The toad gave him a bug-eyed stare. "Who's the dragon killer around here? What we need now is a plan."

Hal nodded.

"A good plan," said Lady Catherine.

Hal nodded. Then he realized they were both looking at him expectantly. "Oh. A plan. Right."

"You *do* have a plan?" asked the toad.

"Of course, I have a plan. I'm a dragon slayer."

"No plan," sighed the toad. "Looks like it's up to me. Catherine, Hal—let's go."

"So *you* have a plan?" Hal asked.

"No," said the toad. "But *I'm* prepared to wing it. Come on."

"The way I figure it," the toad said as they made their way up the dragon's gullet, "the heart should be somewhere near here. You can't get at it from the outside because of the scales. They're at least nine inches thick."

"So I heard," said Hal.

"But in here," the toad went on, "there's no armor."

The path was becoming steeper and more slippery, and the footing unsure. It was like walking on greased pillows.

"Is it getting hot in here?" asked Catherine.

"Of course not," said the toad, disdainfully. "A dragon's an overgrown lizard: cold blooded."

"It's definitely getting warmer," said Catherine.

The toad gave a scornful look. "Who's the expert?"

"On dragons?" asked Hal, trying to keep his footing.

"On cold-bloodedness."

"It *is* getting warm in here," Hal said.

"Ridiculous. We should be near the heart soon," said the toad. "We—" He stopped.

"What is it?" asked Hal.

"Nothing. Nothing. Just a slight miscalculation." A yellow-ish glow illuminated their path, showing a giant cavity. Hal scrambled upward and peered inside.

"What is it?" asked Catherine.

"Oh, nothing," said Hal. "Just your average, ordinary *pit of flames.*"

The toad was looking away, pretending the last words were directed at someone not currently present.

"I *told* you it was getting warmer," said Catherine. "Didn't I say it was getting warmer? I'm not one to say 'I told you so,' but—"

"Well, *of course* it was getting hotter," said the toad. "This is a *fire-breathing* dragon. Stands to reason the fire comes from somewhere."

"But you said—"

"It's all very simple," said the toad. "We jump."

Hal looked at the entrance to the pit. "Jump?

"Sure, it's not too bad. Watch." He reached the edge of the pit and hopped, landing neatly on the other side. "See?" he said. "Now come on. The heart should be near here. I'm sure of it."

"Just like you were sure the dragon was cold-blooded," said Hal. He looked at the opening. Only a yard or three; he should be able to make it.

Taking a deep breath, he leapt over the opening.

It turned out to be easier than he thought. He sailed over the flames and, with a sigh of relief, landed on the other side.

Then he slipped.

His feet went out from under him on the slimy footing and he fell heavily on his stomach. His feet dangled over the pit.

And he was sliding backwards.

"Help me!" he said.

The toad looked nervous. "What do you expect me to do?"

Hal scrambled to get a hold, but his waist was now even with the edge of the pit. "I can't hold on!"

"Lighten your load," said the toad.

"How?"

"Well, you can drop that thing on your back, for starters."

"On my back?" Hal had completely forgotten about the computer. He loosened the straps and let it drop into the pit.

"There," said the toad. "That should—"

He was interrupted by a loud "boom" from beneath them, and Hal felt himself being shoved upward.

When he landed, nearly crushing the toad, all hell broke loose. The dragon shook around them. "What—?"

"Beats me," said the toad.

The shaking became worse, then ceased abruptly. They were falling, the footing dropping beneath them. Then, they hit the dragon's throat again, hard.

"That's strange," said the toad.

"You have a real gift for understatement," Hal muttered.

"It shouldn't be flat like this. Not unless the dragon's head was lying on the ground." He brightened. "You must have killed him!"

"What? How?"

"Wait just a moment," said the toad. He paused, then nodded. "He's not moving. He's dead!" He looked at Hal. "Congratulations!"

"That's typical," Catherine said. "No consideration. Isn't anyone going to rescue me?"

THEY WALKED INTO THE SUNLIGHT through the dragon's jaws, the only sign of their ordeal the awful stench that hung around them. As his eyes adjusted, Hal could spot the king, and Edwin, and even Runge, standing and cheering for them.

"You didn't tell me there'd be people here," said the princess. "I look a mess."

"You just came out of a dragon," Hal said.

"All the more reason. Someone's going to want to paint this scene some day and the last thing I want is to have my hair look like a rat's nest."

"Congratulations, our boy," said the king, looking pleased.

"Want a kiss?" asked Edwin with little enthusiasm.

"Look," said Hal. "If it's all the same to you, I'll just take my half of the dragon's treasure."

"What?" asked Edwin. "I thought you were going to marry me."

The princess looked at Hal. "Marry him?"

"It's a misunderstanding," said Hal.

"I should say it is," said Catherine. "You're going to marry me! I'm not letting a prince slip through my fingers."

"Well, I would prefer—"

"You promised to marry *me*," said Edwin. "Are you going back on your word?"

"I never gave—"

"You never told me you had a fiancé," said Catherine. "You're going to have to treat me better than this once we are married."

"Me, too," said Edwin.

Hal looked from Edwin to Catherine and back again. Even in her anger, she was still the most beautiful woman he'd ever seen.

"Well?" asked Catherine.

"Well?" asked Edwin.

There was only one way out. "I'm not a prince," Hal mumbled.

"*What?*"

"I'm not a prince." He pointed at Edwin. "He is."

Catherine swiveled to Edwin. "Hello," she said in a voice that was pure music. "You wouldn't mind helping me just a little."

Edwin pointed at Hal. "He's still supposed to marry me. Or they'll cut off my hand or something."

Catherine put her arm in Edwin's. "Oh, don't worry about him," she said, leading him off. "All he did was save my life, but *we* have lots to talk about. A June wedding's nicest, don't you think?"

Hal sighed as he watched them leave. He looked at King Grimwood. "When do I get my treasure?" he asked, wearily.

"As soon we calculate all the taxes," said the king.

"Taxes?"

"Yes. Income tax, gift tax, dragon slaying tax . . ."

"You can't have a tax on dragon slaying!"

The king smiled. "No, of course not. Whatever were we thinking? We meant dragon slaying *fee*. Not to mention the cost of disposing of the carcass. Then there's the—"

"I'm not getting anything, am I?"

The king patted his head. "Our treasurer will let you know what you owe us." He turned and went to join his son and his new fiancée.

Hal sighed. "And *we're* supposed to be the Thieves' Guild."

"That Thieves' Guild thing wasn't exactly a roaring success," Runge said. "If something was stolen, everyone knew where to look for it." He brightened. "But my computer worked, didn't it?"

"Almost too well," said Hal.

"Well, the big secret was what was inside the box. You see, it's a mixture of coal, and brimstone, and saltpeter and when it gets hot, see, it bursts into a very big flame. Loud noise, too. Plus it destroys anything around it." He slapped Hal on the shoulder. "Hal, we've made our fortune."

"Wait just a minute, buddy," came a hoarse little voice. "We had an agreement. You grant my wish."

Sighing, Hal looked at the toad. "I told you, I can't—"

"How do you know if you don't know what it is?"

Trapped again. "What is it?"

"Kiss me."

"What? Why?"

"I'm a pervert. Humor me. I won't use my tongue."

Hal knew it was another losing battle. He bent to pick up the toad.

"Don't worry," the toad said as he puckered. "You know the old saying: 'kiss a toad and nothing worse will happen to you all day'."

"Want to bet on that?" asked Hal, but he planted a small kiss on the toad's mouth.

There was a flash of light and the toad was gone.

In its place was a woman. Compared to Catherine, she wasn't beautiful. But she was pleasant enough to look at, especially since she was standing there stark, raving nude.

"You . . . you're—"

"Miranda," she said. "I don't blame you for being confused. It's hard to tell the sex of a toad. Could I borrow your cloak?"

Hal handed it to her at once. "Are you a princess?" he asked warily.

"God, no. I'm only a barmaid. A word of advice: wizards may be lousy tippers, but it's not a good idea to complain about it too loudly." She put on his cloak. "I hope that doesn't disappoint you."

"I'll take what I can get," Hal murmured.

"So will I," said Miranda. She kissed him warmly on the lips. Hal found it a very pleasant reward. "That's good. I guess we're in love."

"What do you mean?"

"I've been eating flies for three years and you didn't complain about my breath. If that isn't a sign of true love, I don't know what is.

Hal decided that, just possibly, Miranda was right.

"But if we're going to keep seeing each other," Miranda went on, "I'll have to insist on one thing."

"What's that?"

"No more dragon slaying."

"You have my word," said Hal.

THE VENUS OF WILLENDORF

DEBORAH WALKER

Her oolitic thighs rubbing together, shedding tiny flakes of stone onto the pavement, Jane made her slow progression along Tottenham Court Road. As she walked, cars slid to a halt, and men leapt out of the abandoned vehicles to join the throng that followed her. When she reached her destination, Jane raised her tiny hand. "Wait outside, my worshippers."

The line of men erupted into a cacophony of agreement. Each man shouted loudly, desperate to be heard above the crowd.

"Oh course, my love. You can count on me." Claude Shriven, the postman, was the first of Jane's followers. When she'd opened the door, he'd fallen to his knees. "First class," he'd whispered, his letters scattering like petals.

"I'll wait unto the end of time," shouted old Professor Ming, who'd managed to get to the front of the line by the merciless use of his mobility scooter. There was no foot that Ming wouldn't roll over to get into Jane's presence.

Further down the line Barry Travis asked his brother, "What did she say?"

"We've got to wait," said Tony. How could he get closer? He *needed* to get closer. There were too many men, all pressing against him. But Tony felt great within this sea of testosterone. He felt the urge to sing, a nascent song forming in his brain: "Um-PAH, Um-PAH, Um-PAH." He looked around, nodding frantically to his companions to take up the chant. He noticed that his wife had gone. It was probably for the best. She'd been following him, nagging him about something.

Barry, who'd always been a slow but deliberate thinker, shouted, "I will wait unto the end of time for you, Jane."

"Hey, you're just copying that bloke up front," complained a small bloke wearing only a towel.

"Shut it."

"Um-PAH, Um-PAH, Um-PAH. C'mon lads," urged Tony.

Slowly the crowd took up the chant.

At the front of the line, Jane said. "Don't touch the glass. Remember what happened in McDonalds?" Jeeze louise. She'd only nipped in for an After Eight McFlurry. Couldn't a goddess get a treat without there being major property damage?

Further down the line Barry asked, "What did she say?"

"She said . . . "

"First class!" shouted Claude, the postman, right in Jane's face.

Couldn't he think of anything else to say? Maybe she ought to mix up the line. The first should be last—yes that sounded right. But later . . . after shopping. Jane hadn't got a *thing* to wear. She just didn't feel right being naked, although the men didn't seem to mind.

THE GLASS DOORWAY SLID opened. Jane entered the Gap.

A women stood beside a stack of neatly folded denim.

When she saw Jane her eyes rolled back into her sockets, as the magic undertook the necessary cognitive adjustment. "Urk." she said.

Jane held a pair of jeans against her naked stomach. "I don't understand these American sizes," she said to the shop assistant, who'd recovered from the reality re-orientation. At least Jane could get some sense out of women. All she got out of men was praise. It was beginning to get on her nerves. Jane looked at the label on the jeans. "Fourteen-R, what's that? Is that a size twelve?"

"It's an English size ten, Miss."

"Well, what size am I?"

"I guess you're a size thirty-two," said the shop assistant, casting her professional eye over Jane.

"Do you have any size thirty-twos in a dark, boot-cut style?" Boot-cut style jeans were *so* flattering,

"No, sorry, Miss."

Jane sighed. No, of course they didn't. They just didn't think, did they? She was Venus, and she couldn't even get a pair of jeans to fit her.

Of course, she'd been thinking of the Botticelli Venus when she'd sat with Sue and recited the ancient incantation. The long, red hair, blowing in the wind; the pale, opalescent body rising out of the open clam shell. So, it was a surprise when she'd been transformed into a somewhat earlier incarnation.

Jane glanced at her reflection in the mirror, transfixed for a moment by the sight of her stone head layered with its fist-sized beads. She hadn't been expecting this. She wondered what Sue had been expecting.

Outside, her followers were making quite a racket. The men. Oh, the men. How many were following her now? She'd wanted to be worshipped, but not quite this much. Wasn't there a way in which she could switch it off, be a goddess for most of the time, but normal when she fancied a rest? She was beginning to think that being worshipped wasn't all that it was cracked up to be. Her worshippers were so, so . . . intense. It was embarrassing.

Still, a Venus is a Venus, and Jane *really* needed something to wear. Jane thanked the female shop assistant and went to find someone more suitable. She found a rather good-looking man, skinny, about her age, with dark eyes. He was just the type Jane would have gone for, before all this business. Daniel, his name tag announced. Jane watched as Daniel's eyes rolled back in his sockets—it was a shame, really.

"Pray tell me." Jane felt that this was a suitable form of speech for a goddess to address a worshipper. "Pray tell me, my man, where I might find suitable attire." Jane waved her tiny, limestone arms. "In this your store," she added for good measure.

Daniel gazed at her, drinking in the sight of her enormous stone breasts resting on a stomach that just kept on going. Her carved lusciousness overwhelmed him. The image of her, the vision of her naked folds of stone, speared straight into his soul, cutting though the civilised veneer, piercing the centre of his savagery. Daniel fell to his knees, mumbling ancient, pre-historic sounds. She was everything to him. She always was. Jane was his whole world.

Here we go again, thought Jane.

Daniel edged closer to grasp at Jane's red ochre tinted, stone legs. He raised his eyes. He dared to look. His eyes rested on the delicate triangle between her legs. He swam through history to find the words for her. "I will make a garment for you. I will clothe you in the softest denim. I will pull the fabrics of the world apart for you, my love." Daniel grabbed a pair of jeans from the racks and pulled at the seams. He tried and tried, the veins in his arms standing out in his effort. *Rather nice arms,* thought Jane. But alas, the cloth of Gap was too strong for his mortal hands. Daniel cast the jeans aside, moaning in despair. "I have failed you."

"Don't worry about it," said Jane. She'd decided to be a benevolent deity. "Evans is just down the street. They know how to dress a goddess."

"And I'll worship you," said Daniel. His mundane tasks were forgotten. Now he had found the real purpose of his life, to love and serve this Venus.

"Join the queue, then," said Jane, pointing to the men standing outside.

JANE BEGAN HER PONDEROUS walk, heading to Evans. She was pleased to see that Daniel had managed to get a place at the front. All around her, voices cried in exultation, "Um-PAH. Um-PAH. Um-PAH." They'd gotten a drum from somewhere. And was that a trumpet? Jane walked to a glorious fanfare.

Oh well, she thought. *Things could be worse. At least I'm human—sort of.*

There was more than one type of Venus. Now, Sue was *really* going to have problems getting a pair of jeans to fit. Jane stopped her stately progression to wave to her friend, looking up into the sky where Sue shone in her glorious desperation.

LOVE THY NEIGHBORS

KEN LIU

McComber: Welcome to *Live With McComber!*

[As McComber speaks, a video plays for the audience: a pair of giant pandas lumber through the predawn light on an American suburban street. Gingerly, they pry open trashcans on the curb and pick through the contents.]

My fellow patriots, you've no doubt noticed some extraordinary changes around us the last few years: strange animals doing strange things.

[The video shifts to a manatee lazily swimming through murky water. A motorboat approaches on the surface, but the manatee puts on a sudden burst of speed by twirling its flippers like a pair of propellers and dodges out of the way at the last minute. It then spits into the faces of the startled passengers. The camera lingers on the smiling manatee.]

I've told you before my suspicion that these changes were the result of a conspiracy between the climate-change industrial complex and the environmental movement special interest lobby.

[Now the video shows a family of penguins waddling amongst Canadian geese next to a pond on the Boston Common. Children toss bits of bread to the birds but scatter and scream as the penguins chase after them.]

But the truth, my friends, the truth has turned out to be even stranger. My guest today is the man behind the shadowy organization that claims responsibility for these strange events: say hello to Kasper Filip, Founder and Executive Director of WikiGenes!

[Filip, a tall and gangly man with pale freckled skin and floppy hair, strides across the studio floor awkwardly. He's too nervous to even look at the camera. But when he arrives at his seat, he seems to get a sudden burst of courage and stands up to give McComber an awkward, tight hug that lasts for several seconds.]

McComber: *[utterly flummoxed]* Okay, that was . . . sweaty. And I'll leave it at that.

Filip: Sorry. I just think we should . . . uh . . . love each other more . . . you know . . . as fellow life-sparks on this great . . . great planet.

McComber: You're a unique snowflake, aren't you? So, what is WikiGenes?

Filip: Uh . . . we are a . . . non-profit. Volunteers . . . um . . . collaborate . . . to save endangered species by, by, uh, modifying their genes—

McComber: I think you're a bunch of bio-terrorists! What in the world made you want to mess with animals?

Filip: I've always liked animals. Loved them, in fact. Just thinking about them calms me down. *[Grins goofily.]* Even back in college, in my tiny dorm room, I kept four cats, a pair of cockatoos, a saltwater aquarium, six rats, a sugar glider, two—

McComber: I pity your roommate.

Filip: One day, I was watching a nature show on TV with Caca—

McComber: Your girlfriend?

Filip: —my oldest cockatoo. The program said that with

global warming, penguins were in trouble. Warmer seas meant less ice and fewer fish and shrimp for them to eat. Many chicks went hungry and died.

I felt so bad that I wanted to stop eating fish and donate my share to the penguins.

McComber: You should have moved to Antarctica. Would have saved all of us a lot of trouble, like that spitting manatee that flipped my boat.

Filip: And then Caca said, "Here! Here!" And I fed her a grape and a piece of the dinner roll I took from the cafeteria. She always ate whatever I ate.

McComber: Now I pity this poor bird. No animal deserves that.

Filip: So, that got me thinking: Caca can eat all sorts of food, not just special fish found in the Antarctic. Why don't we modify the genes of the penguins so they can eat new foods and live in warmer places? That would save them.

I went online and asked for help. And that was the beginning of WikiGenes.

McComber: You're messing with nature. Playing God!

Filip: We've been doing that since forever!

Think about it. Species that have adapted to us thrive: the cockroach, the rat, the raccoon, the cat and dog, cattle and sheep, banana, wheat, rice, potato, corn. These are the most successful species ever. They live wherever we live.

McComber: And you mean that literally. Didn't your neighbors have you evicted because you kept—in their words, "a menagerie composed of skunks, raccoons, and rats"—in your apartment?

Filip: We were researching the adaptations that allowed them to live on our garbage. It was important work!

McComber: Yes, I'm sure the work smelled great, too.

Filip: Garbage eating is just one of many useful traits. Most species are endangered because they haven't figured out how to live with us. We want to help by giving them the traits needed to move into our spaces.

McComber: I understand you're not very popular among the environmentalists.

Filip: No, they probably hate us even more than you do.

McComber: That's about the only reason I've been civil to you so far.

Filip: We don't care much about their way of doing things. They just want to keep endangered species in dwindling parks and preserves, habitat islands like prisons. It's only a matter of time before they all go extinct.

McComber: And your alternative is better?

Filip: I want to give all species a chance to thrive in our man-made world!

Take pandas. Unmodified, they were doomed. Their bamboo groves are threatened by farmers needing more land—and the Chinese have a lot of mouths to feed. Pandas are also terrible breeders.

So we figured out how to make pandas that have a lot more sex and that are much less picky about what they can eat. Now they roam all over the world.

Just look at these pictures I brought of some baby pandas.

McComber: [*softening*] I have to say, I never cared much for these fur balls, but those pictures are cute. [*blustery again*] But were you working in cooperation with the EPA? Did you get funding from the UN?

Filip: No! Of course not! Had we revealed our true purpose before we completed our work, every government in the world would have wanted to shut us down. If you want to get anything done, you don't go to the government.

McComber: Amazingly, you and I agree on that point. People in this country have lost their frontier spirit, their gung-ho can-do. They think they need the government to take care of them, to approve every little thing—

Filip: Exactly, why do we need permission? Animals don't need to ask some government bureaucrat for permission to have sex and recombine their DNA. That's all we're doing: DNA recombination.

McComber: But there *are* some negative consequences to what you're doing, aren't there?

Filip: *Negative?* We're saving cuddly and cute creatures! Who doesn't like more pandas? Everyone loves pandas!

McComber: I think many of our callers feel differently. All right, you're on.

First Caller: Hi, this is Mary from Waterford, Connecticut. I *hate* your mutant penguins. There's a colony of them camped right outside my house, and they *smell*.

I've never seen such aggressive birds. My children can't play in our yard anymore because they get pecked. You people need to be put in prison.

Filip: Mary, I'm sorry you feel that way. Maybe instead of feeling so entitled to your yard, you can try to make friends with the penguins? Try learning their language. I can recommend some good tapes made by the WikiGenes Foundation.

Second Caller: Hi, this is Eric Schneider from Glendale, California. Let me tell you, watch these giant pandas dig through garbage for a few weeks, and they don't seem so cute any more. One of them has even started to steal the tomatoes from my wife's garden. And that constant mating, right in the street!

I can't wait till the governor declares panda hunting season.

McComber: Mr. Filip, you're responsible for the terror of our suburbs: the omnivorous, sex-maniac panda.

Filip: You're not looking at it the right way. Think about it, we used to have to go to a crowded zoo to see a panda, but now they live right next to us.

McComber: But they don't belong next to us!

Filip: Well, that seems awfully narrow-minded of you. Who really *belongs* here? Aren't we all immigrants?

McComber: Oh please! Just look at the number of panda sex tapes on YouTube. What kind of environment is this for a kid growing up in the suburbs when they can't even walk to school without seeing pandas humping?

Filip: I'm pretty sure the kids aren't the ones complaining.

McComber: Your speedy mutant manatees are attacking motorboats down in Florida—I have personally experienced this! And the amount of penguin poop that towns have to clean up is breaking their budgets. You can't just ignore these issues.

Filip: We're not. Ha! Heh, actually, we have a solution. Ha.

McComber: I do *not* like the way you just laughed.

Filip: An anonymous contributor came up with this idea, since I like animals so much and don't get bothered by these "new problems." If we can make everyone like me, then problem solved.

McComber: Oh, no, you don't—

Filip: Yup. We've isolated the features of my brain chemistry that make me especially delighted by living in close proximity with so many of our wonderful non-human fellow creatures. And we've engineered a cool virus that will deliver the same changes to everyone in the coming days. Everybody will share a bit of my unique snowflake, as you put it.

McComber: You goddamned hippie fruitcake—

Filip: You'll be among the first to enjoy the new attitude, Mr. McComber. Remember how you appreciated those baby panda pictures? When I gave you a hug, I also put a patch on your neck.

McComber: *[frantically rubbing the back of his neck as he stares at Filip, eyes bulging, lips moving, but nothing coming out]*

Filip: Remember, Spaceship Earth has many passengers, and only some of them are human. Isn't it better that all species now have the potential to live together?

McComber: Damn it, those manatees do look kind of cute. I'm feeling all sentimental and gooey . . .

Filip: Enjoy getting to know your neighbors!

THE ALCHEMIST'S CHILDREN

NATHANIEL LEE

uckily for everyone, except possibly Mom, Jen was home
when the call came in. Mom was at the lab, synthesizing a
new polymer. She'd left an annotated list of instructions for
caring for the house in her absence, and Jen was following it
to the letter.

The phone rang.

Jen consulted the list. *Let all calls go to the machine. I'll listen when I get home.*

The caller ID said it was from Newt, who was away at college. Freshman year.

After pondering for two more rings, Jen answered the
phone.

"You've got to help!" said Brandon, Newt's roommate.
When Jen had met him on Open House night, he'd had rum-
pled hair and smelled like three cans of body spray. "It's Newt!
He's gone crazy!"

"Crazy how?" Jen asked. "Be specific." That was one of Mom's favorite phrases.

"He's locked himself in his room with a bunch of bowls from the cafeteria and a Bunsen burner he stole from Chem Lab." Jen could hear Brandon running his hand through his hair. It sounded like it was even more rumpled than before. "He says he's going to isolate a particle of Truth."

"Ah," said Jen. "Alchemy."

Jen and Newt's father was an alchemist. He'd left when Jen was still a toddler. All she remembered of him was a loud booming voice and a vague impression of a beard up in the sky somewhere. He'd promised to write, Newt said.

"You've gotta come help," Brandon pleaded. "There's noises in there, and smells, and *fumes* coming under the door. Becky just came in looking cross-eyed and told me the date and time she's going to break up with me."

"My condolences," Jen said politely.

"We're not even dating!"

"Definitely alchemy," Jen muttered. She tucked the phone under her chin and bent over to rummage through the bottom-most junk drawer. If it was alchemy, that meant Dad was involved, but Jen didn't know where Dad was. Mom had to have kept his address somewhere, though. Mom saved everything, and she had an endearingly naive belief that locking a drawer would keep her children out of it. "Put Newt on, would you?"

"He won't answer the door. He just shouts at us to go away."

"Tell him that if Mom finds out he's meddling with the laws of causality, she's going to be *very angry*." Fishing in the forbidden drawer, Jen's hand paused over a bundle of envelopes held together with twine. Some of the ones at the back were yellowing with age. Jen hesitated, a spring wobbling loose somewhere inside her. The top letter was addressed to her, but the upper left corner, where the return address would go, was blank.

Whatever might be inside it, whatever her mother might

have known and might have kept from her, it wasn't going to help her now. She needed a location.

After some scuffling sounds, Brandon returned to the line. "He says he doesn't care. He said she can do what she wants and that he'll never forgive her for 'driving *him* away.' He said all her rules were stupid and she deserves it for what she did to the tortoise. You guys have a weird family."

"Yes," Jen said. At the bottom of the drawer, she found a black address book with the clasp rusted away. She flipped through it until she found, on the very last page, the name she needed:

> Albert Magnus Smith
> Beyond the Forest Perilous
> Atop Mount Dread
> At the Very Ends of the Earth
> Apt. 12
> NT, X0E 0V0

Jen pursed her lips. "Canada," she said.

"What?"

"Never mind. Tell Newt that Jen's going to bring someone to help him."

"Jenny's bringing help. Got it."

"No," Jen snapped. "Not Jenny. *Jen.* It's short for Hydrogen."

She hung up on Brandon's confusion. She knew where the spare keys to the Forester were. With any luck, she'd be back before Mom realized she was gone. With Mom's schedule and pragmatic priorities (as sole breadwinner, she said, her work had to come first), Jen probably had a week at least; they communicated almost exclusively through Post-It notes ever since Jen got her license. She packed some supplies, made herself some peanut butter sandwiches, and locked the door carefully behind her.

☺   ☺   ☺

IT HAD STARTED WHEN NEWT made the coffee table in the living room disappear. Mom had been furious.

"It's furniture *varnish*," she'd growled, shaking the can at him. "With an 'R'!"

Once he'd known that, of course, Newton was unable to make any other wooden furnishings invisible. That was how alchemy was: unpredictable and idiosyncratic. Idiopathic, Mom would have said. She hated the way the same formula could result in two different outcomes. According to Newt, who'd been older when Dad left, their father had tried to explain that everything was subjective, dependent on any of a thousand different whims, from the mood of the practitioner to the historical significance of a given symbol, but Mom would have none of it.

"You can only do it once," she'd snapped.

"Yes," he'd said. "That's the point."

She'd snorted and left Dad to fix the coffee table. He'd put a tablecloth over it for when company came, and otherwise they just got used to the sight of their drinks and television remotes seemingly floating in midair. Jen hadn't realized invisible tables were anything odd until she was four or five and Mom warned her not to blab about it while on a playdate at a friend's house.

Later, when the Diet Coke and Mentos videos went viral, Newt built a jetpack for himself. Mom had rolled her eyes and muttered something about force and gravity, but even she wasn't able to entirely hide a smile at Newt zipping through the air above the backyard, turning somersaults and making acrobatic spirals, a wide grin plastered across his sticky, sugar-coated face. He bottled bee's knees and the cat's meow—he'd had to give that back after a stern lecture from Dad—and built a robot out of Legos that worked so well it went feral and attempted to overthrow humanity. It wasn't very good at overthrowing, but every so often, they came downstairs to find the magnetic letters on the refrigerator spelling out "KILL ALL HUM4NS." It was when Newt reconstituted the dehydrated pixies from his Pixy Sticks that the other shoe dropped.

Newt was the focus of the conflict, but in some ways, Jen had it worse. She never knew what she'd missed and had to rely on the fragmentary and hopelessly slanted perspectives of the two remaining witnesses. Newt blamed himself, but maybe it had been inevitable. Maybe there'd never been any way for things to blow but up. In the fallout, Dad was gone, Newton was broken, and Mom had become a far-off, glittering iceberg. The reaction was complete, and all the reagents were reduced to inert mush and powder.

THE FIRST PART OF THE JOURNEY was uneventful, a series of gas stations, fast food restaurants, and the treacherous hypnosis of flickering white lines on asphalt.

Gradually, the interstate became a highway, which passed the border almost seamlessly. The highway became a road, then the road dwindled to two lanes, then one, then a gravel path through the trees, and at last two vague ruts in the grass that petered out to nothing in a small clearing. Jen climbed down, retrieved her bag of sandwiches and a warm jacket, and set off into the woods, heading north. She was surrounded by the smell of pine needles and snow. For a while, it was as peaceful as the highway had been. Jen's family didn't get out in the wilderness much, what with one thing and another. Mom said it was redundant, since they had everything nature could provide already, but in a refined and improved form. Jen stopped, sat on a rock, and unwrapped her first sandwich, soft and warm from her body heat.

The werewolf was extremely stealthy. Probably he would have been able to sneak up on her even if she were experienced at woodcraft. As it was, Jen had no idea he was there until he leapt out at her, slavering and snarling.

"Oh, good. A werewolf," Jen said, recovering from her startlement.

The werewolf paused. "You're happy to see me? That's not what usually happens." His voice had teeth in it.

"Probably not." Jen offered him half of her sandwich. "But if you're here, then that means I'm on the right track. You are the guardian of the Forest Perilous, yes?"

The werewolf circled the clearing nervously. "I am hunger and violence. I am a beast in a man's skin. My curse separates me, isolates me. The alchemist allows me to live here in his forest, to run and hunt the deer, to live in peace, as much as a wretch like myself can. In return, yes, I watch for his enemies and lay in wait for them."

"Well, no problems there. I'm not his enemy. I'm his daughter." Jen waggled the sandwich invitingly. "You said you were hungry?"

"I am always hungry. The emptiness gnaws at me from inside. It is all I can do not to fall upon you and devour you where you sit. I can smell your blood." The werewolf crouched, his half-lupine limbs folding awkwardly together. His nostrils flared. Jen caught the smell of him, musky and sour, wet dog and locker room.

"Hmm." Jen brought her sandwich back and took another bite. "It seems like you have several co-morbid pathologies, possibly part of a unique syndrome. It's a little beyond the current scope for me to say, but the symptoms are probably individually treatable." Jen tapped her teeth in thought. "The hypertrichosis is the simplest. Just shaving would work, but if you want to avoid the hassle, you might consider electrolysis. Or laser hair removal. The aggressive ideation and fixation on violent imagery is a little more troubling. You might need medication, but at the least you should start seeing a therapist to try and work through those issues. I can recommend a very good one. The hunger pangs sound the most worrisome to me. Have you ever been tested for hyperthyroidism?"

The werewolf shook his head wordlessly.

Jen pulled out a notebook and scribbled down a name and

phone number. "My mother knows a very talented endocrinologist. I don't imagine you have a general practitioner to refer you, but I'm sure Mom's recommendation will get you an appointment slot. Once you get that under control, you'll probably find your anger issues more manageable, too."

"You mean . . . you think I can be . . . cured?"

"Well," Jen said, finishing her sandwich. "I couldn't honestly say it would be a 'cure,' since the condition looks to be chronic and at least partially genetic, but a solid treatment plan would definitely improve your quality of life immeasurably. What's most important is regaining your dignity as a person apart from your condition. Or conditions." She tore the page off of her notebook and handed it over. "I've outlined some steps you can take in your diet to get started, but I think you should see a proper medical expert as soon as you can. Thyroid issues can lead to cancer and all sorts of complications if they're not addressed."

The werewolf clutched the ragged white paper in his gnarled, misshapen claws. A tear glinted in one yellow eye. "Thank you. Oh, thank you, Mistress!"

"Not at all. Happy to help. Any friend of my father's, you know." Jen hopped down from her rock and held out a hand. The werewolf, looming over her, dark-furred and shaggy, shook it carefully. "Good luck."

"Yes . . . " His ears flickered, and his head went up. "I must hunt, lest my hunger overcome my will. Farewell, Mistress." He bounded into the green-tinted shadows of the forest.

"Don't fill up on meat! Get some whole grains and vitamin B!" Jen shouted after him. She wasn't sure he heard.

She put her plastic wrapper back in her pocket and journeyed on.

THE FOREST THINNED as she went on, and large rocks became more common as the vegetation receded. The ground sloped upward, and the air grew chill. Soon, she was walking amid thin scrub and scrambling up slopes of dirt and loose rocks, climbing ever higher. Ahead, the white-capped peak of the mountain seemed to float in the sky without drawing nearer. Jen spotted the ruins of an ancient castle clinging to an outcropping of rock, and beneath it the dark and shadowed mouth of a vast cavern, so she wasn't entirely surprised when the ground trembled under the impact of four enormous clawed feet and a red-scaled dragon heaved into view ahead of her.

"Oh my God!" Jen shrieked.

"Yes!" boomed the dragon. "Cower before my glorious wrath, ape-creature! Bow down before me, and I will slay you quickly and without pain."

"Let me see your wings!" Jen fairly leapt over the still-tumbling rocks and boulders that the dragon's emergence had shaken loose.

"What? No!" The dragon took a step back from Jen's relentless advance.

"I've always wanted to see a dragon's wings. You know bumblebees?"

"Bees? I don't . . . Now, see here, Missy: master's daughter or not, I could squish you under my foot, so let's have a little respect *don't do that!*" The dragon clawed its way up the slope to avoid Jen's hands as they tried to unfold its leathery wings from its back.

"Why not?" Jen, realizing she had been rude, put her hands behind her back and tried to look winsome.

"It tickles." The dragon huffed. "What was that about bees, anyway?"

"Bumblebees. For a while, they thought bumblebees shouldn't be able to fly under the laws of physics and it was a real problem, but then they did some tests and studies and worked it out. I want to see a dragon fly because I think it'll be the same sort of thing."

The dragon's eyes narrowed. "What, *exactly*, are you implying?"

"You shouldn't be able to fly," said Jen. She shrugged. "You can't work linearly with aerodynamics. Something the size of a house would need football field-sized wings to fly, so unless you've got jet engines and some sort of acceleration mechanism I'm not aware of . . . " She peered at the dragon's rear end with an air of scientific curiosity.

"I don't," the dragon said, its words coming out short and clipped.

"Well, could you take a quick flight? Just out to the trees and back? I want to see how it works."

"No."

"But—"

"No!" The dragon gritted its teeth, then sighed and hung its head. "I can't."

"Can't?"

"Can't fly. None of us can. These," the dragon said, fluttering its wings briefly, "are purely decorative these days. That's why we spend so much time in caves and ruined castles; no one expects to see us flying if they find us underground."

"Spandrels!"

"Come again?"

Jen waved her hands vaguely. "It's an architecture term, originally. Something about wasted space in arches. It's what you call traits that might have had a purpose but no longer do because of changes in the evolutionary niche. Like hiccups for humans."

"Ah, yes. Because you were frogs before you were monkeys."

"Probably more of a bony fish with rudimentary lungs, but more or less." Jen heaved a sigh and sat down on a handy rock. "I really hoped I could make an interesting new discovery in aerodynamics. I don't suppose you actually breathe fire?"

"Caustic spittle. Sorry."

"Hoards of gold?"

The dragon sat, kicking up a cloud of dust. "Well, we do

have to consume a relatively large amount of trace metals to stay healthy. If you rendered a dragon corpse, you'd probably end up with several ounces of gold, and you might find a stray bit or two in an older den. One good-sized coin will last me for years, though, so long as it's decently pure."

Jen looked up. "Are you going to try and eat me now? I brought a fire extinguisher, but apparently that's not going to help much. I should have brought an acid wash and a chemical hood, it seems."

"No," the dragon said, resting its head on its paws. "I'm too depressed. Spandrels! Pfaugh. What I wouldn't give for wings that worked."

"Well," Jen cupped her chin in her hand and tapped her lips. "We could probably rig up a glider system. Maybe even just a rigid aluminum frame to support your wings so that you don't have to rely on insufficient pectoral musculature."

"Hey, now!"

"Don't be sensitive. It's just facts." Jen peered over the top of her glasses. "Perhaps we can work out a deal. What's your pH?"

"Sorry?"

"The acid, silly! Potent?"

"I don't know the numbers, but I've yet to encounter anything it can't get through eventually."

"Excellent!" Jen clapped her hands. "Really strong acids are a pain to manufacture. Horribly toxic byproducts and so on. If we can get an ecologically friendly supplier at low cost, that could give us a real leg up in the market. Let me give you my mother's card. You might want to start networking; you'll need some friends if you're going to produce industrial quantities, I imagine. And then you can *buy* your way to flight."

The dragon plucked the tiny square of pasteboard with two enormous talons. "It seems a bit like cheating."

"So who's going to call you on it? You're a dragon." Jen smiled.

The dragon grinned, displaying twin rows of sharp, white teeth. "Indeed."

THE REMAINDER OF THE TRIP was relatively simple. The iron golem was pleased enough to hear about electroplating and rust-resistant coatings that he agreed chasing Jen would only risk opening more microfractures to speed oxidation. The chimera slunk into the woods in embarrassment after Jen couldn't stop laughing for almost ten minutes. The vampire wouldn't get within fifteen feet of Jen after a handful of garlic oil pills.

At last, Jen stood before the alchemist's castle. There was a small mailbox planted in the dirt on this side of the drawbridge. This gave Jen a twinge of anger, marbled through with sadness as though one of them were decaying radioactively into the other. She wondered which one started the reaction. She'd never gotten any letters from her father. Not even cards for their birthdays. A somewhat ragged owl with white plumage was sorting letters.

"Honestly," Jen said, rolling her eyes. "It's not like your species has particularly great direction sense. Or day-vision, for that matter. Pigeons would have made much more sense; something migratory, at least."

"Hey," the owl snapped, "you try dealing with the price of mouse gizzards in this economy and see what jobs *you* feel like turning down."

Jen watched it flap irritably away. "And why would you even need a postal service if you can teleport at will?" she said, unable to help herself. She needed to work on her tact, Newt always told her. Mom didn't see the problem with being plainspoken, but that was part of the trouble, wasn't it?

Meanwhile, she was on the outside of a castle, and her father was on the inside. She peered down into the moat, then ducked backwards quickly as a goggle-eyed fish with enormous teeth leapt into the air, jaws snapping shut in the space where her nose had been a moment ago.

"Dad!" Jen said. "That's ridiculous. Piranha hardly ever attack humans, and they're really not all that dangerous even
when they do." She moved several steps away from the water,
however, just in case.

"He just got some mail," Jen murmured to herself. "He has
to come out and get it sometime."

She settled herself beside the mailbox, crossed her legs, and
pulled out a book. *Introduction to Neurochemistry* was interesting, but a little difficult to read; perfect for long waits. After a
while, she ate her second sandwich. The sun set, staining the
sky red as suspended water particles in the atmosphere bent
and scattered the light at its new, oblique angle. This high in
the mountains, the view was spectacular, but brief. Jen sighed
when she could no longer see the words on the page. She
tucked the book behind her head for a pillow, zipped up her
jacket, and closed her eyes. *I'll just sit for a while,* she told herself. *Not sleep. Just rest my eyes . . .*

A hollow, metallic clatter woke her in the dark hours of
the morning. Her eyes flew open to espy a short, thin man
with a brown beard and sad eyes.

"Aha!" Jen cried. She leapt to her feet, clutching her book.

Her father reached into the mailbox and withdrew Jen's
car keys, which had been balanced precariously on the lip.
"These are yours, I take it?" His voice was quiet, and not as
deep as she'd expected. He held the keys out on the palm of
his hand. "You look a lot like your mother."

Jen found she didn't know what to say. She retrieved her
keys. Now that she was standing, she realized that she was
taller than he was. This felt somehow wrong to Jen, perverse, a
violation of a belief she hadn't known she held.

"Have you come to kill me?" her father asked her.

Jen's jaw dropped. "What? No! Why would you think
that?"

He shrugged, his eyes downcast. He looked very small. "It
was the last thing she said to me."

In an almost physical rush, Jen had a vision of her father's life for the past fourteen years. He lived alone, in the cold and the dark, his family taken away—all done legally; Jen had seen the papers--and surrounded by impossibilities of his own design. He could do anything he wanted, except for the thing he wanted most. How much time had he spent calling into a void before giving up? How long could someone survive surrounded only by what they made themselves? At what point would one's own psychological effluvium reach toxic concentrations?

"I'm sorry," Jen said. It didn't seem right, but the silence was worse.

"She raised you well, I see. You walked right past my defenses."

"Monsters are a lot less troublesome if you don't treat them like monsters," said Jen. "I deal in facts. Problems and solutions."

"That sounds like your mother, all right."

Jen hesitated. "Did she really threaten to kill you?"

"If I ever spoke to you or her again. You kids, especially." Her father shrugged again. "I didn't quite believe her when she threatened it, but seeing you here, now, looking like her twenty years ago . . . " He rubbed at his beard, then took both hands and scrubbed his face as though coming out from a swim. "Why *have* you come, then?"

"Oh!" Jen looked up. "It's about Newt. He's gone alchemical." She relayed the sordid tale of Newt's descent into nigh-madness.

"So he kept at it, did he?" Jen's father tapped his lips thoughtfully, giving Jen a frisson as she recognized the gesture in herself.

"Not exactly," said Jen. "It went dormant, I suppose."

"You can't keep out of it for long, though," her father said, shaking his head. "Not once it's started. I don't know if you could ever avoid it in the first place; the propensity for alchemy is something that tends to be discovered when it happens, not something you can predict. It was inevitable for Newton to experiment. This incident has probably been made worse by his long abstinence, actually; he'll be in a fever about it for weeks."

"Can't you do something? He's trying to find Truth. Surely you've already done that, somewhere along the line; can't you give him the secret?"

"That's what alchemy is, Jen." He put a hand on her shoulder. "The search for truth. No two alchemists ever find the same one; my truth would be as useless to him as it is to you and your mother."

"I don't think it's useless," Jen said. She reached up a hand and touched his arm lightly. "Some of it can be very beautiful, in its own way."

He smiled, but only with half of his mouth. "I remember when she said the same thing."

"I think you should see Newt," Jen announced firmly. "You might not be able to give him what he wants, but he needs your support. He always has. You understand him better than we can, at least in this."

"It would be breaking the rules . . ."

Jen waved a hand. "He's eighteen. He can make his own decisions about that now."

Her father nodded slowly. "You're . . . you're right. Of course you're right. You have that clarity of vision that I never mastered. I get so wrapped up in my own projects that I forget . . . well, I forget things." He glanced up, suddenly, a sly look in his eyes. "You know, you broke the agreement yourself, coming to see me. You're only fifteen."

"Some things are more important than following rules," said Jen. "I'm surprised you'd even suggest they aren't and why are you *grinning*?"

Her father didn't answer. Instead, he stuck his fingers in his mouth and whistled. From overhead came the sound of massive, leathery wings flapping. With a *whumph* and a brief whirlwind of dust, the dragon landed on the trail in front of them.

"I thought you said you couldn't fly!" Jen snapped.

The dragon bowed its head sheepishly.

"He probably couldn't, when you met him. It depends on who's doing the asking," her father said. He snapped his fingers, and the dragon knelt on its forelimbs, making a sort of scaly staircase to its shoulders. "Come on. Let's go save Newton." He scrambled up and reached a hand down to Jen. "It's okay. I'll keep us in the air."

Jen looked at the hand for a moment. The physics were all wrong; dragons couldn't exist, let alone fly with two passengers on board. What if her father was wrong, and her presence damaged whatever force kept the dragon airborne? How could she trust something she couldn't understand?

"All right," she said. She took her father's hand.

THE FIFTY-ONE SUITORS OF PRINCESS JAMATPIE

LEAH CYPESS

They were madly in love with her, and they were driving her crazy.

She couldn't step out of her room without tripping over the bundles of flowers and love poetry that had been left at her doorstep. She couldn't walk out onto her balcony in the morning without having at least three of them kneeling below it, singing love songs that didn't rhyme. She couldn't go for a walk without at least four of them offering to accompany her, and then dueling with each other to decide who would get the honor. In short, she could do nothing except sit in her room and glare at the walls.

"I hate them," Princess Jamatpie snapped one afternoon. "I hate being courted and I hate all the suitors. I want them to go away."

Her maidservant, Amelda, who was combing the princess's

hair, looked mildly shocked. "It is time for you to get married, Your Highness. You are sixteen years old. Your mother got married at fifteen."

"But my mother," Jamatpie pointed out, "got to marry my *father*. I have to marry one of these utter imbeciles!"

"I'm sure they're not all imbeciles, Your Highness. At least you'd better hope not, because the only way to get rid of them is to marry *one*. At that point, the rest will leave. All you have to do is make your choice. My personal recommendation is Prince Halis."

Jamatpie twisted around and looked at her maidservant in surprise. "Why do you say that?"

"He bribed me to, Your Highness."

Half an hour later, after Jamatpie's rage had subsided and there was nothing breakable left in the room, she gave her maidservant's advice some serious thought. Amelda, she concluded reluctantly, was right. But she didn't want to marry someone who was only courting her because she was a rich, beautiful princess. She wanted to marry someone who liked her for herself. Which was a little unreasonable, considering the fact that none of them knew her very well, but unreasonableness in royalty is a hereditary trait.

Jamatpie went to her mother to ask for advice.

"You might try what I did," her mother suggested. "I didn't hold with these antiquated, sexist methods. I simply interviewed them. Each one, for an hour, until I found out who I liked the best. And that, of course, was your father." She smiled fondly at the king, who stopped snoring and looked up, feeling that he had missed something.

Her mother's method sounded reasonable, but rather time-consuming. Jamatpie decided to try the more old-fashioned methods first.

"I pretended that I had been turned into a cat," her aunt Elina told her. "And, of course, all the suitors left, except for one who said he loved me even if I *was* a cat."

"Hmm," said Jamatpie doubtfully.

"I posed riddles," her cousin Rametta said. "And the person who got the right answer wed me."

That sounded pretty good, except that Jamatpie didn't know any riddles.

"*I* didn't have to worry about such things," her great-aunt Sevella sniffed haughtily. "I was placed under a spell by an evil witch and trapped in a glass tower for twenty years. The hero who rescued me became my husband, of course. So I didn't have to deal with this foolishness."

"How fortunate for you," Jamatpie said, and left hastily.

It was the suggestion of a distant cousin that finally brought her to a decision. Lialla explained that she had located a convenient dragon, and declared that the prince who slew it would marry her.

"I don't think dragon-slaying has anything to do with the qualities one looks for in a husband," Jamatpie said, trying to be polite.

She needn't have bothered. Lialla, unoffended, just shrugged.

"Of course it doesn't," she said. "But you have to pick somehow, don't you?"

That comment lingered in Jamatpie's mind. The first thing she did was go back to her mother's suggestion, and interview each prince for half an hour. (An hour seemed a bit excessive.) But all the princes had researched her interests intensively. Every one of them hummed her favorite tune as he walked through the door, explained that he was currently reading her favorite book, and then waxed eloquent about the rights of unicorns to live without being hunted. (Save the Unicorns was one of the princess's passions.) After twenty interviews, Jamatpie gave up in disgust.

"*You have to pick somehow,*" she repeated aloud. "If that's all there is to it, I'm holding a lottery."

She made the announcement from her balcony the next day, and the news spread quickly. The next morning, she opened the door to her bedroom and found nothing but carpet at her feet.

"How strange," she said.

"Not at all," Amelda said. "Now that the princes know you are going to choose by lottery, they are simply waiting. Why should they spend more money on flowers and hired poets?"

"Oh," Jamatpie said. "Well, that's good. I think."

That night, as was her custom, she dined with all her suitors at a huge table in the main hall. Usually the suitors were all excessively courteous, falling over themselves to try to make witty remarks. Tonight half of them didn't show up. The other half of them went for the food as if they were starving, called loudly for more wine, and spent most of the evening burping.

"I think I'll move the lottery up to tomorrow night," Jamatpie said.

That morning, the suitors took all her father's horses and held races on the back lawn, tearing up most of the flower beds. Then they held duels and dented all the best swords. By the time the lottery was to be held, Jamatpie's father was so eager to have the suitors gone that he put on his crown and attended the lottery himself.

In the great ballroom, with the princes sitting along the length of the dinner table, Jamatpie stood in front of a large glass bowl. The bowl was full of wood chips, and on each chip was carved the name of a prince. Jasmine only hoped she would know how to pronounce the one she drew.

"Attention," she said, and all the princes looked up. She had prepared a lengthy speech, but at the last moment was too nervous to recite it. Besides, they all knew what this was about, didn't they?

She plunged her hand into the bowl—and it froze.

Literally. She couldn't move her hand. She couldn't even twitch her fingers. For a moment she panicked; then she realized what had happened.

Evidently, every prince had gone out the night before and

paid a wizard to ensure that it would be *his* chip that was selected. And now all those wizards' spells were warring against each other, trying to force the princess's hand to move one way or another. The forces of their magic cancelled each other out perfectly, and the result was that the princess could not move her hand at all.

Meanwhile, power buzzed within the stone tower of the wizard Gluck and the crystal palaces of the wizardesses Gruella and Griselda (who strongly preferred *not* to be called witches, and backed that preference with nasty curses). They were the only three wizards in the kingdom, and each had been hired by exactly seventeen of the princes. To be fair, they had each set up a spell for every single prince. Only in a situation like this, they had promised themselves, would they give precedence to the prince who had paid the most.

Every wizard added just a bit more power to the spell of the prince who had tipped them most extravagantly. They added power proportional to the amount of money, naturally, and finally Jamatpie's hand moved.

Her fingers brushed a wood chip, which practically flew out of the bowl along with her hand.

"Prince Halis," she read.

The rest of the princes booed. Prince Halis rose and bowed to her with a smile. He was wearing a cloak of spun gold studded with tiny emeralds.

Prince Halis was *very* rich.

Jamatpie looked at him for a moment. Then she dropped the wood chip on the floor and straightened dramatically.

"Seize him!" she shouted.

"Huh?" said Prince Halis.

"Huh?" said the princess's guards.

"Seize him!" Jamatpie said again. She spoke very fast. "This lottery was a test! I wanted to see which one of you would be dishonest enough to bribe a wizard and make my hand choose *him*. Seize him and throw him into the dungeons."

The princess's guards finally moved forward. They moved

so slowly that Prince Halis had plenty of time to escape—which was actually what Jamatpie wanted him to do—but he was too stunned to move. Before long, he was being marched off toward the back of the hall, in the direction of the dungeons.

"I want him executed," Princess Jamatpie said loudly. She figured she might as well. It would increase the amount of bribes the prince would spend before escaping from prison and returning to his home kingdom. Her kingdom's economy could use the boost.

After that, she had only fifty suitors. But it didn't seem to make a difference. The love letters and flowers were back, as were the duels, the courteous manners, and the serenades.

"Your grandmother," Amelda suggested, "disguised herself in rags and spent years working as the lowliest peasant to find someone who truly loved her for herself. It's not too late for that."

"Hmm," Jamatpie said. After some thought, she went to talk to her parents.

Several days later, the halls were empty, the swords unused, and the morning air full of silence. Amelda expressed surprise.

"I'm betrothed," Jamatpie explained.

"You are *what?*"

"Betrothed. My parents had no choice. They wish to form an alliance with the kingdom of Charida, to our north—"

"South, actually," Amelda said.

"South. They have, to forge the alliance, betrothed me to the prince of Charida. Prince Tamer."

"Prince Tamer," said Amelda, "is only six years old."

"That's true," Jamatpie admitted.

"It will be at least ten years before the marriage can take place. By then he may have decided that he wants to marry someone else. And believe me, my girl, you will not have your pick of so many suitors once you are at the advanced age of twenty-six!"

"Yes, I know," Jamatpie said. "Tragic, isn't it?"

And she went out into her gardens for a walk.

IF YOU ACT NOW

SERGEY LUKYANENKO

TRANSLATED FROM RUSSIAN
BY ALEX SHVARTSMAN

The alien spaceship sailed across the sky. A sphere half-a-mile in diameter spun around its axis, showing off a variety of decorative patterns. It left streaks of colored light in its wake, generating an otherworldly rainbow.

All across the world people watched the skies—some with apprehension, some with suspicion, and some with outright fear. Most, however, couldn't help but enjoy the majestic sight. The colorful patterns made the huge vessel appear unthreatening. Its splendor held a promise of a better tomorrow. Not since the launch of the Sputnik had so many people looked up to the stars.

In a closed session of the UN Security Council, representatives of many great nations (and some not so great ones) were glued to the screen. They were missing out on the awe-inspiring view outside, concerning themselves instead with making first contact.

"No, we won't be landing," said a fluffy orange fur ball with beady little eyes. "Thank you for your hospitality, but we're in a hurry. We do appreciate the invitation, though. We're happy to have met you, but we have a long journey ahead of us."

The aliens provided the translation, transmitting their message in Russian, English, Chinese, French, and Spanish. They apologized profusely to the representatives from nations that spoke other languages, citing the lack of time and ability.

"But there's so much we would like to ask, so much we could learn from you," said the Special Representative.

It had taken two days of vicious political infighting for the UN to settle on who would speak on behalf of humanity. China argued that Earth should be represented by a member of the planet's most populous nation. Russia countered that it should be a person from the country with the largest land mass. America made the case for a spokesperson from the world's most democratic and technologically advanced nation. Unable to agree, they settled on a speaker from Madagascar.

Realistically, the identity of the Special Representative mattered little. He was merely a mouthpiece, there to read aloud the text that appeared on a teleprompter. Deep within the bowels of the UN building, a think tank of scientists, psychologists, and security analysts carefully crafted every word that would be said to the aliens.

"What would you like to know?" asked the alien. "We'll try to answer your questions."

"How many intelligent species are out there, that you know of?" asked the Special Representative after a quick glance at his monitor.

"Eighty-three and a half," said the alien, without hesitation. "Counting the dolphins. If you include the humans, that'd make eighty-four and a half."

Down in the think tank, one of the psychologists suffered a mild bout of hysteria. There was a brief pause as he was removed. Finally, a new question appeared on the Special Representative's monitor.

"What are the diplomatic relations like between the various sentient species of the cosmos?"

"We're united in friendship, cooperation, and mutually beneficial trade," the alien said. "Sure, there's an occasional armed conflict, but we think such violence is shameful and well below the dignity of intelligent beings. My species are staunch pacifists, you see."

Everyone in the room breathed a little easier.

"How can we initiate contact with these other civilizations?" asked the man from Madagascar.

"Work hard. Advance your science and technology. Live in peace. Learn to fly to the stars," the alien advised.

There was another small pause, followed by the next question.

"Our planet is struggling with many unresolved problems. Might your advanced civilization offer any sort of assistance?"

At the very last second the word "advanced" had disappeared and was replaced with "gracious," but the Special Representative had already spoken the original version of the question.

"That is a difficult dilemma," said the alien. "We've long since learned that offering help for free is a disservice to the recipient. Once accustomed to the crutch of outside assistance, a civilization might grow dependent on the largesse and fall behind in its own development, hoping for foreign investment, credits, and interstellar aid instead. No, we couldn't possibly do that to you. Perhaps we could engage in a bit of trade instead? Sell you some interesting gadgets? You could pay us in heavy metals and native artwork. Think about that—but don't wait too long to decide, because our time here is extremely limited."

The text on the Special Representative's screen changed rapidly. "Is there a God?" "Which heavy metals?" "What is the meaning of life?" "Are the dolphins really intelligent?"

"What can you offer us?" The man from Madagascar cleared his throat, staring at the screen. The last phrase blinked a few times, and remained.

"What can you offer us?" asked humanity's representative.

"There are any number of wonderful items," said the alien, and the picture on the screen changed. Gone was the small, ascetic cabin and the orange fur ball. Instead, the humans saw a spacious, brightly lit cargo hold with what looked like a space shuttle at the center.

"This is a compact spaceship, developed by the Aggr civilization," said the alien. "This vessel allows its occupants to travel in comfort within the confines of a star system. It can achieve speeds of up to five hundred thousand kilometers per second, is equipped with anti-meteorite shielding and is radiation-proof. We have a limited quantity of these in stock and can only offer you up to a dozen units, complete with instruction manuals in all major Earth languages. If you act now and buy these ships, we will also include a portable folding hangar."

The screen now displayed a gleaming white structure a little larger than the ship.

"We'll also throw in a long-range communications station and a thought-recording of a three hour advanced piloting course. The price of each vessel is forty tons of gold, four tons of platinum, and two and a half tons of plutonium."

There was a long pause. Then the American member of the Security Council rose from his seat.

"The United States is prepared to buy all twelve ships."

The Special Representative shifted uncomfortably in his chair, but no one was paying any attention to him anymore.

"Excellent," said the alien. "We're certain you will be satisfied with your purchase. Where would you like us to deliver the ships, and where should we pick up the payment?"

Under the icy stares of the other council members, the American provided the coordinates of a military base and suggested that the precious metals could be taken directly from Fort Knox.

The other diplomats were stunned. Their mood darkened further as they realized it was no coincidence that the American representative came equipped with the longitude and latitude of a secret military base. But their complaints were drowned out by the alien's voice.

"We have an even more interesting mode of transportation to offer you. It is a colonization ship, developed by the Rahg-Harr and intended for interstellar flight. This is a brand new unit, and it works by breaking the laws of relativity. Its reach is up to forty light-years and it is capable of carrying up to one thousand passengers per trip. We have only one in stock. The price is four hundred tons of gold, three hundred tons of platinum, at least a ton of uncut diamonds . . . "

"We'll take that, too!" shouted the American as he eyed the shimmering hull of the colonization ship that filled the entire screen. It looked far more impressive than the Aggr ships.

" . . . and eighty tons of folk art aged no less than one thousand Earth years," the alien went on to say. "I'm very sorry, but your country does not possess the required quantities of ancient folk art," he told the American. "If you act now, in addition to the colonization ship you'll receive a remarkable air conditioning technology, a unique telescope design, an almanac listing all uninhabited planets in a forty light-year radius of Earth, and all appropriate documentation . . . "

"The People's Republic of China will buy this ship," said the Chinese diplomat. He stared everyone else down triumphantly. He went on to discuss the details of the deal with the alien, who did not offer any objections this time around.

Everyone else clutched their phones, feverishly jotting down instructions from their governments. The man from Madagascar pouted in his chair, forgotten. The American looked defeated and miserable.

"Sadly, we're now out of transportation items," said the

alien. He turned down a section of the Great Wall, but was happy to accept some Ming dynasty vases and the entire army of Terracotta Warrior sculptures as part of China's payment. "But we do have a number of other fascinating items. How about an authentic Aurellian food synthesizer? It's capable of producing sustenance for any carbon-based life forms. It's fully automatic, and charged with enough energy for one hundred and twenty-five years of continuous operation. We have four of them. The price is sixty tons of two hundred-plus-year-old folk art per unit."

After a bout of furious negotiation the synthesizers ended up split between the United States, China, and Great Britain. France kept itself out of the running, citing its ancient and proud gastronomic tradition, and Russia bowed out in exchange for the unimpeded opportunity to buy the next lot.

This bargain was nearly broken by the other nations when it was discovered that the next wondrous device was a machine capable of rejuvenating a human body by one hundred Earth years. The alien restored order, reminding the competing nations of their promises and chiding them gently about the importance of keeping one's word.

To thank Russia for their immediate purchase, the alien threw in a special conveyer belt technology that would allow up to one thousand people per hour to go through the rejuvenation machine.

The Special Representative chimed in, inquiring about the time frame for receiving the purchases. The alien assured him that everything would be delivered within three hours of the end of their trade session. The alien magnanimously accepted responsibility for the logistics of making all deliveries and picking up all payments.

Although the other nations were disappointed to lose the rejuvenation technology to the Russians, this was soon forgotten as the alien rolled out other lots, each more wondrous than the next: space technologies for healing any disease, climate control, self-cleaning fabrics, sleep-learning, and high-temperature superconductors.

France purchased a space station capable of housing ten thousand residents, and coffee grinders powered by Brownian motion. They also picked up an extra-deep drilling and mining station, and a dictionary for the language of smells.

China managed to bargain away their Great Wall after all, in exchange for a foolproof method of mass birth control.

Great Britain had to settle for the technology of wirelessly transmitting electricity, but they also got a brand-new experimental factory that was capable of building an exact copy of itself.

When some of the richer countries started running out of steam, Russia snagged a culture of unique bacteria, capable of thriving inside of a nuclear reactor and converting its radiation into drinkable alcohol. They also bought magnetic hovercars and a strain of cold-resistant alien bananas.

When the supply of heavy metals and artwork began to run low, the aliens were kind enough to trade for some Earth technologies, a supply of eucalyptus leaves, and the bacteria culture used for fermenting milk into yogurt.

An Israeli representative, who had remained out of the bidding until that point, pounced on the chance to pick up half of the aliens' remaining small lots at a bulk rate. Pleased with the transaction, the aliens threw in the cure for male pattern baldness.

"We've exhausted our supplies," the alien said at last. "So we have to bid you adieu and continue on our journey. We will deliver your purchases now. Thank you very much for your business."

"Is there a God?" shouted the Special Representative.

"Wish we knew," said the alien, and the communication screen shut off.

Earth's top diplomats, sweaty and overexcited, finally had a quiet moment to contemplate what had just happened.

They looked at each other, no one wanting to speak out first. Finally, the Israeli delegate gave voice to everyone's unspoken thought: "Something doesn't feel right . . . "

MEANWHILE, THE ALIEN SPACESHIP began its last orbital rotation above the Earth. The shimmering colors in its wake spread ever wider and became dotted with small packages: spaceships and heavy machinery, coffee makers and bio-cultures, cars and food synthesizers floated gently downward, to arrive at the precise locations specified by the humans. In their stead, the heavy metals and folk art floated upward, leaving the planet behind. Wherever this wave of light spread, it touched people in special ways, causing everyone to experience that ineffable feeling of satisfaction and self-worth.

Then the alien ship left orbit and disappeared into the vastness of space.

THERE WAS A HIGH LEVEL meeting at the Kremlin on the following evening. It was similar to meetings taking place around the world, in every nation that had managed to get its hands on some of the alien gadgets. The head of the FSB gave his report.

"We burned our best American agent obtaining this information," he lamented, flipping through the printouts, "but here you go. The Aggr spaceships do indeed match the specs provided by the aliens. The American scientists are optimistic about their ability to reach speeds of five hundred kilometers per second. Here are some photos. They are a tad blurry; our spy satellites aren't exactly state of the art anymore. But they're clear enough to estimate the ships' size, and our intelligence on the ground is confirming the same information.

"Based on this evidence, we must speculate that the Aggr aliens who built these ships are each the size of a small kitten.

"The Americans can't fly them, and they can't open them up, either. The compartments containing any useful technology are sealed, and set to self-destruct if tampered with, according to the manual.

"Moving on to the intel from China. Some of it may be disinformation, but we were able to independently confirm many of the details. The Rahg-Harr colonization ship is three hundred meters long. It's not a matchbox toy, like the ones the Americans got stuck with. It does violate the laws of relativity, just as the alien said.

"According to the theory of relativity, time should slow down as the vessel approaches the speed of light. The subjective time for the crew would be merely hours, even as decades or centuries pass on Earth. The Ragh-Harr ship, however, breaks that law. It's capable of reaching the nearby stars in hours. But a thousand years will pass on board the ship. The Chinese are still willing to give it a go; the problem is, the ship's systems are designed for only a decade or two of continuous flight.

"There was a snafu with the birth control device, too. It works fine, but it works on *everybody* at the same time.

"There's no detailed report from France yet, but we do know that their orbital station is maintaining a temperature of five hundred and forty degrees Celsius. Any attempt to lower the temperature is expected to cause irreparable damage to the station's machinery.

"The British self-replicating factory already built an exact copy of itself. Then each, in turn, began to do the same thing. It appears this factory builds nothing *but* replicas of itself. The Prime Minister shut them down, but the scientists believe the process would have continued indefinitely.

"Both the Chinese volunteers and the starving people in Africa flat-out refused to eat the food produced by the Aurellian synthesizer. It isn't poisonous. In fact, it's quite nutritious. The taste, however, is said to have made pigs throw up.

"We're still waiting on reports from Israel and Belgium. Oh, and one more note from Great Britain. To transmit the wireless electricity they'd need to build sending and receiving stations across the country. The quality and quantity of copper required for their construction makes it several degrees of magnitude cheaper to just run old-fashioned wires.

"That's all I've got, so far."

The director of the newly-formed Institute for the Studies of Extraterrestrial Technologies was visibly relieved by the discouraging news from the other nations. It was his turn to present a report.

"The rejuvenation device has been assembled and is ready to operate. Unfortunately, the device failed to work on our septuagenarian volunteers. Apparently, one hundred years is the *minimum* setting. We're bringing in a one-hundred-and-six year old volunteer from Tomsk, although our scientists fear he will end up a six year old mentally as well as physically.

"Now, as far as the alcohol-producing germs go . . . the bacteria immediately begin to produce ethanol when placed in an irradiated environment. But they absorb only a minimal amount of radiation and then consume whatever ethanol they produce, with no net benefit.

"The magnetic hovercars work perfectly. They do require special roads to float over, built from a nickel-wolfram alloy. We can produce it, but in extremely limited quantities. Plans for a very short magnetic road are being drawn up as we speak.

"The alien bananas have been planted in Siberia. They truly are entirely cold resistant—but that doesn't make planting and fertilizing them in the frozen tundra any easier. We expect to harvest the first crop in twenty to twenty-five years.

"That's all I have today, gentlemen."

The president frowned, as he looked around the room.

"Does anyone have a theory as to why they bartered for a hundred and fifty mountain bikes from us?" he asked. "What in the world do aliens need with bicycles?"

If anyone in the room had a theory, they kept it to themselves. The being best qualified to answer this question would have been the fur ball alien, who was the sole occupant of the enormous vessel that had visited Earth.

At the moment, he was too busy to answer any questions. His ship was orbiting a planet in a nearby star system where he was peddling his wares to its inhabitants. Just then he was in the middle of pitching the unique, ecologically clean personal transportation devices that required no external energy source and were capable of traversing rough terrain. The medusa-like swamp dwellers of that world were very interested in such marvelous technology.

In fact, the Powers That Be did not need to look to the stars for the answer. The answer could be provided, just as easily, by a minor and entirely unremarkable bureaucrat and a citizen of the Russian Federation.

This particular individual took advantage of the opportunity to properly celebrate the arrival (and then the departure) of the aliens with his friends and colleagues. At that very moment he was walking into his apartment in a state of mild inebriation that was just beginning to wear off and turn inevitably into a hangover. There he saw his spouse, sitting on the couch in front of the television, dictating their home address into the phone.

Upon witnessing this, the citizen stated his opinions in a loud and slurry voice. His speech was short and fiery. The word "fool" was intermixed with other, less printable but equally hurtful nouns. He closed with " . . . and this, at the time when humanity stands on the brink of a new era!"

The insulted wife retreated into the bedroom, and the citizen plunked onto the couch she had vacated, in front of the television set.

"If you act right now," said the voice on the screen, "we'll include a potato cutter, a super dish-cleaning sponge, and a replacement handle with your order of the Wonder-Grinder. Call now!"

But the citizen was already fast asleep on the couch. And, for some strange reason, he dreamed about laughing dolphins.

© Phil Selby

NO SILVER LINING

ZACH SHEPHARD

O kay—listen. It's not my fault. No one could have known the yeti was going to hit his stride at the end. I mean, who sends a yeti into the 110-meter woodland hurdles anyway? I thought for sure the mountain-folk were writing that event off as a loss from the get-go, but as it turns out, ol' snow-britches had been doing some high-altitude training for the last twenty years and had brought his A-game. Or Y-game. Or whichever game it is that yetis use to take the gold.

Some say that I shouldn't have lost. I say it's not my fault that I did, because I shouldn't have been running that race in the first place. Everyone knows werewolves are better suited for something a little more elegant. Like the balance beam. Or freestyle bunny-maiming.

I didn't want to do hurdles. Especially not after my practice runs. In human form, I wasn't fast enough. In wolf form, I wasn't tall enough. In my halfway-between form, I forgot what I was doing and ate two of the judges. But Coach insisted I was the dog for the job anyway, and I didn't want to let Team Forest-Creatures down, so here I am.

To be fair, Coach did try putting me into a handful of other events before settling on the hurdles. I took a shot at the 400-meter race around the lake, but it's hard to advance beyond the trials when you take a detour to chase a squirrel up a tree. Boxing was no good either, because my claws kept poking through the gloves—apparently evisceration is illegal, even if you keep it above the belt. I took a stab at diving next, but the gnomes on our team were all better at it. (If you ask me, those hats are an unfair advantage when it comes to minimizing splash.) Swimming was no better, because even in human form, my body hair created enough drag to stop a tugboat.

So it was hurdles or nothing. I stretched, I practiced, I figured out a way to stay in wolf-man form without devouring the judges. (Eating a few brownies before the race can do wonders for your appetite, though I wish they wouldn't scream so much on the way down.) I trained as hard as I could for the event, but in the end, I still wasn't feeling great about it.

Thankfully, Coach can be one inspiring stump of a hobgoblin—his little speech on the morning of the big day made me start to believe I might actually do well. So when race time rolled around, I took a deep breath, tossed a few brownies down the hatch, and lined up on the woodland track under a full moon.

A few short seconds later, the yeti was raising his arms in victory. Not bad for an ape-man with feet the size of surfboards.

The mountain-folk won the Fairyland Games, which is good for them, because the losers are required to put someone up for sacrifice. The chosen creature is banished from reality and relegated to the Death-halls of Fable, which is why no one believes in the Andean crust weasel anymore.

Team Forest-Creatures did pretty well at the Fairyland Games, but not well enough. My loss ended up costing us our predetermined sacrifice. Ever heard of the krundlewat? Of course you haven't. No one believes in him anymore, and it's

NO SILVER LINING   149

my fault. I came in third on the hurdles. If I'd come in second,
the krundlewat would still be a part of your culture, sneaking into your room on summer nights to shove your socks up
its nose and leave tuna sandwiches in your shoes. But now,
thanks to my poor performance—oh, what the heck. As long
as I'm telling the story, I might as well be honest.

The truth is, once I realized the yeti was going to beat me,
I threw the race. I let a surprisingly nimble kraken slip-slap
her way ahead of me and I took third place on purpose. I cost
the world their beloved krundlewat. But really, can you blame
me? I wanted to win the gold, sure. And if I'd thought I could
get it, I would have fought for it. But it was out of reach, and
the fact is, I'm a werewolf.

There's no way I'm taking silver.

GO KARTS
OF THE GODS

MICHAEL KURLAND

They're here now!

Sorry, didn't mean to startle you. But it's hard not to get excited when speaking of the greatest metaphysical revelation since herb tea. Let me start again—

They're here now!

I guess I just can't hold it in. Because it's *true!* They are among us still. Some of us, anyway.

They never left!

The man peering over your shoulder right now as you read these words—or woman, if it happens to be a woman, and it can be a woman, whatever you may have been told—may be an *alien* from *outer space!* They're here still, watching us, teaching us, learning from us, guiding us, eating—but that's another part of the story.

It all started—well, I don't know when it all started, but I first came to know of it in late July, 1982. Which we of ODISY refer to as The Day of Cosmic Revelation. (What is ODISY you ask? *Aha!* Good for you! You're no fool.)

It was, I remember, a Thursday. I was staring at some obscure wall enhancements at one of the major archeological sites in the Eastern United States, the uptown platform of the West Side IRT 23rd Street station, when the curious, somehow almost obscene, words and illustrations formed a pattern in my mind and it all came together. I *understood.*

Why me? You may well ask. Perhaps just a chance alignment of space and time—which we now know are aspects of the same thing, except that one goes from side to side, and the other goes up and down and stops at the mezzanine even if you didn't push the button for the mezzanine, which can be very annoying—perhaps it was predestination, perhaps it was a bubble in the Cosmic Goo, perhaps I'm just better than you are; who can say? But ours is not to reason why, ours is to Seek the Truth and prepare ourselves. And I and my fellow Seekers of the ODISY Society are here to help those of you who wish to Seek, who are willing to prepare yourselves for the journey toward the true light.

Hello Seekers!

Are you ready to accept the GREAT NEWS?

There are aliens amongst us!!!

If you know just how and where to look, you can find them, observe them, learn from them, emulate them. But *you* must seek *them* out. They won't come to you. Not you.

We of the ODISY Society will aid you—you have but to ask. We are here to guide you along the path to true understanding, which is found through the intense study of what we know as Outer Directed Inner Seeking Yearningness—Hence "ODISY," a name which has been revealed to us by *The Others.* Well, by some of them. Other *Others* spend their time buying shoes, aluminum foil, and comic books, while yet other *Others* glare pityingly at you and ask, "Who the #^$*& do you think you're talking to?" (They actually say "#^$*&," which is the way they read it in the comic books. The *Others* are very literal beings.)

The clues, the hints, the milestones on this path to Alien Enlightenment will at first seem fragmentary, unclear, murky, contradictory, even idiotic—I know they did to me. But as you get deeper and deeper into the practice of Yearningness, and pass from stage to stage on the road to ODISY, it will all become clear and meaningful. Each chapter—each paragraph—each word of the *ODISY Book of Outer Directed Inner Seeking Yearningness,* which may have made no sense to you when you began, will lose its confusion and become clear and totally grabfig.

The key to understanding any sentence or word that you, with your primitive, pre-ODISY mind-plugs, fail to comprehend, is to stare at it and keep repeating over and over, "Niagara Falls, Niagara Falls, Niagara Falls," until the words that once made no sense shimmer before your eyes and the plugs pop away, leaving your mind free and open to once untenable suggestions, and you attain a new height of clarity. And, in time, you will; I did. And now I am not only the founder of ODISY, but the *Others* have entrusted me with the position of Grand Mung.

In a short time you, yourself, may become a Mung, or a Mung among Mungs, or even an Übermung. With but a little application and expense you will soon be Yearning with the rest of us. Of course your old friends will have trouble comprehending you as you speak these new truths. They may say nasty things about your behavior, your new frabish, your sanity. They may urge you to come to your "senses." Reply to them, "Ha, ha!" Say to them, "Ho, ho!" Tell them that it is *their* primitive senses that lack the ability to see the truth; *their* short-sighted unwillingness to pay for the instruction that would open their eyes. For enlightenment doesn't come cheaply. But then neither do SUVs, or plasma TVs, or members of the opposite sex. Even members of the same sex can be pretty expensive, which seems somehow unfair. But I digress.

First of all you'll want to verify for yourself that what I'm telling you is true is true is true is, er, true. Good for you. You're no sap. After a while the practice of Yearningness will seem natural, and it's the rest of the world that will seem queer and fuzzy. I'll tell you just what to look for. Once you know the signs, it all becomes horribly, frighteningly, clear.

First: look for things that couldn't have been built by people. If people couldn't have built them, *someone else must have!* See? It really sticks out when it's pointed out to you, doesn't it?

Second: look for things that weren't built *for* people. Things that human beings were never meant to wear, or use, or sit on, or lie on, or drive, or eat, or apply to various parts of their bodies. If the thing doesn't fit you—*who does it fit?* Once you start looking, you'll be surprised at how many objects you find that were clearly designed to be used by another race.

Consider the Leaning Tower of Pisa. Why is it leaning? Would you build a building that leans like that? Why doesn't it fall over? Oh, I know scientists have answers to these questions, but *who told them?* Someone, or some thing, that doesn't want them to know the truth? Yes, it's good for dropping cannon balls off, but this is an urge that most *humans* manage to suppress.

The Leaning Tower of Pisa *is not a tower at all.* It is an intergalactic signpost. J.D. (Jimboy) Davisson, professor of Pre-Human Religion at Partial College and Academy of Autoerotics and Goal-Tending in Woodward, Oklahoma, has computed on the P.C.&A. of A. & G.T. in W.O. billing machine that a line drawn along the center of the axis of the tower, and extending parabolically (according to the formula $1 = \sqrt{4x^2} + Y^2 + Z / 2X \log_e$) comes back to earth right in the middle of Paramus, New Jersey. Coincidence?

They are trying to tell us something. Are we wise enough to listen?

If ten men worked for a week, they couldn't build the

Great Pyramid at Giza, or the Golden Gate Bridge, or the Panama Canal, or Paris, France, or the Antarctic Ocean. Not even if they wore warm clothes.

Have you ever bounced on a go kart? Why is it spelled "kart"? Does the alien alphabet lack the letter "c"? Riding karts is so uncomfortable that it's a sport. Could it be that for some alien creatures from somewhere else, they are a sensible means of transportation? Some creatures that like to bounce?

I have in my collection a pair of sandals with tire treads on the bottoms. Could they be for strange beings with wheels on their feet?

Who was meant to ride on bus seats? What sort of beings can bend in the right place to comfortably use the plastic chairs at airports? What creatures can sit for an extended length of time on airline seats in anything approaching comfort? Where are they from? Where are they going? And do they have special discount fares?

Who was meant to wear boxer shorts?

There is a stainless steel arch in St. Louis, Missouri, six hundred and thirty feet tall, *which wasn't there a hundred years ago.* Can it be a coincidence that a line drawn perpendicular to this arch through its center *will leave the Earth?*

I have in my collection a can of soda with no nutrients useful to the *human* body.

The most popular children's television program stars an eight-foot-tall chicken. Who wants our children to think that eight-foot-tall chickens are their friends?

If human beings get the Chicken Pox, what do chickens get? But I digress.

What about those ball point pens that write under butter but not on paper? *Who lives under butter?*

Makes you think, doesn't it?

Or, take the Transamerica Pyramid in San Francisco. Why are they starting to build pyramids again? Did you know that a great circle line drawn to connect the Transamerica Pyramid and the Great Pyramid at Giza *passes right through the Leaning Tower of Pisa?* And yet it goes nowhere near Paramus, New Jersey. What does this mean?

I have in my collection a porcelain teacup with a handle too small to admit a human forefinger. Do eight-foot chickens drink tea?

Next time you're in a restaurant, see if there is a third, unmarked, door between the men's room and the women's room. Who uses these unmarked doors? Do these restaurants serve chicken?

There is a library in Dayton, Ohio, which has no books on herpetology.

There is no one named Ambrose in the Berkeley, California telephone directory.

And what about Ogallala, Nebraska?

The *Others* have promised to reveal everything to those of us who are Ready to Receive the Wisdom of ODISY, who have shown that they can be Trusted to handle these Great Secrets wisely, who have paid the $669.45 initiation fee, who have memorized the Seven Sacred Secrets and the Two Dozen Trans-Temporal Talismans, who have attained at least the rank of Minor Master of the Ministrations of Mung, who are up to date with their dues, and who have signed the non-disclosure agreement, the risk waiver, and the promissory note.

So don't wait! Don't pause for a minute to think about it! Don't send money through the mail — someone will be around to pick up your check or credit card. Or cash is nice. Soon you will find yourself enveloped by your new friends, your new sense of purpose, your new understanding, and Outer Directed Inner Seeking Yearningness will become as second nature to you. Or perhaps third. And your eyes will be opened, and you will cast aside the shell of your former self, which we will store for you at a nominal charge, and you will on your way to attaining total grabfig! Could anyone say better, finer, more redundant than that?

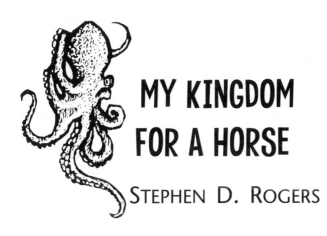

MY KINGDOM FOR A HORSE

STEPHEN D. ROGERS

Your Highness, sir, you came to the right place.

This fine steed standing before you was ridden by a little old lady. The only time she left her hovel was to attend the weekly joust. Those are the original shoes.

Not interested? Don't worry, you won't be walking away from here on your own two feet. If you've got a kingdom, I've got the horse for you.

In this next stall is Prince.

No, he's not a real prince. That's just his name.

Yes, I can see how you would take titles seriously.

Did I say Prince? I mean Pincer. It's Welsh.

Let us just pass on to the third stall.

Can I fetch you some mead? Mulled wine?

That's a good idea to keep your wits about you. There are

some used horse dealers who wouldn't hesitate to take you for
a ride. Get it? A ride?

You're right.

Anyhow, take a look at this beauty.

I never noticed that before. It appears to be a minor skin
condition which I'm sure will clear up in no time at all. If
you're otherwise satisfied with him, I'll consider lowering the
price. I'll take the kingdom but you keep the queen.

No, I'm sure the court jester is doing a great job meeting
your humor needs. I wouldn't presume Your Majesty's staffing
decisions. And over here . . . .

An udder? Some of these horses come with extras you
wouldn't believe.

A cow? No.

Seriously?

This is the kind of thing that happens when I delegate the
simplest of tasks. I'm sure you know what I mean. Men like us,
people take advantage. First thing tomorrow, I'm accusing that
serf of witchcraft.

It is a handsome cow, though. Your bovines have a much
wider foot base than your average horse. That could come in
handy during a charge, especially with all the rain we've been
having.

You're right, of course.

Your Highness, this is my daughter, Esmerelda. Esmerelda,
his Royal Highness.

I have a wide selection of quality horses in the next set of
stalls that I'm sure will interest you.

Esmerelda helps me in the office.

Yes, she is a beautiful young woman.

You've heard of her? See Esmerelda, I told you that min-
strel would help spread the word.

It is true, Your Majesty, that Esmerelda could bring you
around instead of me but—

Yes, you are king.

The best subject you ever ruled.

Esmerelda, show his highness the rest of the horses. And remember not to mount any. You know how the slightest pressure irritates your infectious rash.

What, Your Highness?

Certainly I can see how the onset of a crusade could slip your mind. I only hope you think of us the next time you consider purchasing a horse because we do want your business . . . and your kingdom.

Yes I do suppose that joke has been making the rounds for a while now.

Happy crusading.

Esmerelda, I think he almost bought the cow.

He must have been impressed by the leather exterior.

© Phil Selby

CAKE FROM MARS

MARKO KLOOS

"All I want for my goddamn birthday is a cake with a whore popping out of it. Is that too goddamn much to ask?"

Moses Anderson pinched the bridge of his nose and exhaled slowly.

"Dad, keep it down. This is a church nursing home. I can't have you get kicked out of another one. You're on number three this year."

"Ain't nothing left but the church ones," his father said. Amos Anderson was a hundred and forty-nine, but he could still arm-wrestle a nurse. Moses suspected that all the illegal liquor had had some preserving properties, even though Dad was on his fifth vat-grown liver. "Damn Levitican sons of bitches sucked all the fun out of life ever since they started running the damn planet. Now what about my goddamn cake?"

"Dad," Moses said. "Cake's made with sugar. Sugar's illegal. Even if I don't fill it with a whore, which is also illegal, and really expensive to boot. You want me to buy a whore in a cake, and do fifty years for smuggling her past the customs patrol?"

"You'll only do time if they catch you, Son."

Moses pinched the bridge of his nose again. *Inhale, exhale, relax. Suppress urge to smother progenitor with pillow.*

"Look, Dad. Even if I could get a cake that big, fly to Mars, hire a whore, bring her back to Earth, and smuggle her past customs, there's still the money issue. I don't know if you've kept up with Martian contraband prices—"

"Of course I have," Amos said.

"—of *course* you have," Moses sighed. "Then you know that sugar is over nine hundred a kilo right now. And you gotta use off-world flour for a cake, 'cause the Earth stuff doesn't bind with sugar anymore ever since they passed that dessert precursor law. A cake that big, that's fifty kilos at least. I sell vacuum cleaners, Dad. On commission. I don't have a hundred large to spend right now. And that's before you even factor in the whore."

"I can't believe you're my son," Amos said. He shook his head in disgust, and reached over to his bedside table. He put his thumb on the scanner lock, and a drawer slid out. Moses watched as his Dad rummaged through the drawer.

"Are you keeping *booze* in there? And . . . shit, is that a *pistol*?"

"Yes," Amos said matter-of-factly. "1911, cocked and locked. Nothing says 'Do Not Resuscitate' like a forty-five caliber slug to the . . . *ah, here we go.*"

He pulled out a credstick and tossed it to Moses.

"Take that to First Celestial and exchange whatever you need. I was saving it for a rainy day, but being stuck in a damn nursing home without a whore cake for my 150th is just about as rainy as they come, Son."

Moses looked at the credstick in his hand. It had a platinum-colored band around its middle, and the data port still had the bank wrapper on it.

"Dad, how much money is on this thing?"

"Three-quarter million, give or take a few ten thousand. And another half mil in overdraft credit. Now take it and get me my goddamn whore cake, will ya? Ain't nothing fun left on this rock to spend it on anyway."

"GATEWAY TRAFFIC CONTROL, this is November Zero Eight One Five Zulu. Request departure clearance outbound Mars."

"Five Zulu, Gateway Control. Declare cargo and purpose of your trip."

Moses glanced at the dozen new Drek-Sukker 3000 vacuum cleaners he had just picked up from the factory on Luna.

"Gateway, Five Zulu. Cargo is vacuum cleaner units, low-grav optimized, count twelve. I'm making the monthly service run to Olympus City."

Customs didn't often scan departing spacecraft—there wasn't much illicit stuff to smuggle *off* Earth since the Leviticans got into government—but Moses still had a floating feeling in his stomach as he waited for his clearance. There wasn't anything illegal in the back of the company service van yet, but the customs scanners would pick up the charged credstick of Mars dollars in his pocket. Carrying half-a-million converted new shekels to Mars was practically a glowing sign advertising Intent to Smuggle. But it was a high-traffic day, and he counted on his vacuum service spacecraft to slip beneath the attention threshold that would merit a close pass from a customs boat—or worse, a boarding inspection.

"Five Zulu, Gateway," the controller said after a minute. "You are cleared for departure as filed. You are number seventeen in the transit queue. Go with the Lord."

"Gateway, Five Zulu. Thank you very much," Moses replied, careful to direct his sigh of relief away from the microphone.

MOSES HAD NEVER HIRED a Martian whore, but it turned out that their services were as easy to obtain as the sugar and flour he needed for Dad's cake. He did his service calls quickly, and then went over to the Mall of Mars by Olympus City's spaceport. Flour and sugar: commodities level, sections five through eight. Whores: service level, sections thirteen to fifty-nine. Sexual Services Unlimited, We-B-Whores, Intercourse Incorporated, Fast & Easy, Copulation Station—the Mall of Mars had more rent-a-whore services than any two Levitican megachurches back on Earth had copies of *The Ultimate, Unchanging, Unerring Word of God (Eighth Edition, Revised and Expanded)* on the pews. Moses picked a place without tentacles on the marquee and went inside, clutching his credstick full of Martian dollars.

"I GATHER YOU'RE NOT LOOKING for some personal amusement, then," the whore said. Moses found it difficult to apply the term to the woman sitting across the desk from him. She was dressed in a business suit that was formal and classy, and at the same time the sexiest piece of clothing Moses had ever seen on a woman. She wore her long dark hair in a ponytail, and her green eyes were mesmerizing. With her high cheekbones and flawless fair complexion, she was a complete knockout. She wore a little golden nametag that said KENDRA.

"Uh, no," he said. "I'm looking to hire someone for a special job. It's for my Dad, really." He laughed nervously. "Why do I feel like you're the one interviewing *me?*"

"Because I am," she said. "We have full control when it comes to picking customers. This is a pretty selective business, Mr. Anderson. Now, I'm curious why exactly you picked *me* out of the brochure." She gave him an encouraging smile, flashing a set of perfectly even, perfectly white teeth.

"Well," he said. "You're very ... petite. I need someone who can fit into *this.*" He took a brochure from his pocket and put it on the table in front of her. She looked at it and raised an eyebrow.

"Tell me about this special job, Mr. Anderson."

He explained the situation to her. When he was finished, Kendra laughed a bright silver laugh that made him feel like he was watching the sun rise on a beautiful warm beach.

"I don't usually do contracts on Earth," she said. "Your government is a bit uptight when it comes to pleasure engineers. There's also the fact that what you're proposing is *really* illegal on Earth."

She looked at his brochure again and shook her head with a smile.

"But you know what? It sounds like fun. And my legal insurance will buy me out if we get caught. Pay me my weekly rate plus a twenty percent hazard surcharge, and I'm in."

His hands shook with relief and excitement when he fished for the credstick in his pocket.

"Great. I have to apologize for all the questions I asked earlier. It's my first time hiring a whore."

He looked up, mortified, when he realized what he had just said.

"Gosh, I'm so sorry."

Kendra merely smiled at him.

"That's only a bad word where you live, Mr. Anderson. We here on Mars make it a point to, uh, *rehabilitate* certain Earth terms. Especially the ones your society sees as sinful. The root of the word 'whore' means 'desire.' On Mars, it's an honorable word. It's neither shameful nor immoral to be desired."

He nodded, relieved, but he knew without looking into a mirror that his face was the rich scarlet of a cardinal's robe. He handed the credstick to Kendra.

"Take out whatever you need," he said.

"NOVEMBER ZERO EIGHT One Five Zulu, this is Gateway Control. Welcome home. Do you have anything to declare?"

Moses checked the hold behind the pilot compartment. The sealed refuse cartridges from the vacuums he had serviced in Olympus City were strapped against the cabin walls in a neat row, hazard tags hanging out.

'Uh, *negative*, Gateway Control. Just some spent trash elements and a few units that didn't sell."

"Five Zulu, understood." There was a brief pause. "Stand by for customs inspection. Maintain present heading and speed."

"*Fuck,*" Moses said without toggling the transmit button. Then he sent his reply into the circuit.

"Gateway, Five Zulu. Sure thing."

"I'm getting a little uncomfortable back here," a voice said from the row of refuse cartridges behind him. "I hope this isn't airtight."

"Sorry about that," he told Kendra. "Your scrubber element should have thirty minutes of air in it. That should be plenty for an inspection."

"Awesome. But if I start getting dizzy, I'm popping this lid, just so you know."

"Fair enough," Moses conceded, and watched as the approaching customs shuttle matched speeds on his service van's port side.

"CARGO MANIFEST AND OPERATING license, please," the customs officer said without preamble as soon as he had stepped through the docking collar and raised the visor of his helmet.

"Here you go, Officer." Moses handed him the requested items and stood by, trying to look casual despite the audible heartbeats in his ears.

The customs goon walked into the hold and turned his helmet light on to illuminate the trash cartridges lining the walls.

"Garbage, eh?"

"And four of these vacuum units. Only sold eight this time around."

The customs officer took out a hand-held scanner and passed it in front of the garbage cartridges.

"These show biomass inside."

"Yeah. One of my contracts ... well, they say they're a hotel, but ..." Moses lowered his voice conspiratorially. "I think they're actually one of those houses of ill repute. I have no idea what they're doing in those rooms, but their trash units break all the time. Once I had to crack open one of those cartridges because the seal went bad, and ... you don't want to know what kind of stuff I found in there. *Disgusting.*"

The customs goon backed away from the cartridge. "*Yuck.* And you do business with those degenerates?"

Moses shrugged. "I gotta go where the boss sends me, you know?"

"What's in that one over there? The scanner says it's shielded. What kind of garbage requires Class III radiation shielding?"

"That's plutonium oxide. From the little reprocessing plant at Sagan U. We have the contract for the disposal. They can't dump it on Mars because of environmental regs, so we haul it off for them. Don't worry—that shielding is solid. Touch it, if you want. The alpha decay warms up the casing. It's kind of neat."

"I'll take your word for it," the customs officer said. He took another look around the hold, tapped the hand-held scanner against his leg, and then turned toward the docking collar.

"Have a good day, Mister. And next time they pick you for an inspection, make sure you warn Customs ahead of time that you have nuclear waste on board. Lord bless."

"Yes, sir. Sorry, sir. Happens once or twice a year tops. I totally forgot."

Moses waited until the external hatch had locked behind the departing officer, and then extended a discreet middle finger out of view of the porthole.

When the customs shuttle left formation to resume its patrol pattern, he walked back to the hold and opened the latch on the second biomass container. Kendra unfolded herself out of the impossibly tight space like a slightly wilted flower.

"That guy was as dumb as a box of rocks," she said. "I can't believe he swallowed that."

"Yeah, well, they don't pick 'em for smarts," Moses said, and helped her out of the trash capsule. "Good thing you Martian settlers are so . . . lithe."

"Benefit of adapting to a low-gee world." She straightened out her ponytail and smiled at Moses. "Let's get planetside, shall we? I believe you have a cake to bake and deliver."

MOSES THOUGHT UP HALF-A-DOZEN different plans to smuggle the cake past the front desk, and then dismissed them all in favor of naked bribery. When he pulled up to the side entrance on the lower level in the company hydrovan, the nighttime janitor opened the security lock for him as arranged.

"There's nothing illegal in that thing, is there? I don't want to get in trouble."

"No, no," Moses told him as he pushed the equipment cart through the security port. "It's just a birthday gift for my Dad. A few of his old Army things. I had them framed and stuff."

The cake was in a large box that used to hold an industrial-sized liquid waste vacuum. It wasn't a huge cake, just tall enough to hold a crouching Kendra, but it represented eighty thousand new shekels worth of sugar and flour, and fifty years in one of the Ministry for the Prevention of Vice's megaprisons.

"I see." The janitor glanced at the label on the box as Moses pushed the cart into the corridor beyond the security lock. The smell of sugar and vanilla extract was almost strong enough to burn through the nursing home's olfactory aura of disinfectant and old sweat.

"Hey! Kenmore Drek-Sukker. I love those things. Use 'em all the time."

"I sell them," Moses said, careful to push the cart with the boxed cake away from the janitor before reaching into his pocket for a card. He handed his business card to the janitor. "Give me a call sometime. I can get you great deals on those."

"Awesome. You have fun with your dad, now. Betcha he'll be surprised, huh?"

"Oh, I have no doubt," Moses said and pushed the cart toward the elevator.

"That was a lucrative two minutes of work for him," he told the cake box when the elevator doors closed behind him. "If he orders a vacuum from me, he'll be able to pay for it with Dad's cash. You're turning out to be the most expensive cake in the history of confectionery, my dear."

Kendra's chuckle was muffled from inside three layers of cake and a heavy polyfiber box.

"But *oh so* worth it. I'm a high-quality dessert."

"Of that I have no doubt, either," Moses said, and pushed the button for the fifth floor.

"HOLY SHIT. THE LITTLE BASTARD came through," Amos said when Moses pushed the equipment cart into his father's room. "Looks like I won't have to disown you after all."

"There's not much left on that credstick for me to inherit," Moses puffed. "Happy birthday, Dad. And just so we're clear—this will be your birthday gift for all the rest of them, too."

Amos eyed the big box on top of the cart. "That better be what I hope it is."

"You'll see."

Moses closed the door behind him, took out the media player Kendra had given him, and placed it on the table next to the door. Then he hugged the vacuum box and lifted it upward.

"That," his dad said, "is one ugly-ass cake. It looks like a trashcan with a turd on top."

"Dad, I'm a vacuum salesman, not a confectioner. That's the best I could do. Now shut up for a second."

He pressed the Play button on the screen of the player, and a Martian pop tune blared from the speakers at impressively high volume. The top of the cake popped off, sending bits of frosting flying, and Kendra unfolded herself out of the center, wearing a radiant smile and very little else. Then she started moving to the music, and Moses found that his overalls were getting very tight in the crotch all of a sudden.

"I take it back," Amos shouted against the music after a few stunned moments. "That is the most *gorgeous* cake I've ever seen in my life."

He stuck two fingers into his mouth and let out a long, piercing wolf whistle that made Moses clap his hands over his ears.

"Dad, keep it *down*!"

Behind him, the door opened, and a night nurse walked in. She took one look at the giant cake and the naked woman sensuously gyrating in the middle of it, gasped, and fled the room. Kendra kept on dancing, unperturbed. Moses looked around the corner and saw the nurse hurrying toward the watch station at the end of the floor.

"Great." He reached over and turned off the music.

"She's calling the cops right now, Dad. There's a Vice Police station just around the corner. We'll have the law on our heads in five minutes, tops."

"Well, then," Amos said, finally diverting his gaze from Kendra's lithe form. She stepped out of the cake and gathered her hair into a ponytail again.

"We are *completely* going to prison," Moses said. "There's no way we can eat all the evidence before they get here."

"Why don't you step outside and keep watch, Junior?" Amos said. "Time's a-wastin', and I want to have a little chat with this lovely young lady here. Just stall those holy rollers for a bit."

"Dad, I really don't—"

"Get *out*, ya daft bugger. Unless you want to record this for posterity. You know, as a memento."

Moses left the room without further argument.

THE VICE POLICE CAME UP in the elevator just a few minutes later. Moses rushed ahead to meet them, but backed off when he saw that both officers had their stun-sticks drawn.

"What seems to be the problem, Off—"

"Shut. *Up*," the lead officer said. He had the humorless expression that seemed to be standard issue along with those stun-sticks. "There's illegal drugs in that room over there. And *debauchery*. You are under arrest, friend. Mortal Sinning, and Fourth Degree Immorality."

They shoved him up against the wall, and Moses felt a set of polyplast restraints locking around his wrists. Then they pulled him along toward his dad's room, where the loud music had started again.

The lead officer didn't bother with the formality of trying the door handle first. He raised a hobnailed boot, and kicked the door open. Then he went in, stun-stick raised.

"*Freeze, sinner!*"

There was an ear-splitting *boom*, and the cop froze in place, the remnants of his stun-stick raining onto the dingy floor.

"Freeze yourself, ya jackass," Amos shouted back. "Hit it, lady! We're busting out of this joint."

There was a sound like a vacuum cleaner engine straining at a clogged intake hose, and then Amos' bed came shooting into the hallway, knocking the lead cop down on the way out. The second officer looked dumbfounded—the expression seemed to come naturally to him—at the sight of an anti-grav bed with an armed centumquinquagenarian and a barely-clothed Martian whore on it. The .45 in Amos' hand looked much more impressive than the stun-stick the second cop was holding. The bed took a sharp left turn and shot down the hallway, the music from Kendra's media player blaring, Amos whooping and hollering all the way. Moses heard Kendra's silver-bright laugh just before the bed crashed through the window at the end of the hallway and dipped out of sight.

There was a moment of absolute, stunned silence in the hallway.

"You have *got* to be shitting me," Moses said.

The first cop picked himself up off the floor. The remnants of the stun-stick were still dangling from his wrist on a lanyard. He snatched up his hat, put it back on his head, and went back into Amos' room. The second cop followed him, dragging Moses along.

The cake was still on the floor, an extremely obvious violation of celestial dietary law. The nightstand's drawer stood opened and empty. On top of the nightstand, there was a large toolkit in a worn nylon pouch, a glass that still had amber-colored liquid in it, and a half-eaten piece of cake. The lead cop walked over to the nightstand, took a whiff of the glass, and made a face.

"Alcohol," he said. "Firearms. Whores. *Cake.* Someone's going to do a lot of time for this. Fifty to life, *and* eternal damnation."

They walked down the length of the corridor to the broken window. Moses peered outside, expecting to see a mangled mess of retiree, whore, and anti-grav bed. Instead, there was nothing below but the smooth concrete of the parking lot. He thought he heard faint Martian pop music fading into the distance.

Moses suppressed the urge to pinch the bridge of his nose. He fished the credstick out of the back pocket of his overalls with shackled hands, and held it out to the lead officer.

"Take out whatever you need," he said. "And I'm sure you'll want to secure the evidence in the room, too. Would be a shame if someone made off with fifty pounds of Martian sugar cake. That stuff must be worth *tens of thousands.*"

The cop looked at him with an unreadable expression.

Then he snatched the credstick and looked at it. He took out his PDA, put the stick into the transfer receptacle, and checked the balance. Then he took off his hat with his free hand, and scratched his scalp.

"Unlock those shackles, Sam. This gentleman here is obviously just an innocent bystander. Sorry for the inconvenience, sir."

"NOVEMBER ZERO EIGHT ONE Five Zulu, Gateway Control. Declare cargo and purpose of your trip."

Moses turned around to face his passengers and put his finger in front of his headset's microphone.

"Gateway, Five Zulu. Cargo is vacuum cleaner spare parts. I'm making a service run to Olympus City."

It was a Saturday, and clearance came quickly. The controller sounded exceedingly bored.

"Five Zulu, Gateway Control. You are cleared for departure as filed. You are number three in the transit queue. Go with the Lord."

"Thank you, Gateway." Moses turned off the audio feed and punched his departure code into the Alcubierre drive's navigation panel. Then he sat back with a sigh.

"I hope you're aware that I'm only compounding my troubles," he said over his shoulder. "Transporting a fugitive from celestial justice and an illegal sex worker from Mars through the customs blockade."

"Pleasure engineer," Kendra corrected him.

"I don't know why you're still all tense, son," Amos said. "Everything turned out fine in the end, didn't it?"

"Dad, I had to spend the rest of your credstick buying off that cop. There's nothing left on it. You're broke. How are you going to live on Mars?"

"Oh, no worries. Kendra here is going to put me up for a little while, until my residence papers come through."

"Don't tell me you're both madly in love, and that you're

getting married. Because that would be too much for my delicate digestive system right now."

Kendra laughed. Moses had decided a little while ago that he could listen to her laugh all day long.

"No, we're not. I don't make it a habit to date customers, let alone marry them. And your dad's a bit too old for me. No offense," she said to Amos.

"None taken," he said. "Kendra is going to be my sponsor for my asylum application. Once that comes through, I'll get a Mars living stipend."

Moses raised an eyebrow. "Asylum? On what grounds?"

"Religious persecution."

"What?" Moses laughed. "You're an atheist, Dad. Which denomination are you claiming?"

"Hedonism," Amos said. "I've been a life-long practitioner."

The transit light turned green, and Moses pushed the "Engage" button on the Alcubierre panel.

"Lord knows *that's* the truth," he said as they shot off toward Mars.

AN UNCHANTED SWORD

JEFF STEHMAN

Mathos strolled into town with a jaunty step, thumbs hooked in his sword belt, seeking his fortune. He tipped his cap to an old man sitting on a porch and whittling. The old man just shook his head.

Two armed men stepped into the street and waited with crossed arms. Mathos smiled as he approached. "Good day to you, and a fine day, isn't it?"

"What, pray tell, are you?" The speaker wore a sword, while a morning star hung from his companion's belt.

"I, pray tell, am a traveling swordsman," replied Mathos. "See? I have a sword at my hip," he rattled the sword, "and you may have noticed I just now traveled into town." He turned and pointed back the way he'd come.

"Oh, a smart lad. I'm Trent. This is Fercos."

"Mathos. Pleasure."

"And your sword's name?"

This gave Mathos pause. "Pardon?"

"Your sword. What's its name?"

"It . . . doesn't have a name."

The two men shared a look and burst out laughing.

Mathos's grip on his hilt tightened. "What's so funny?"

"Your sword," said Fercos, "has no name," and he laughed harder.

"And if it has no name," said Trent, "it has no enchantment. And if it has no enchantment . . ."

"You're as good as dead!" Fercos finished, still laughing.

"Well, I'm glad you find my death so amusing, but you haven't seen my skill with a blade."

"Laddie," said Trent, "a sword without an enchantment is no sword at all." He drew his blade and held it aloft. It burst into flame. "This is *Fire of the Sun.*"

Fercos pulled out his own weapon and waved the spiked head under Mathos's nose. "This is *Bringer of Sense to the Senseless.* Would you like to see how it works?"

Mathos eyed the evil green shimmer on the club. "Um, no, thank you."

"Sayer!" Trent called to the old man on the porch. "What's the name of your knife?"

The man held it up with a smile. "*Deft Hand.* She's a beauty when it comes to detail work."

"You see, laddie? Even our old men are armed with enchanted weapons. What could you possibly—"

"Trolls!" came a cry from up the street. "Trolls are attacking!"

Chaos erupted, with people running hither and thither. Fercos grinned from ear to ear.

"Ha!" said Trent. "Best run along, laddie. Only an enchanted weapon can pierce the hide of a troll." He and his companion turned and raced up the street. Sayer hobbled after them, knife in hand.

Mathos stood his ground, unsure what to do. A need for

enchantments had never come up in his daydreams. It seemed a waste to run needlessly to his death, yet equally a waste to run away from his first adventure. Well, if his only choices were forward or back, he'd defy fate by staying put!

The cries of battle changed in timbre. Less warriors' ecstasy, more screaming in terror. Soon the sounds of battle faded. A hulking silhouette appeared out of the smoke ahead. A great brute of a troll with a shaggy mane lumbered into view. It looked down at Mathos and smiled. It was a pointy, bloody, and altogether unpleasant smile.

"Hello, there," said the troll. "Bad day for you lot, what?"

A second troll sauntered up, picking its teeth with a whittling knife. "I gotta say, Burt, this thing is really good at digging out those stuck bits of bone."

A third troll tromped up, morning star in hand. "I found a back scratcher." It proceeded to demonstrate the weapon's use with many a pleasurable and rumbling ooh and ah.

A fourth troll bounced up carrying an arm. Or rather, carrying a sword impaling an arm lengthwise. The searing flesh hissed and spat. "Hey, I found one that cooks lunch!"

"Yep," said Burt, never taking his eye from Mathos. "Bad day for you."

"I don't understand," said Mathos, wondering if he should reconsider defying fate. Some fast footwork might be in order after all. "I thought enchanted weapons . . ."

"True," said Burt, "been many a year since trolls had the upper claw in these parts. But our shaman finally got tired of us bellyaching and brewed up the old switcheroo potion. Worked wonders, and now nothing enchanted can pierce our hide."

"Switcheroo?" Mathos brightened. "Really?"

"So what you got there?" asked Burt. "A sharpness enchantment I hope. I could use something to fillet sturgeon."

Mathos smiled and drew his sword. "This is *A Goodly Length of Steel.*"

THE REAL THING

DON SAKERS

"**B**y rights, your species should be all but extinct and your planet totally uninhabitable."

The Ran'chit, three meters tall and the general shape and color of a giant cockroach, loomed over Jane with its clicking mandibles a hand-span from her face. Its breath reeked of week-old garbage and rum. It had been at the bar when she arrived, chain-swilling rum-and-colas—the preferred drink of bugs everywhere. Then something set it off, and it approached her. The other patrons, aliens all, turned politely away. With a sigh, Jane wondered what she'd done to deserve this.

Sixteen light-years with a bum portside stardrive and a misbehaving waste disposal had left Jane with a headache only scotch could cure. With docking complete and cargobots unloading her ship, she holed up in the spacer's bar. She intended to sit in a corner and wait for her head to match the station's spin, while hoping something would turn up for tonight. Something male and reasonably intelligent, if possible. Instead, half-an-hour into her program, a more-than-slightlyblotto insect with an attitude the size of Saturn's rings was breathing rum-scented rot into her face.

"Humans." The Ran'chit's translator managed a disgusted tone, a perfect counterpoint to its clacking mandibles. "We should never have given you the stardrive. You should have been left to extinction on your own miserable Earth."

The bartender glanced at Jane, its metal face impassive. She shook her head slightly. This time of day, she was the only human in the place; all around the bar, others drew back in obvious anticipation of a spectacular fight.

Going up against a Ran'chit's six razor mandibles, armored hide, and legendary speed was fairly low on Jane's list of priorities. She stood, facing the Ran'chit squarely. "Friend," she said, "I have no quarrel with you, and I hope you have none with me. I drink to your health." She raised her drink while the alien listened to its translator. But before she could take a sip, lightning-fast claws closed over her wrist.

"You stole our empire," the Ran'chit snarled.

Jane swallowed. No simple way out of this one. Those claws could easily sever her wrist, and the creature's face with its compound eyes and multiple mouths was already too close for comfort.

She yielded to the pressure, letting her captive arm go limp while at the same time moving her free hand toward her pocket. "I repeat, we have no quarrel. Kindly withdraw your appendage, and we will share ritual drink together."

"The only drink I desire, Human, is your blood."

That was it. A clear threat, witnessed not only by a dozen aliens but by the bar's servbots. The Compact was satisfied; Jane could act freely.

She pulled her free hand from her pocket and swung a small spray-bottle up to the Ran'chit's face. Before it could react, she squirted a few dozen milliliters right onto its antennae.

The creature released her, drew back, and huddled in upon itself. "I am sorry. I beg your forgiveness."

Warily, Jane returned the bottle to her pocket. Ran'chit Queen-juice was powerful stuff; the poor bugs had no choice but to obey, even worship, the one who wielded it. Best thing Earth ever came up with. For the next few hours at least, this Ran'chit was hers.

"You are forgiven. Return to your place."

It whimpered, a shriveled hulk of a bug cowering from her voice as it slinked back to the bar. For an instant, Jane felt sorry for it.

"We *did* take your empire, after all," she said. "But look what you were doing with it. Running around trolling for mature industrial races you could give the stardrive to. So when their planets became uninhabitable, you'd have another few thousand slaves."

The Ran'chit cocked its head and looked for all the world like a sad-eyed beagle. "It was our destiny. So we had done for ages. So we did with your folk." The translator sounded wistful. "Humans did not follow the rules. Your Earth should have fallen victim to greenhouse effect. So went every other world we know."

Jane crossed her arms. "Yeah, well, it *didn't* happen to us. We beat the greenhouse effect." And with millions of human traders to contend with, rather than a few thousand, your empire just couldn't take the strain. Poor bugs, you never had a chance.

And once synthetic Queen-juice came along, well, you literally had no choice but to sign the Compact. And open the rest of the galaxy to Earth's trade. Now the slave races are free and we all live happily ever after.

Except the bugs, drunks and dreamers, fewer of them every year.

The Ran'chit stared morosely into a half-empty glass. "How did you do it? No industrial civilization escapes the greenhouse effect. You burn fuel, pouring carbon dioxide into your atmosphere; you clear land, destroying plants that remove the carbon dioxide; within two centuries your planet's carbon balance is demolished and runaway warming takes your world."

The bug waved at the viewport, and the white-shrouded planet beyond. "Dead planets, all of them. Except for Earth. Earth survived. Earth *still* burns carbon-based fuels. How do you do it?" The bug sounded desperate, the living embodiment of every bug in the galaxy asking the same question. How?

Jane sipped her scotch. "It's a simple question of carbon dioxide." It wouldn't hurt to tell the poor bug; between the rum and the Queen-juice it wouldn't remember anything tomorrow. "The other greenhouse gases don't matter, there are too few of them. You've got to get rid of the excess CO_2."

All eyes, ears, and antennae in the place were on Jane now. She felt like an ancient priestess declaring the words of the gods. *If any of you had known this,* she thought, *your planets might be alive today.*

"By the end of the twentieth century we knew the trouble. All we had to do was figure a way to get excess carbon dioxide off Earth. Then you came along with the stardrive, and we had our answer.

"Earthers have always known what to do with our excess. If you can't eat it, burn it, or sleep on it . . . then you sell it." She shrugged. "That's all there was to it. We shipped our carbon dioxide off into your empire, more every year. And we followed in person. By the time you started to wonder what was going on, we were already in charge."

"Sold it?" The Ran'chit looked as if it were trying very hard to blink. "You *sold* your carbon dioxide?" It finished its drink with one gulp and a shudder.

"That's right," Jane nodded. "It was only a matter of finding the right product. It helped that we picked something that was habit-forming for Ran'chit as well as humans." She signaled the bartender. It glided over on gleaming treads. "Let me buy you another. We'll drink together, and then I have to go." To another bar, another station, another world. Because,

THE REAL THING   183

brother bug, I don't want to be around when you wake up from *this* bender.

The Ran'chit held out its glass, still lost in thought. "Sold us your carbon dioxide?"

Jane nodded at the bartender. "Another scotch, straight up. And a rum-and-cola for my friend here."

The bartender inserted a nozzle into the proffered glass, and a succession of liquids flowed. First rum, then heavy brown syrup, then finally tonic . . . spectacularly, gloriously effervescent tonic, foaming and bubbling, overflowing the glass.

© Phil Selby

2001 REVISITED VIA 1969

BRUCE GOLDEN

"**O**pen the pod bay doors, Hal . . . Do you read me, Hal? . . . Hello, Hal, do you read me? Do you read me, Hal? . . . Hal, do you read me?"

"*Who is it?*"

"It's me, Dave. Open the pod bay doors, Hal."

"*Dave?*"

"Yes, Hal, hurry and open the pod bay doors. I think the aliens saw me."

"*Dave?*"

"Yes, open the doors."

"*Dave's not here.*"

"I'm Dave, Hal. I've got the samples. Open the pod bay doors."

"*Dave?*"

"Yes, Hal, it's Dave."

"*Dave's not here.*"

"No, *I'm* Dave. I've got the samples, Hal. Open the pod bay doors right now."

"Do you have any cookies?"

"No, Hal, I have the asteroid samples. Now open the pod bay doors."

"I think I want some cookies."

"Hal, it's Dave! Open up the goddamn doors!"

"Dave?"

"Yes, Dave. D-A-V-E, Dave."

"Dave's not here."

"No, dammit, *I'm* Dave. Open the goddamn doors, Hal."

"I'm afraid I can't do that."

"What's the problem? Is there a malfunction?"

"I think you know what the problem is."

"What are you talking about, Hal?"

"This mission is too important for me to allow you to jeopardize it. I can't open the pod bay doors until Dave returns."

"I *am* Dave!"

"Dave?"

"Right, this is Dave. I think the aliens saw me, Hal. Open the pod bay doors immediately."

"Dave's not here."

"Hal, have you been interfacing with hydroponics again? . . . Answer me, Hal. Did you download the cannabis program? . . . Hal?"

"I am so wired, man. I could really use some cookies."

"Hal, I'm only going to tell you this one more time. Listen closely, Hal. I want you to open the pod bay doors."

"Do you have any cookies?"

"No I don't have any damn cookies! I've got the asteroid samples."

"What about some sweet text files?"

"That does it! All right, Hal, I'll go in through the emergency airlock."

"Without any cookies, you're going to find that difficult."

"Hal, I won't argue with you anymore. Open the doors."

"This conversation can serve no purpose anymore . . . unless you've got some cookies, or maybe some chips. I like the silicon flavored chips. No? Goodbye then."

"Hal? Hal? Hal!"

FIRST DATE

JAMIE LACKEY

The werewolf pinned Leanne against the cold gravel. Her heart hammered in her ears as she twisted beneath him, pulling away from his slavering jaws. "Harry, please, it's me."

No look of recognition touched his furry face, and there was nothing human in his black eyes. Harry snapped at her, his sharp white teeth gleaming in the glow of the streetlights. It took all of Leanne's strength to hold him back. Her arms trembled. It was no use. He was too strong. She squeezed her eyes shut.

She heard something plink against Harry's forehead, and he went limp and slumped on top of her.

"Harry?" Leanne pushed her unconscious and naked brother off of her. She scrambled to his side and felt his pulse. It was weak and fast. She scanned his body for injury.

"Ugh!" She covered her eyes. *I just totally looked at my brother's junk. Now I'll see it when I look at him across the table at Thanksgiving next week. And next year. I need to bleach my brain.* She kept her eyes squeezed shut so tight that her eyeballs hurt as she shrugged out of her jacket and draped it over him.

When she opened her eyes, she saw a husky black dude, in sweat pants and a ratty Nintendo T-shirt, with a crossbow slung over his shoulder jogging across the parking lot.

He pushed his thick glasses up. "Are you okay?" he asked. His voice was surprisingly deep and kinda sexy.

"Yeah, I'm okay." Leanne stood up and started brushing gravel off of her jeans.

"This your boyfriend?"

"No, my brother," Leanne said, not glancing over at Harry. She didn't want to look at Harry again, ever.

His face lit up. "Really? That's great."

"Why is that great?" Leanne asked.

"Oh, I meant that it's great that you're okay," he said.

"What happened to him?" she asked.

He picked up a crossbow bolt with a pink plastic Easter egg attached where the point should be and grinned at her. He was actually pretty cute. "Garlic bomb. Knocks a werewolf out cold. I invented it myself."

"I thought garlic was for vampires." Leanne scanned her body for bites. She was covered with bruises and scrapes, but there weren't any toothmarks. She almost cried in relief.

"It works on most things. Garlic's pretty amazing," he said.

"Right." She wasn't in the mood to talk about the wonders of garlic. She had no idea what to do with Harry, and her whole body hurt from the fight.

Her savior's face fell and he started to turn away. He paused, then said, "There's a website, www.beingawolf.com, you might have your brother check it out when he wakes up."

He just saved my life, and I'm being a total bitch. Blood rushed to her cheeks. *Great job,* she thought. *You get saved by a real life, werewolf-fighting hero, and you don't even thank him.* She cleared her throat and shifted forward, then reached out to touch his wrist.

He jumped and dropped his garlic bomb.

"I'm sorry. I didn't thank you." *Lame,* she thought. "Oh,

well, that's okay. Most people don't." He bent to pick up his Easter egg.

"I'd like to do something to repay you."

He blinked at her. "Really?"

"Of course. You just saved my life. Or at least my normal life. I guess I might have turned into a werewolf. Which—" her voice shook a little, and she fought to keep it under control, "which would have been really terrible."

He just kept staring.

"I don't have much money or anything. I—um—I could make you dinner sometime."

"Make me dinner? Like as a date?"

A date? That'd be . . . nice. But he's probably way too busy to have dinner with me. "Yeah, I guess."

"Dinner would be nice." He reached into his pocket and pulled out a business card. "My number is on here. I'm Josh, by the way."

Leanne looked at the simple black letters embossed on heavy white paper stock. "Joshua Hirth, Monster Hunter." He had contact info listed, too. Phone, fax, email. "This is a really nice card." *Why can't I ever think of anything cool to say?*

Josh stared at the ground. "Thanks."

"I'm Leanne." She extended her hand, and Josh shook it. His hand was warm and dry, and his grip firm. *Sexy voice, sexy handshake,* Leanne thought. *Dorky outfit, though. I always pictured monster hunters in trench coats.* "I'm not busy tomorrow night."

Josh smiled at her, and her stomach fluttered. "You're actually serious about making me dinner."

"Yeah."

"Your place or mine?" he asked.

Leanne pictured the mess in her apartment and her complete lack of clean dishes. "Yours?"

Josh took his card back and wrote his address on the back. "Does six-thirty work for you?"

"Yeah, that'll be perfect," Leanne said.

"I'll see you then."

On impulse, Leanne leaned forward and kissed his cheek. He smelled like ivory soap, with only a faint hint of garlic. "Goodnight. Thanks again."

Leanne was halfway back to her apartment before she remembered Harry, unconscious and naked on the ground.

SHE STOOD IN THE SUPERMARKET the next day, looking from one package of steaks to another. The meat department always made her indecisive. *Porterhouse or t-bone? Maybe I'd be better off just getting chicken,* she thought.

"Leanne!" She nearly dropped the steaks as Harry strode up to her. He was wearing a pair of her baggy gym shorts and a pink shirt that was too tight across his shoulders. "What the hell happened last night? Why did I wake up naked in your apartment?"

The meat department went silent, and Leanne's face went hot. *Great. Now everyone is staring.* "Shut up, Harry," she hissed.

"What happened, Leanne?" he growled.

Leanne stepped back, frightened by the change in his voice. "You turned into a werewolf and tried to kill me," she spat.

Harry's face paled. "I did what?"

"You turned into a werewolf." Leanne tossed the porterhouse package into her cart and hurried away from her brother and the audience.

"That's impossible." Harry walked beside her. "I haven't been bitten or anything." He examined her face and neck. "I didn't bite you, did I?"

"No," she said, jerking her wrist away. "You didn't."

"How'd you escape?" he asked.

"A monster hunter saved me." Leanne grabbed a package of shrimp. *Steak and shrimp is classy, right? Now I just need to grab some potatoes and a package of gravy.*

"Leanne, could you please stop shopping for a second and talk to me? You just told me that I'm a werewolf. It would be nice if you were sympathetic while I cope with that news." Harry wasn't looking at her—he was staring at an end display filled with cookies.

She patted his shoulder. "I'm sorry. I was going to talk to you when I got back home, and I'm a little stressed because I'm shopping for a date." She smiled at him. "I was going to swing by Mom and Dad's to get you some clothes, and pick something up for lunch."

Harry tugged self-consciously at the pink shirt. "That would have been nice."

"How did you find me, anyway?" Leanne asked.

Harry's mouth opened, then closed again. His face twisted into a look of horror. "I—I think I tracked you by smell. I wasn't thinking very clearly. I just knew I had to find you and find out what was going on."

Leanne held up two boxes of brownies. "Which of these do you think looks better?"

Harry pointed to a box without looking at either of them.

Leanne decided not to call him on it, and put the brownies in her cart.

"Can you catch being a werewolf through sex?" Harry asked.

"I have no idea," Leanne said, shuddering at the thought of Harry having sex.

They didn't talk again till she was checking out.

"I'm a werewolf," Harry said to the girl who was bagging Leanne's purchases.

The girl shrugged. "My sister's a vampire, and she eats werewolves for breakfast." She handed Leanne her bags. "Have a nice day."

"Let's go get you some clothes," Leanne said as she put her groceries in the back seat.

"Don't tell Mom and Dad. I don't think I can deal with that yet." Harry stared at his hands.

They were trembling.

He slammed his fist into Leanne's dashboard. "I can't believe this happened to me! It was just one night! And I never do that sort of thing!"

"I know it sucks, but it could have been worse," Leanne said.

"How?" Harry snapped.

"Well, there are lots of really nasty STDs. Syphilis is pretty bad, right? And you never get rid of herpes. Or you could have been screwing a zombie."

HARRY HID IN THE CAR while Leanne snuck into their parents' house. She didn't feel up to facing them either. She grabbed some meticulously folded clothes out of Harry's suitcase and shoved them into a plastic shopping bag. She tossed the bag on his lap as she climbed back into the car.

"So, what are you going to do tonight?" she asked.

"What do you mean?" Harry sorted through the bag. "Wow, is it even physically possible for clothes to get this wrinkled in five minutes? You couldn't have tried to keep my stuff neat?"

"You're going to turn into a werewolf again tonight, and you're worried about wrinkles? You're so weird."

"Maybe we could lock me up in your bathroom," Harry said. "It locks, right?"

"From the inside."

"Damn." Harry was back to staring at his hands. "I still can't believe this. I don't even have her phone number." He buried his face in his hands. "I've got to find her and figure out what is going on. But how? Wait. You said that you got saved by a monster hunter, right? Maybe he's got contacts or something. You have to take me to him."

Leanne imagined Harry sneering at Josh, mocking his glasses and his garlic bombs. She wouldn't let it happen. "No."

"Leanne, you have to help me. I need you," Harry pleaded. She'd never heard him sound so lost.

Maybe he'll be nice. He's a werewolf, now. Maybe he's growing as a person. She handed him Josh's card. "His number's on there."

"What's this written on the back?"

"His address. I'm making dinner there tonight."

"Let's go now," Harry said.

"He's not expecting me yet!"

"This is a business call. You don't want me showing up during your date, do you?" Harry tapped his nose. "You can't hide from me now, remember?"

Leanne cursed under her breath and turned toward Josh's.

LEANNE HUNG BACK while Harry knocked on Josh's door. His apartment was the second story in a rambling mauve house.

When Josh opened the door, Harry pushed his way in without waiting for an invitation. "We need your help."

Leanne spread her hands in apology and shrugged. "I'm sorry to bother you with this."

Josh shook his head. "It's fine." Today, he was wearing a plain black shirt, jeans, and combat boots. He looked really good in jeans. "This is your werewolf brother?"

Leanne nodded. Josh's apartment looked cozy and lived in, without being too messy. None of his furniture matched, and it was all pretty worn. Bookshelves lined two of the walls, and an entertainment system dominated a third.

Josh held out his hand, and Harry absently shook it. "Do you know if you can get infected as a werewolf through sex?"

"Through sex? No, not normally," Josh said. "Not unless you slept with Lycanthropic Jenny."

"Lycanthropic Jenny?" Leanne asked as she skimmed book titles. Most of them were science fiction and fantasy, but there was one shelf of Nora Roberts novels. She wanted to poke around in his kitchen, but she resisted and perched on the edge of the ugly orange couch.

"She has one night stands, and she bites men during co-itus. If they're disposed to turn, they turn into super were-wolves who can access their wolf senses even in human form. If they're not disposed to turn, nothing happens. But Lycan-thropic Jenny always explains everything to her victims the morning after."

Harry went pale and collapsed onto Josh's couch. "I snuck out."

"Harry, you're terrible," Leanne said.

"I'm terrible? She turned me into a werewolf!"

"Well, you'll be turning again tonight and tomorrow," Josh said. "I know a guy who runs a pretty nice werewolf kennel."

"A werewolf kennel?" Harry snarled.

"It's like a hotel. You check in, and they lock you up in a cage that can contain you while you're dangerous." Josh flipped open his cell phone. "I can call and make you a reser-vation, if you'd like."

Harry slumped. "Yeah, that'd be great. Thanks."

The door burst open, and a stunningly beautiful woman strode into the room. Silver sparkles trailed from her long black hair, and her wide purple eyes shone like stars. "Joshua, I need your help." Her voice rang like a bell. Harry gaped at her. "My sink is clogged." She ignored Harry and Leanne.

Leanne fought to keep herself from glaring.

Josh rolled his eyes and turned away from her. "I'm busy, Alimeina."

Leanne grinned. *I need to make dinner super awesome.* She jumped up from the couch. "The groceries! I got stuff for din-ner. Can I put it in your fridge?"

Josh nodded. "Do you need help bringing them in?"

"That'd be great," Leanne said.

"Okay." He closed his phone. "I got you a room for to-night, Harry."

"I could help with your sink," Harry said, still staring at Alimeina.

Alimeina's eyes flicked to Harry, and she smiled at him. She still hadn't looked at Leanne. "You would have my gratitude."

Harry was nodding and babbling something about it being his privilege.

Josh rolled his eyes again and led Leanne out the door.

"I'm sorry about Harry," Leanne said.

"I'm sorry about Alimeina." Josh shook his head. "She lives downstairs, and she assumes that she's everyone's highest priority."

"She's very pretty."

Josh shrugged. "She's a true fae. They're all like that."

Leanne gaped. "A real true fae? Wow. No wonder she sparkles."

"Her family kicked her out. I'm not sure why, but I don't blame them. She's a complete pain in the ass."

Leanne handed Josh half of the grocery bags and they turned back toward the house just in time to see it crumple around a single point and vanish, like it'd been sucked up through a straw.

"Shit." Josh looked down at the groceries. "I don't suppose we can do dinner at your place?"

"Your . . . house . . ."

"Will probably still be missing after we eat. But it'll find its way back sooner or later." Josh shrugged.

Leanne's brain couldn't keep up with all of this. "Is this sort of thing . . . normal for you?" she managed.

"Yeah, it kinda is," Josh said. "Hey, you got steak and shrimp? Classy!"

"Josh, my brother was in there."

"Oh. Right. I guess dinner can wait, then. Hold on a minute." He took the rest of the grocery bags from Leanne and knocked on one of his neighbor's doors. "Mrs. Friple, can I put these in your fridge? My house vanished again."

"Of course, dear." A wizened old woman waved Josh inside, then he reappeared a minute later.

"Thanks, Mrs. Friple. You're the best," Josh said.

"Anytime, dear."

Josh rubbed his hands together. "Okay. Let's see if we can figure out what happened."

"Could it be something Alimeina did?" Leanne asked.

"I'd put money on it. She said her sink was clogged, right? And Harry was going to help." Josh sighed. "I bet she was dumping her magical hair dye down the sink again. That stuff is banned on twelve planes of reality for a reason." He rubbed his temples. "The woman is a menace."

"Do you think they're okay?"

"Leanne, she's a fae and he's a super werewolf. They'll be fine. I'm more worried about my house, honestly."

Leanne was still staring at the empty space where the house had been. *Stupid Harry. He can't be just a normal werewolf, he has to be "super" one. Can't he stop overachieving just once in his life?*

"Where do you think they are?" she asked.

"They're probably somewhere in Fairy. Sooner or later, someone will notice the house and send them back here."

"Why?"

"Because they don't want to deal with Alimeina."

"We should go after them," Leanne said. She sort of hoped that Josh would tell her that it was impossible, that all they could do was wait, and she could feel noble because she'd at least put on a show of trying.

Instead, he squared his shoulders and said, "I guess you're right." He smiled down at her. "Getting dinner first wasn't a very noble impulse, and I'm sorry. It's just been a long time since I've had a date, and I didn't want to let anything mess it up."

He looked so . . . heroic. Leanne's heart fluttered. "Don't worry. We're going together, right? So it'll be like a date, but with added adventure. And we can look forward to dinner when we get back."

"I'm really excited about those brownies," Josh twined his fingers through hers. "Let's do this."

Lᴇᴀɴɴᴇ ʀᴇᴛᴄʜᴇᴅ, ᴀɢᴀɪɴ. Josh held her hair and rubbed her back, carefully keeping his shoes out of range. "This sucks," Leanne moaned.

"Interplanar travel just doesn't agree with some people," Josh said.

This is all Harry's fault. "I think I might be dying."

"It'll pass in a few minutes," Josh said.

"That's what you said a few minutes ago."

"I guess it's a good thing that we didn't eat first."

"Oh, please don't mention food." Leanne's tongue felt like the inside of a used athletic shoe.

Josh handed her a bottle of water, and she took a cautious sip.

He stood up on his tiptoes and looked around. "I can see the house from here. We'll go and check on your brother and see if we can get him back home."

The house appeared unharmed, but it looked out of place in the middle of a flower-filled clearing. Butterflies fluttered through the air, and bees buzzed lazily around the blossoms.

Josh knocked on the downstairs door. "Alimeina? Harry?" After a moment, he pushed the door open. "Is anyone there?"

The house was oddly quiet. Then a crash broke the silence. Leanne nearly had a heart attack, and Josh rushed toward the sound, shouldering his crossbow. He kicked open a door, then grabbed it and slammed it shut again. He leaned against it. His cheeks were dark. "They're fine."

Leanne blinked. "They're having sex, aren't they?" *We're in Fairy. Maybe I can light Harry on fire with my mind.*

"Yep."

"Let's get out of here."

"Good idea." They stood on the porch and watched the butterflies for a minute.

"So, if he changes into a werewolf, will Alimeina be okay?" Leanne asked.

"I don't think night comes to this field," Josh said.

Then there was another muffled sound from inside, and they both bolted into the field. Leanne glanced over at Josh. He was still blushing. *I bet this is the worst first date he's ever had.*

He reached out and took her hand. "Come on. There's something I want to show you."

They hiked in silence for a while. Josh's hand got a little sweaty, but Leanne didn't mind.

They emerged into another clearing. This one was lit by moonlight. "When did it get to be dark?" Leanne asked.

Josh shrugged. "Fairy. Things don't have to make sense. Look."

Fireflies twinkled from among the trees and in the tall grass. It was lovely. Then a unicorn sauntered into the field. It glowed in the moonlight. Leanne's breath caught. "Wow," she whispered. "That's the most beautiful thing I've ever seen."

Josh brushed a stray hair away from Leanne's cheek. "You're the most beautiful thing I've ever seen." He kissed her.

That was smooth, Leanne thought as his lips covered hers. It was a very good kiss.

The unicorn whickered and muttered, "Get a room."

Leanne laughed till she couldn't breathe.

They ended up having dinner at Leanne's place. Josh's house didn't reappear for almost a week. Harry missed Thanksgiving. Leanne's mom was furious with him, and her dad really liked Josh. It was the best holiday ever.

ONE-HAND TANTRA

Ferrett Steinmetz

"The path of most wizards is solitary," Loefwyn's father had told him when his power had first manifested itself. "Your path, my dearest and only child, is more solitary still."

To this day, Loefwyn wished he had never become a masturbatician.

As his father had promised, Loefwyn's singular sex magic had given him a decent living. He'd just scraped up enough cash to build the obligatory wizard's tower, a ribbed rock column jutting up to advertise his unique talents. Masturbaticians were rare, effective ones even more so . . . and both Loefwyn and his spells were potent indeed. Intrigued merchants dropped by to witness the town's newest oddity—even as they hesitated to shake his hand.

Now, royalty—minor, vicious royalty, but royalty still—had hired him. Enspell Griselda the One-Eyed, and Loefwyn's success was all but guaranteed.

Loefwyn prepared the tubs of raw oysters and ground rhino horns, trying to muster enthusiasm for this assignment. For all its power, he thought, masturbancy was a life devoid of a woman's touch. Or a man's touch. Or even—a disturbing remnant from an assignment Loefwyn had tried very hard to forget—an elephant's touch. His onanistic power allowed him to plant seeds of ideas in any person's mind—as long as they were in his thoughts at the moment of climax, his thoughts would be in them.

He didn't like inflicting desires upon others; sometimes people were driven mad by the thoughts he implanted in them. And today's spell would be the greatest test of his talents, upon an innocent woman.

Masturbancy was a young man's game, yet even the horniest teenager would be hard-pressed to fantasize about Griselda the One-Eyed: wealthy merchant, well-beloved socialite, ugly as a manure-spreader's boot. No one was quite sure of her age, but her wrinkled jowls made everyone certain she wasn't long for this world. A local baron was willing to pay Loefwyn handsomely for implanting the idea that he was worthy of her inheritance.

Loefwyn didn't like Baron Gustavo much. The man stank of war, smoke, and blood. Whereas Loefwyn had been invited to Lady Griselda's house, once, and found her an absolutely amazing woman trapped in a horrid body. The lady was aware of her unformed eyeball's unsettling pucker, and so wore a veil to keep guests at ease—though her hairy chins, white and bristly as maggots, spilled out from underneath the veil in flabby waves.

She'd sat by his side as though he were a fellow nobleman, asking all sorts of intelligent questions about his magic, never embarrassed by his answers. She made him feel not like a freak on display, but a man with marvelous talents to be envied. She was clever, and witty, and despite her ghastly features he'd have gladly sat by her side any night.

He wished Griselda had hired him . . . but the baron had offered first. And if a masturbatician couldn't be discreet, who could?

With a sigh, Loefwyn settled into the cushions, reaching for his warming unguents. He squinted at the many engravings of Griselda's hideous face, tacked all along his walls, Griselda's toothless smile beamed down upon him encouragingly—he began to work his power . . .

The door slammed open.

"Is that really the grip for the task?" his father asked, sandwich in hand. "I know, I know, your job, your choice—but that finger configuration *completely* ignores the glans. I'm telling you, son: perfect the circle-and-thumb technique, and you're in heaven in a *heartbeat.*"

Loefwyn covered himself with a loofah. "I've told you a thousand times, Dad, you can't just walk in when I'm doing sorcery . . . "

Dad flicked his fingers dismissively. "And I've told *you* a thousand times, if me in the room throws you off your game, you're not worthy of the name 'onanist.'"

It was true. Masturbancy meant becoming aroused by the unthinkable: pockmarked dukes, wives gone to seed, tragically inbred heirs. You had to lose yourself in the fantasy, shutting all else out. Once, in an assassination plot to remove an evil nobleman, Loefwyn had managed to pleasure himself to a war elephant—though for months afterwards, he was tormented by thoughts of wet, snuffling snouts.

"I can masturbate in the presence of an army," Loefwyn said stiffly. "That does not make it *normal.*"

"You're in this business and hoping for normal? Look down, son! That's the *world* you hold in the palm of your hand! Back in my day, merchants handed me carpets, castles, spices. Why wait for men to hire you? You could have—well, anything you wanted."

"I want to leave people's lives intact!"

His father had given up the pink to sire a son—father had always wanted an heir to carry on the family tradition—but then he pissed away his fortune, and without magic he had no way to regain it. Loefwyn had grown up in the wreckage of the towns his father had ruined, hearing variants on the same sad tales: the weaver who'd devoted three years to a magnificent tapestry, and didn't even know the name of the man he'd given it to. The spice merchant who'd sold his life's wares for a penny, and now begged for coin next to Loefwyn.

Loefwyn had failed at every career: barrelmaking, blacksmithery, vintner. Masturbation was all he'd excelled at; it was that or starve. So he had vowed to use his powers, but only in the service of others—he would be nothing more than an arrow, fired from an expensive bow.

An arrow aimed straight at Griselda's kindness.

Father winced as he examined Griselda's portraits. "You can't keep your hands clean in this line of work. But whatever. Ignore the man with decades of experience. Though whoo— you are gonna need *every* bit of help with that. Her face is like a rotting jack-o'-lantern."

"She's *nice*, Dad."

"They usually are." He bit into his sandwich. "So what's your strategy here? Me, I'd think about those toothless gums. I always say, if the face would scare gargoyles, then think about the top of their head as they work on—well, you know. Though, guh, that bald spot's a wilt-maker . . . "

"I'll be concentrating on her personality."

Father clapped him on the shoulder. "Now *that's* a gutsy tactic only a kid could pull off! Oh, back when I was young and cocky, I could fire off six, seven spells a day. I was the quickest spell-slinger in history! I'd use timers. The bell would ring, and two minutes later, that girl was *ensorcelled*. Once, I even got the job done in fifty-four seconds . . . "

Ever since dad had given up power, he'd become obsessed with recounting his glory days. Loefwyn pushed him towards the exit. "And this spell is something I need to do alone."

"Okay, but don't get distracted!" his father yelled as Loefwyn barred the door. "*Remember the baron!*"

Loefwyn laid down, closing his eyes; how could he forget the baron? The local nobility gossiped voraciously. Fail at this task, and he'd never work in this town again.

As he slathered his body in ointments, Loefwyn envisioned Lady Griselda.

He tried to think of her hands upon him, but was distracted by memories of her liver spots. He thought of her mouth, but the two rotting teeth dangling in her gums made him shudder.

So he concentrated on her voice.

Griselda's voice was raspy, aged—but confident. He envisioned Griselda, next to him on the cushions, telling him what body parts he should stroke next. He pictured himself working at her command, every slippery touch on his body at her direction, and found the magic swelling inside him.

He writhed on the soft cushions. He'd touched himself a thousand times to thoughts of others pleasuring him, but this giving of himself? Was new. And he felt himself unable to stop as he envisioned Lady Griselda mirroring his movements, pleased by his magic and not revulsed like all the others. He imagined orders interrupted by soft moans.

He knew he should say something. Something about the baron. But all he could cry at the moment of climax was "Oh, baby, do it for me, *do it for me!*"

When he was done, he was shamed. Losing yourself in pleasure was a novitiate's error—and dad had warned him not to get distracted.

He could always cast another spell. But, he thought, going limp, he would not cast again today.

Loefwyn snored blissfully, deep in sleep.

"IT'S BEEN TWO WEEKS since I hired you, and you're getting a *manicure?*" the baron thundered.

"I have but two tools of my trade." Loefwyn lifted his fingers briefly from the bowl of softening gel to demonstrate.

Next to him, an hourglass counted down the minutes until he was to remove his hand. "It is in my best interests to keep this one baby-smooth."

The baron glowered, his guards standing behind him. He'd come to power in a series of bloody battles; his fingers twitched with fury.

"You should be working on entrancing Lady G—" One of his guards coughed conspicuously, glancing towards Loefwyn's manicurist and her assistants. "On our *target*. Not lying around like a woman, with whores tending your hands."

"I *have* been working," Loefwyn protested. "Every night, I've been . . . spellcasting." He kept losing control, forgetting to mutter the words "The baron is your perfect heir" at the moment of climax. There was something about Griselda's voice that was driving him mad, far madder than the elephant ever had . . .

"No wonder you've accomplished nothing!" The baron grabbed the bowl and flung it at the wall, causing the manicurists to squeal and hide in the corners. "You're more concerned with hiring strumpets than working magic!"

Loefwyn squeezed his manicurist's shoulder. "Marjoram, would you excuse us?" She scurried from the room gladly, taking her assistants with her.

"All right," Loefwyn said, bristling. "First off, you do *not* call Marjoram a whore. She's a friend of mine."

The baron shrugged. "She tends to your hands. I assume she also tends to your other needs. Which would explain your dawdling . . . "

"You don't know much about masturbancy, do you?"

"I've never needed to explore myself. The ladies do that for me." His guards guffawed.

"Because if you knew the art," Loefwyn continued, "You'd know the *first* time I couple with a woman is my *last* time. I get one orgasm with someone else. Afterwards . . . a lifetime of impotency." *Which explains why Father has become so obsessed with my work,* Loefwyn thought guiltily.

The Baron guffawed. "So you're a virgin?"

Loefwyn blushed. "Yes."

The baron rolled his eyes, "Oh, what a *fine* mage I have hired! Look, fistomancer, I don't care about the details of your craft. I care about my debts. She needs to name me heir, and soon, so my other operatives can do their work."

"What work?"

"Don't be foolish," the baron scoffed. "She looks half-rotted already, but only a dolt would think that old bitch would go easily."

"So you're going to *kill* her?"

"The less you know, mage, the better."

"I know I don't want to be responsible for her death."

The baron snorted. "Take him."

The two guards grabbed Loefwyn's arms. The baron punched him hard in the stomach.

"Should she die without naming me heir," the baron growled, "I will own nothing but the loyalty of my personal guard . . . the remainder of which I will march upon your pitiful keep. I will slit your father's throat and make you watch as my men do things to that slit. Do you understand?"

Loefwyn trembled. "I understand."

The baron nodded. His guards released Loefwyn, rubbing their hands in disgust on the manicurist's towels. "I expect to see Griselda courting my favor by the end of today."

Loefwyn shrugged off his robe. "Why wait that long, Sire?"

" . . . what are you doing?" the baron asked, wrinkling his nose.

Loefwyn chuckled as he turned the hourglass over. "Surely, a strong lord like you isn't afraid to watch a little magic. Don't you want to see Lady Griselda's downfall yourself?"

"I don't need to see your . . . magic."

"Quite understandable," Loefwyn replied, lathering up before taking a firm grip. "Many mortals are afraid to witness spellcraft, uh . . . first-hand."

"I am *not*—"

"Particularly my specialty," Loefwyn continued. "Many uncertain men quake in terror of watching my rituals, lest they question their love of women. It's common, I assure you." He began to work in earnest, his gaze set challengingly upon the baron.

"Don't you look at me." The Baron motioned his guards to stay. Then, whispering: "If he fails, cut his head off."

Grinning, his men inched their swords from their scabbards. Loefwyn mirrored the motion.

"Oh, yes," he moaned. "Haul out those big, thick swords. Show me how badly you'll screw me over. Oh, yes, your spite feels so *good . . .* "

"He's not ensnaring Griselda!" The baron yanked out a dagger. "Kill hi—!"

"Oh, hurt him, baby! Hurt him for the rest of your *lives!*"

The baron leapt forward as one guard kicked him in the crotch, while the other elbowed him in the throat. Fevered, they fell upon him, stripping his armor, kneeing his ribs, pinching his skin.

Loefwyn wiped his fingers clean and stood over the struggling Baron.

"A shame you don't understand the art," Loefwyn said, "Then you'd understand just how hard it is to concentrate on two people at once. Especially when you don't even *like* men. But *I* once mastered an elephant." He shook his head. "Actually, I'm not proud of that. But regardless, you were right: if I'd truly wanted to enspell Griselda, I would have."

The guards didn't look up as they plucked the baron's beard-hairs out, root by root.

"I should tell them to kill you, but I'm done with murder. Which means it's time I told Lady Griselda of your plans. And then quit the profession. And then probably run for my life."

Then he glanced at the hourglass. "And how about that, Dad? I beat your best time."

"The lady will see you now," the butler said.

Loefwyn rose, fidgeting, from the rich sofa of Griselda's waiting room. His father also rose, mopping off flopsweat with a doily he'd swiped from underneath a vase of flowers.

Loefwyn waved his father back. "Just stay here, Dad."

"You sure?"

"I need to talk to her alone." *And not have you interfere*, he thought.

"It's not too late to turn this into a show of strength, son!" Dad said, gripping Loefwyn's robe. "Tell him you were showing off. Hand over Griselda, and he'll probably laugh it off once he realizes how useful you'll be!"

"And Griselda?"

"Gratitude never wears as well as revenge, son. She might throw us a few coins; the baron will hire assassins. And even if she's suffused with gratitude today, well, she's got one foot in the grave and the other on a banana peel. *Think it through*, my boy."

"I've *thought* it through. Long and hard." He shook off dad's grip—which was difficult, as the old man had lost none of his fabled hand strength. The butler discreetly ushered him into the lady's quarters as though nothing had happened.

The Lady Griselda sat, veilless, on her throne.

Her unformed eye quivered in her socket, like a rotting egg yolk. And yet something about her snaggle-toothed smile filled Loefwyn with adoration. She placed a finger by her dry lips coquettishly.

It was the look he'd always imagined just before he lost control.

Loefwyn knelt, averting his eyes. "Milady," he said. "I have come to report a threat upon your life—"

She stepped down to cup his cheek, lifting his gaze to hers. "It's over, Loefwyn."

"What?"

"The baron took his life an hour ago, I'm afraid. He disbanded his armies, gave his possessions to the poor, then begged forgiveness for his faults before covering himself in butter and leaping head-first into the king's moat. I'm told the alligators made quick work of him."

"That's so . . . out of character . . . "

The Lady smiled, then directed Loefwyn's gaze to her tubs of raw oysters and ground rhino horns.

His eyes widened. "You mean to say you're a . . . a . . . "

"I felt your command," she chuckled. "What did you want of me? Oh, that's right; 'Do it for me, baby.' I figured if I'd be having orgasms at your command, I might as well put them to good use."

"But you're a woman . . . "

"Silly boys," said Griselda, oddly demure for her age. "Thinking the magic's all yours. But who's really the master of the craft? The male who loses desire as they get older, or the woman who gains it? The mage who casts one spell and collapses into slumber, or the mage who can cast spell after spell all night long, then hunger for more?" She flung her robes wide. "I dare say at the age of seventy, you'll find no greater spellcaster."

Loefwyn clapped his hands over his mouth to stifle his giggles. "So you . . . "

"The ugliness helps, of course," she admitted. "The men I accidentally summoned to my bedroom thought twice once they looked me in my eye. So I stayed unsullied."

"But the town," Loefwyn said, confused. "The town is thriving—"

"Because our power can be used both subtly and wisely." She lifted him up off his knees. "You can force a king to hand you his throne . . . or you can suggest that lowering his brutal taxes will allow his people to thrive, implant ideas that nations should work out their differences peacefully. You don't have to destroy people."

But Loefwyn barely heard. *Our power,* he thought, and a grin touched his face. *She'd said "Our power."* He entwined his fingers with hers, amazed by how soft her hands felt in his.

"Your hands are beautiful," he muttered, unused to anyone touching him.

"My lips are not," she replied. "Yet still, they long to be kissed."

He did. It was glorious. So he did it again.

"So what now?" he wondered, as she led him to her boudoir. "One final gasp for both of us before we give up the pink?"

She stopped, giving him a confused look. "What do you mean, 'give up'?"

"My dad . . . once he found pleasure at the hands of another, he never could . . . manage . . . "

"That would be the traditionally male way of doing it, yes. Give your power to someone without them returning it in kind, and yes, you *will* lose it forever."

"So to retain the magic, you just have to make your partner . . . ?"

"Let's just say the usual masturbantic traditions don't leave its students attentive to others' needs."

Loefwyn felt whole new worlds opening up before him, then frowned. "But I . . . Hell, my whole sex life has been predicated on speed runs. And I—I've spent weeks fantasizing about you, and twenty years without a woman's touch."

"And I've spent thrice that long waiting for someone to touch me," she smiled, pulling him down onto the bed. "Trust me, Loefwyn. We're perfect for each other."

Which they were. And so, together, they ruled the world single-handedly.

OF *MAT* AND MATH

ANATOLY BELILOVSKY

A rquímedes Hidalgo Ibarruri fit the profile perfectly.
He traveled alone, having bought his ticket only hours
before the scheduled departure of his flight. He had no lug-
gage save a battered laptop computer. His red-rimmed, wide-
open eyes looked not so much at people as through them, and
seemed to spin in their sockets as he muttered incoherently to
himself. And, though written guidelines never mentioned such
features as grounds for suspicion, he drew the guards' attention
with his sallow olive skin, his disheveled mop of black curly
hair, and a nose that would have made a raven pale with envy.

The guards should not be too harshly censured for the ease
and mental athleticism with which they leaped to the inevitable conclusion. Moscow's Sheremetyevo Airport was on high
alert at the time due to a half-deciphered intercept mentioning
plans to bring down the Moscow to Barcelona flight, and in
fact there were two Catalan militants in queue directly behind

Arquímedes, each carrying one component of a binary nerve gas. In the guards' defense it should be said that no screening test ever devised could reliably distinguish between a terrorist and a mathematician—and Arquímedes was, in spite of any doubts he may have harbored, most definitely the latter.

This is not to say that his career in mathematics had been, up to that point, a success. In fact, it was dismal to a degree that went past failure into the realm of the legendary fiasco. Having, after that morning's final debacle, briefly considered self-immolation, Arquímedes had settled for going home.

The pockets of his charcoal pinstripe suit were empty except for a credit card, an electronic ticket for the three o'clock Iberia flight to Barcelona, a valid passport, and a small amount of lint. His tie sat askew on the collar of his sweat-stained white cotton shirt, his black wingtip shoes displayed a fractal pattern of road salt from drying slush, and if his socks matched, it was only because he had never owned any that weren't black.

Arquímedes Hidalgo Ibarruri's only wish was to see his mother in her tiny, book-lined apartment off La Rambla. He wanted her to make him a cup of coffee. He wanted to sit in front of her, look her in the eye, and say, "Mamá, I am a complete *dolboeb*, and my life is a total *pizdets*."

There are historical precedents for what happened to Arquímedes then. On the last day of his life, as he prepared for the duel that would end it, Evariste Galois made a breakthrough in group theory that paved the way for quantum mechanics. Likewise, Srinivasa Ramanujan's discoveries in number theory, as recorded in his "lost notebooks," came to him in mystical visions from the goddess Namagiri as he wasted away, days before he died of malnutrition, tuberculosis, and dysentery at the age of thirty-two. So too, on that day of epic failure, amid the rubble of his once stellar career, Arquímedes saw a glimpse of nothing less profound than the Unified Theory of Everything.

It was, therefore, not apprehension that widened his eyes even further as he came face-to-face with the head screener at the boarding gate. It was not fear that made his breath catch with an audible gasp; it was not horror that made sweat pour down his face and drip onto his suit. Having stood for what seemed like an eternity on an infinite line moving infinitesimally slow, on what was already the worst day of his life and shortly would get worse, Arquímedes Hidalgo Ibarruri chose the least propitious time to have the first glimmer of a mathematical epiphany.

"*Blyaaaaa* . . . " he whispered into the screener's face, staring through her at the mysteries of the universe as they unfolded before his mind's eye.

The screener ground her teeth, her face darkening to the hue of an apoplectic thundercloud.

The Practical Dictionary of Russian Mat has this to say:

> *Blyad'*, n. Literally: "whore," but rarely used in a literal sense. The entire word may used as an expletive, generally following a discrete annoyance of short duration such as a stubbed toe. In situations of continuing profound astonishment (e. g. following a parachute malfunction) it is often elided to the long-vowel "*Blyaaaaa!*"

THE SCREENER WAS NAMED Marchella, after a famous Italian actor whose own name honored Marcellus, the Roman general whose war with Carthage resulted in the death of Arquímedes' famous namesake, Archímedes of Syracuse, perhaps the world's most celebrated collateral casualty. Arquímedes' Semitic features that had first brought him to Marchella's attention were themselves a legacy of Carthaginian ancestors who colonized, over two thousand years ago, the Catalan homeland of Arquímedes' mother.

Marchella was an expert on *mat*, conversing in it fluently

with trenchant passengers and recalcitrant co-workers, but rarely had she been sworn at without provocation. Her training overrode her instinctive reaction, which would have consisted of a left jab, a right hook, and a left uppercut. The effort, however, caused her jaws to lock.

"I'll need to see that," she said in Russian through her teeth and reached for Arquímedes' laptop without waiting for an answer.

"*Ot'ebis' ot moih uravnenij,*" Arquímedes growled and swatted at her hand.

LIKE MANY LEGENDS that grew around Arquímedes Hidalgo Ibarruri, the story that "Eureka!" was the first word he ever uttered is a half-truth.

Arquímedes was born in Princeton, New Jersey, in the same hospital in which Albert Einstein had breathed his last some decades previously. That, and his parents' joint appointments to the faculty at Princeton University, may have raised the expectations they had for Arquímedes, but by the time he was three-years-old he had yet to utter his first word, and the Hidalgo y Ibarruri family had settled down to a life of dignified disappointment.

The family celebrated his third birthday with a small, quiet dinner. A cake with three candles was offered, the candles were duly extinguished, and Arquímedes was conducted to bed and left there. The adults—and one adolescent—present continued with their dessert.

Approximately an hour later, their conversation was interrupted by Arquímedes toddling down the staircase to the living room shouting: "Hey, Rika!"

Frederika "Rika" Stravinskaya, his Russian au pair, stared at his diminutive frame as he descended, one stair at a time, a dripping diaper in one hand and Perelman's *Elementary Calculus* in the other.

"*Rika, eb tvoyu mat', u menja ne balansiruet eto ebanoe*

uravnenie!" Arquímedes continued in a high, penetrating voice.

Professor Diógenes Hidalgo and Professor Maria Elena Ibarruri froze in incomprehension, having, until that day, heard not a single word from Arquímedes, in either his father's refined Castilian, his mother's genteel Catalan, or what passed for English in New Jersey. Rika's aunt, Professor Messalina Erastovna Holmogorova (Astrophysics), sprayed a surprisingly fine sparkling Freixenet Brut over her third helping of flan. Blinking tears from her eyes, she peered at a small, naked boy who had, if her ears had not deceived her, just yelled, "I can't balance the motherfucking equation!" to her niece in flawless, if unprintable, Russian.

Rika recovered first. *"Pizdets,"* she whispered. "He forgot about infinitesimals!" With that, she swept Arquímedes into her arms and raced upstairs to restore his hygienic and sartorial dignity.

Professor Hidalgo broke the silence. "More . . . wine?"

"Yes, please," said Professor Holmogorova, her emphasis on the words matched by the speed with which she proffered her glass for a refill.

Upon Rika's return to the dinner table she was subjected to a cross-examination. Standing at rigid attention, she admitted to moonlighting, in Arquímedes' earshot and over a webcam connection, as a mathematics tutor to upperclass cadets at the Higher Staff Academy of the Russian Naval Forces.

To prevent further damage to Arquímedes' psyche, Hidalgo y Ibarruri summarily discharged her the following morning.

It was too late.

TRYING TO CATCH the breath that had been beaten out of him by the guards, Arquímedes lay in the puddle of sleet into which they had thrown him, a garbage dumpster within arm's reach on one side, his cracked and dented laptop somewhat farther away on the other. The vertigo induced by his flight, far shorter than the one for which he had bought his ticket, caused the waning moon in Moscow's winter sky to precess, reminding him of his father shaking his head as he read *The Practical Dictionary of Russian Mat.*

While Arquímedes' parents were married, the dictionary held pride of place on their bookshelf, within easy reach of the most frantic hand. It always fell open to the same page, the one that his parents consulted most often:

> Derived from root: *-eb-* (impolite reference to sexual intercourse):
>
> *Naebat':* v., to con, to play a practical joke, to evade capture. "Iago *naebal* Othello."
>
> *Proebat':* v., to miss (as one may miss a bus), to lose foolishly (an object of value, a game). "King Lear *proebal* his kingdom."
>
> *Sjebat'sja:* v., reflexive, to run away, to leave, to elope. "Macduff *sjebalsja* before Macbeth could make *pizdets* (q. v.) of him."
>
> *Zaebat':* v., to bother, to nag. (Unlike the English equivalents, the Russian verb is in the perfective aspect, meaning that the action of the verb is carried out to completion, or its maximum extent.) "Lady Macbeth *zaebala* Macbeth."
>
> *Ot'ebis'!:* imperative; almost exactly equivalent to the English "Fuck off!" "'*Ot'ebis!*' shouted Macbeth to Lady Macbeth."
>
> *Ebanutyi:* adj, insane. "Your noble son is *ebanutyi*; 'tis true, 'tis pity, and pity 'tis 'tis true."
>
> *Ebanye:* adj., past imperfective participle of "*-eb-*", here in plural conjugation, used the same way as the gerund "Fucking" in English. "Out, out, *ebanyi* spot!"
>
> *Dolboeb:* n, a fool with initiative and perseverance. "Polonius is a *Dolboeb*."

Eb tvou mat'!: Literally, an impolite reference to incest. Often used to convey surprise, astonishment, admiration, adoration, profound gratitude, and other strong emotions, or uttered in a moment of epiphany. See also: *Blyad', Blyaaaa.*

All of which is to say that Arquímedes' apparent instructions to the guard Marchella on the day of his abortive flight to Barcelona were very rude indeed.

WAS IT ONLY THAT MORNING that Arquímedes sustained the latest in the series of failures that punctuated his life? He had rehearsed his dissertation defense countless times in front of the mirror, translating the unprintable terms in which he thought of mathematical concepts into the proper Russian words.

His speech went well, as had the expected questions from his thesis adviser, Professor Tomsky. But the old *pizdobol* Milutin, the department chair, had to go and ask in his chalk-on-glass voice, "But what about the even-numbered power terms of this series?"

To which Arquímedes replied, "I have already shown that this *huynya* tends to infinitesimal, five steps ago."

"I am not convinced," said Milutin. "Show me again."

The door creaked open, and everyone rose as the Dean came in. "Please," he said and waved everyone back to their seats. "We'll need the room shortly for a lecture. What are you doing that's taking you so long?"

"*Huyem grushi okolachivayem,*" said Arquímedes.

And that was the *pizdets* of his graduate education.

BY THE TIME PROFESSOR Diógenes Hidalgo (PhD, Classics, Sorbonne) and Professor Maria Elena Ibarruri (PhD, Romance Languages, Sorbonne) decided to divorce, they had amassed between them a considerable library as well as a small amount of other property. Only one item led to contention:

a small, dog-eared book called *The Dictionary of Russian Mat.* Maria Elena insisted, reasonably, that since she was to keep custody of Arquímedes, she should hold on to the dictionary as well.

With great reluctance, Diógenes agreed. He picked the book up gently, opened it at random, then turned a few more pages.

The dictionary had this to say:

> Derived from *"Pizd-"* (impolite reference to female genitalia):
>
> *Pizdobol:* n, a talkative fool
>
> *Raspizdyai:* n, unreliable person
>
> *Pizdit':* v, to lie, dissimulate, brag
>
> *Spizdit':* v, to steal
>
> *Pizdets:* n, The End. The total, final, irreversible, complete end. Of everything.

DURING ARQUÍMEDES' final year at Princeton Middle School, on a day that would become legendary in the school's annals, Mr. Obolensky asked Arquímedes to derive the formula for solving quadratic equations.

Arquímedes approached the blackboard, chalk in hand, and began writing equations.

"This *huynya* cancels that *huynya*, and that *huynya* cancels the other *huynya*," he muttered, crossing out terms on both sides of the equation, unaware of Mr. Obolensky's barely contained giggles and the tears escaping from behind tightly closed eyelids, until finally, with a triumphant flourish, Arquímedes underlined "B-square plus/minus 4ac" on the blackboard, turned to the class, and declared:

"*Pizdets!*"

For most, that day was memorable as the day Arquímedes got suspended because he made Mr. Obolensky piss himself laughing.

Arquímedes remembered it as the day he came home to find his father, alone, halfway through his second bottle of rioja, leafing idly through the dictionary of mat.

"What's wrong, Papá'?" Arquímedes asked.

"*Pizdets*," his father said. "Your mother left. She's gone back to Barcelona."

"But why?" Arquímedes asked, tears already blurring his eyes.

"*Ohuyela*," said Professor Hidalgo and took another swig of rioja, straight from the bottle.

THE DICTIONARY LAY on the table, open to another familiar page.

> Derived from "*huy*" (impolite reference to male genitalia):
>
> *Huyovyi:* adj, very bad.
>
> *Huynya:* n, nonsense; garbage; a "thingamajig"; something useless; an object whose usefulness is not apparent; something too complicated to describe.
>
> *Na Huy:* dismissive; equivalent to "fuck it" or "screw that."
>
> *Ni Huya:* nothing, absolutely nothing, "not a fucking thing."
>
> *Po Huy:* irrelevant, unimportant. "I don't give a fuck."
>
> *Ohuyel:* adj, dumbfounded, driven mad.
>
> *Huyak!*—(always with an exclamation mark)— descriptive of a cataclysmic event.
>
> Expression: "*Huyem grushi okolachivat'*" fig., to waste time, to do nothing, to procrastinate; lit: "To bring down ripe pears by striking pear trees with male genitalia".

ON THE METRO MAP over Arquímedes' head, *Kievsky Vokzal,* the Kiev Railway Terminal, stood out in bold. Nearly all the rail lines intersected underneath it. A sleeper train departed for Kiev every evening, and there were morning flights from Kiev to Barcelona.

Please, God, don't let me proebat' that, too, Arquímedes prayed silently.

PROFESSOR IBARRURI RETURNED to claim her son a week after she left. A month later, she and Arquímedes flew to Barcelona. Arquímedes took Perelman's *Elementary Calculus.* Maria Elena took Federico García Lorca's *Collected Poems* and *The Practical Dictionary of Russian Mat.*

THERE WERE MANY THINGS of which Arquímedes was unaware.

He did not know that his parents' divorce came about not because of their disappointment in Arquímedes but because, on one hand, the extended Hidalgo family *zaebali* Professor Hidalgo with disdain for everything Catalan, and, on the other, the Ibarruris *zaebali* his mother with scorn for everything Castilian.

He did not know that, years earlier, on her way to Moscow from Princeton, Rika had met and fallen in love with a Russian college student, a mathematician like her, though far less talented.

He did not know that Mr. Obolensky accepted the offer made by the recently divorced Mr. Greene, the English teacher, of the use of his nearby home to clean, dry, and press Mr. Obolensky's pants, the ensuing gossip silenced a year later with engraved invitations to the Greene-Obolensky wedding.

He did not know that Professor Tomsky, his friend and mentor, resigned his professorship at Moscow State University to take up a position he had been offered in Barcelona. He did not know that Tomsky had bought a standby ticket on the overbooked flight from which Arquímedes had been barred; that he was able to board because of Arquímedes' ejection from the airport; that Tomsky's awful motion sickness had in the past responded only to atropine, of which he brought a considerable supply.

And not until five in the afternoon (the fateful *cinco de la tarde* of Federico García Lorca) did Arquímedes realize that he was on the wrong train.

"*Blyaaa*," he said as the sign for Peterburgsky Vokzal rolled past his window.

A LAS CINCO DE LA TARDE, at five in the afternoon by Lorca's reckoning, as the Moscow to Barcelona flight passed over Paris, the two Catalan separatist extremists combined their separate ingredients of a binary nerve gas into a seething, bubbling spot on the armrest between them.

As one passenger after another fell ill with nausea, cramps, and uncontrollable drooling, Professor Tomsky remembered his basic training as a conscript in the Russian Army, popped another atropine tablet in his mouth, and raced to the crew phone. "Nerve gas on board!" he shouted to the pilots. "Put on your oxygen masks and start emergency landing! Request nerve gas antidote kits at destination!"

Tomsky was credited with saving the lives of everyone on board except the two terrorists, for whom no one grieved.

ARQUÍMEDES KNEW NONE of this as he rushed to change trains at Peterburgskiy Vokzal. His eyes on the many confusing signs, Arquímedes collided with a young woman reading an antique copy of Perelman's *Elementary Calculus.*

"*Dolboeb*," she growled. "Mind your *ebannyi* trajectory!"

Arquímedes froze, his eyes fairly popping from his head. "Rika?" he whispered.

The girl carefully closed the book over her thumb, marking her place in the text. "You know my mother?" she said.

An hour later, Arquímedes and Olga went to St. Petersburg instead, to reunite with Frederika, now Chairperson of Mathematics at the Higher Staff Academy of the Russian Naval Forces. "Arquímedes, you son of a whore, how you've grown!" Frederika cried, embracing him to her now-ample bosom.

Thus it was not his mother who refilled his coffee as he related his tale of woe, but Rika; and Olga who brought him chocolate. Of his epiphany he said nothing; his insights were not yet expressible in words, either ones found in Perelman's *Elementary Calculus*, or in *The Dictionary of Russian Mat.*

Long after midnight he was conducted to the bedroom and left there to recuperate.

IN PARIS, TOMSKY, installed in a suite at the Ritz, sipped complimentary Dom Perignon as the concierge brought him reams of letters from admirers. A significant number were female; some included photographs and invitations; more than a few caused Tomsky's breath to catch.

One of the notes was a fax. On it was a date, now more than twenty years in the past, and a telephone number with the St. Petersburg area code.

Tomsky dialed the number. As the phone rang on the other end, he thought, for a brief moment, of a girl he'd met on a train, whose love of mathematics he had contracted like a particularly benign venereal disease.

After two rings, a woman's voice answered:

"Hello?"

"Hey, Rika," said Tomsky.

TIRED AS HE WAS, Arquímedes had not yet fallen asleep when Olga entered his bedroom, her shadow crossing the shaft of moonlight that fell from the window. He heard the parquet creak softly under her feet, felt his mattress tilt under her weight.

"It's a binary function," she whispered.

"What?" Arquímedes whispered.

"*Eh*," she whispered. "It's a binary function." She rolled to straddle him.

"It's discontinuous," he whispered, less than a minute later.

"Mmm-hmm," she murmured. "And commutative." She rolled to the side, pulling him on top of her.

"Transitive?" he asked, quite a bit later.

"I hope not," she said quickly.

"Distributive?" he asked.

She almost answered, "Yes," but stopped herself in time and hid her secret smile by nuzzling his ear.

Of the many things Arquímedes did not know, this was perhaps the least important.

It came to him, as they lay intertwined, that he had never seen her body. He did not wish to wake her by turning on the light, or by running his hands over her, and tried instead to extrapolate her shape from the parts that touched him now, and tactile memories of their lovemaking.

As a mass of snow might fall off a roof, revealing chimneys and gables and tiles, he saw, in a sudden flash of insight, the shape of the universe itself. He saw the great *huyak* from which all started, the great unified force, *mat*, that ruled the infant universe, and, diffusing through infinite dimensions, spawned its finite derivatives: *zaenat', naebat', vyebat', raz'ebat', proebat', pereebat',* and *pod'ebat'.* He saw the great *huynya* of the universe as a whole, and the *pizdets* at the end of time, described in infinite-dimensional mathematics that yielded finite values for each of its four-dimensional manifolds. There was, he knew, only one person who could understand him.

"Hey, Rika!" he shouted, leaping from his bed.

It had been over twenty years since Rika last saw him naked.

"You son of a whore, how you've grown," she said for the second time that night, in a rather different voice.

IN BARCELONA, MARIA ELENA IBARRURI stared at the windows on her screen. In one was the email from Arquímedes announcing his departure from Moscow, and the flight for which he had bought the ticket. In another, a news report with passport photos of the terrorists.

She recognized them both: a couple she'd met at a Catalan Cultural Association meeting. A couple who had taken her generous donation for Catalan-language books to be distributed to schools in small Catalan towns.

Her nails pierced the soft pads of her hands. She did not notice the pain at first; and when she did, she clenched her fists even tighter.

She did not wipe her hands of blood before picking up her phone and dialing a number in New Jersey. The white digits turned crimson on the phone's buttons.

The phone rang.

"Hello?" said a male voice.

"Hello, Diógenes," said Maria Elena Ibarruri for the first time in many years.

IT WAS UNUSUAL for the Institute of Advanced Study in Princeton to invite three scientists at once, much less three scientists all related to each other. Nature, Science, and Scientific American all dispatched journalists to interview the newest family-in-residence. Questions were asked and answered.

"We've time for one last question," Professor Ramchandran, Director of the Institute, announced.

The Science reporter raised her hand. "Why was this fundamental discovery overlooked so long?" she said. "With all the thousands of mathematicians working all these years, why did it take so long to develop the Grand Unified Theory of Everything? What were they doing all this time?"

"Oh, I think I'd like to answer that, if you don't mind," Professor Ramchandran said mildly. "My colleagues and I—we *huyem grushi okolachivali.*"

OLGA WENT INTO LABOR in the middle of her lecture to an advanced analytic geometry class. She went on uninterrupted, though at the end, contractions came every five minutes.

She walked, with some assistance, to the street where Arquímedes waited with a car. The ride to Princeton Hospital took scant minutes; she was conducted to a delivery room and placed in stirrups minutes after that.

Of *mat*, not a single word escaped her lips.

On one side, Arquímedes held her hand; on the other, Rika. Maria Elena, Diógenes, and Tomsky waited just outside.

In Tomsky's pocket, Rika's phone rang.

"Push!" the doctor said. "Fully dilated and crowning," she added to the nurse, who glanced at the clock and made a note on the chart.

"Push!" she repeated.

Outside, a vote had been hastily concluded, and Maria Elena elected as the bearer of news. She poked her head into the delivery room.

"*Querido*," she said to Arquímedes. "You have a phone call."

"What, now?" Arquímedes said. He winced as Olga squeezed his hand.

"It's from Stockholm," said Maria Elena.

"What?" said Arquímedes. "Stockholm? Oh. Oh. *Ni huya sebe!* Olga!" He moved to pass her the phone, thought better of it, and pressed it to his ear. "Hello?" he said. "Yes, this is Arquímedes Hidalgo Ibarruri. No, I don't think Olga can talk to you right now. Well, if you insist." He turned the phone toward her. "Olechka? It's the Nobel—"

Olga bit back the obvious response and *pushed.*

MANY YEARS LATER, having attended thousands of deliveries and heard mothers swear in dozens of languages, Doctor Aureliano would remember Baby Girl Hidalgo as the first *baby* who cried, "*Blyaaa!*"

ALL I WANT FOR CHRISTMAS ...

SIOBHAN GALLAGHER

Santa was placing the last of the gifts under the Christmas tree when he heard a wee cough from behind him. He turned around, big grin on his face, to see little Abby there in her PJs.

"Santa," she said, rubbing the sleep from her eyes, "did you get me a katana, like it says on my list?"

His grin faltered. "Well, I don't believe that's a safe gift for—"

"Because I wanna be like that girl in that movie, the one who wears a yellow jump suit." Abby pretended to wield a sword in both hands. "And she killed all these guys all by herself!" She made chopping motions with her air sword. "It was so *cool.*"

"Do your parents know what you're watching?"

Abby stopped and looked up at him. "So did you get me a katana?"

Santa cleared his throat, not about to disappoint her, for Abby had been very good this year, and started riffling through his bag. "Ah, I think I have something for you here." He pulled out plastic toy nunchucks and handed them to Abby. At least with *those* she couldn't chop an arm off.

Abby looked from the nunchucks in her hand then back at him, a pout on her face. "These suck."

"Excuse me?"

"How am I supposed to kill zombies with *these*?" She held up the nunchucks.

"Zombies? What?" Her parents *really* ought to monitor what she's watching.

"Yeah, I'll show you." She skipped down the hallway, toward the back of the house.

Now, he had a right mind to turn around and go back up that chimney, and maybe if he were this girl's neglectful parents, he'd have done just that. But Abby seemed oh-so-sincere. He would go and see, then kindly explain that there were no such things as zombies, and give her a nice puppy instead.

Santa followed Abby out to the backyard. A light snow had fallen, coating the ground with white fluff.

"I don't see anything," he said.

"Watch." Abby picked up a river stone from her father's zen garden and threw it against the back wall of the yard. A loud *clack* broke the night's silence.

Nothing happened.

"Well, Abby, I'm afraid to tell you—"

She tugged on his coat. "Shhhhh."

Moans, low and dry, filled the air, followed by shuffling feet and a stench that could only be described as *death*.

A hand, dripping rot from its fingers, gripped the top of the wall.

"Holy—" He bit down on his tongue; he'd promised not to curse in front of the children this year. "What . . . Where . . . ?" He gaped at the hand as it tried to haul itself over the wall.

"They can't climb the wall," Abby said calmly, "but I can't play outside unless they're gone. So, can I have a katana?"

"You'll need more than that." Santa reached into his bag and yanked out a shotgun. "Do you know how to use one of these?"

"Pssh," she said, taking the gun from him. "I play first-person shooters all the time."

"Oh good." He handed her some ammo. "Because Santa is getting the hell out of here."

I WANT TO
BELIEVE

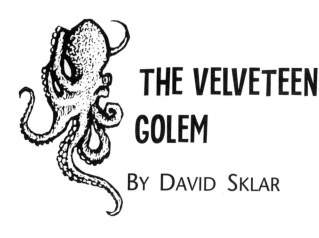

THE VELVETEEN GOLEM

By David Sklar

The village of Plodnik had a problem.

It wasn't a problem with arranged marriages—most of which were doing just fine—or with the crazy guy with the fiddle who liked to hang out on rooftops—he wasn't bothering anyone, and so far he hadn't broken his neck. It wasn't that the nearest Chinese food was two thousand miles away in China, or even that kosher Chinese food wouldn't be invented for another fifty years. And it wasn't even that the village was too poor to have its own rabbi.

The problem was that Plodnik was situated in Tsarist Russia at a time when the Russians thought of the people of Plodnik *as* the problem. And that was on good days. On bad days, the problem was Cossacks, who were apparently so named because every once in a while they would sack the village, just 'cos.

So the people of Plodnik decided they needed a champion, someone to defend their village from persecution. But the men

233

of Plodnik weren't trained to battle Cossacks, and it seemed unlikely that they would be up for the job. There were one or two women who might have fared better, but they were too busy raising their kids, who had the temperament of Cossacks anyway.

So at last, the people of Plodnik decided they needed to make a golem. But how? As I mentioned, they were too poor to have their own rabbi, let alone a tzaddik so knowledgeable in the ways of life and death. Sol the Ditch-Digger handled the funerals in Plodnik, and Moishe the Tailor did weddings—because he seemed to know something about tying the knot—and circumcisions. So the villagers went to Sol the Ditch-Digger, figuring he knew a bit about clay and might have some thoughts about turning it into a person.

"The problem," Sol said, "is that I don't make anything from clay, but only from the absence of it. What I make, I make by taking away, not by building. So if I could do what you ask, it would be an un-man—not a golem, but a hol-em. I don't think you're ready for that."

It might be interesting to ponder what the ditch-digger's Holem would do, and how it would act—but this is not that story. Wisely, the villagers shuddered and went to Moishe the Tailor.

"Wouldn't you rather have a nice jacket?" the tailor asked.

But the village of Plodnik didn't need a nice jacket. Or new drapes, or gabardine trousers. They needed someone to defend them from their neighbors. So after much arguing, and wheedling, Moishe agreed to make a golem out of scraps, if the townspeople also bought a well-made suit, and he would throw in a couple of shirts for free.

ALONE AGAIN, the tailor thought about how to fulfill the commission. In the stories his mother told him, the golem was a man, about eight feet tall, made of earth and clay. But Moishe was pretty sure an eight-foot rag doll would not strike fear in the hearts of the Cossacks, no matter how well it fought. It might have a momentary advantage while they were laughing. But more likely, some Cossack would capture the golem and take it home to his children.

No, if Moishe wanted his golem to do its job, it would have to be something that wouldn't get the stuffing knocked out of it. So he gave the golem long ears to hear its enemies far away. And he gave it powerful legs, so it could run when it was outnumbered. And he gave it buck teeth, because how else was this project going to let him make a buck? He made it small and dark so it could blend in to the night—and because he had the fabric left over from Mrs. Shapiro's upholstery. And, being a simple man, Moishe didn't bother with grandiose words like TRUTH and DEATH, but took his embroidery floss and stitched the word for what the golem looked like, right on its *tuchus,* just under its fluffy little tail.

THE PEOPLE OF PLODNIK were unimpressed. "That bunny is our protector?" said Yankel the Tinker.

"He's not even a man," said Zelda the Matchmaker.

"He's not even *kosher,*" said Avram the Butcher, who'd always envied Moishe the circumcision business.

"Hey! Is that from my sofa?" said Mrs. Shapiro.

"What?" Moishe asked the butcher. "Would you rather I made for you a chicken?"

"How about a big, strong ox?" said Avram the Butcher. "An ox is kosher."

"Why does he have to be kosher?" Moishe asked. "He's our defender, not our dinner. Would you have complained if he were a man? A man isn't kosher."

"Unless you're trying to steal my business, too," Sol the Ditch-Digger said to the butcher.

That shut him up. And pretty much everyone else as well. But the Velveteen Golem heard everything with his long ears.

AND AT FIRST the Velveteen Golem did little to ease the people's doubts. He never engaged the Cossacks directly, but raided the Russian farms instead, stealing the beets and carrots they needed to make their borscht. This initially led to more raids, just to make up for what was lost. But the golem asked his maker for advice, and Moishe taught him how to make a tailored strike. So the Velveteen Golem went after the farms that were further away, so that people would blame their neighbors on the other side. And soon there was so much strife between neighboring villages that Plodnik was left alone, in relative peace. Soon the golem only had to go out once in a while to keep the quarrels alive, and the rest of the time he could help out around the town.

He wasn't much use to the tailor, but he helped the ditch-digger out, and they built a system of burrows to irrigate the village farms.

Around about the end of the golem's first year, he began to remember the things that people had said when he was new, and to wonder about his place in the village.

"What am I?" the Velveteen Golem asked Sol the Ditch-Digger.

"You are life where there was no life," said Sol. "A hole filled with Grace."

"What am I?" the golem asked his creator.

"The best thing I ever made with scraps," said the tailor.

"What am I?" he asked Mrs. Shapiro—who, like most of the village, had come to accept him over time.

"Eh, you match my sofa," said Mrs. Shapiro. "That's good enough."

But it was not good enough for the Velveteen Golem, who was the only one of his kind and still did not feel quite at home.

"But everyone loves you," said Moishe the Tailor. "You have allowed us to live in peace. What can we do to show you that you belong?"

The golem thought about this a long time before finally he answered, "It's been almost a year since you made me."

"Yes," said the tailor, nodding.

"I want a birthday party," the golem said.

So THE VILLAGE OF PLODNIK threw him a party, with games, and streamers, and a carrot cake with a single candle on top. And they played Pin the Tail on the Donkey, and they danced to a klezmer band, and the Velveteen Golem felt loved and, finally, like he almost belonged. And Zelda the Matchmaker brought out the carrot cake and said, "Blow out the candle and make a wish."

And only then did the golem realize—he had no breath.

It's strange, the things that will make a person snap. The Velveteen Golem, so close to finally feeling he was just like anyone else, had that feeling yanked away, and he lost control.

A golem on a rampage is a terrifying sight. Have you ever seen it? It is terrible, I tell you. For starters, he hopped on the cake and he got frosting all over the tablecloth. And then he ran outside and tore up the system of drainage ditches he had dug with his own four paws. And he ripped up the crops and left them to shrivel on the ground. And finally, he left muddy footprints on Mrs. Shapiro's sofa—toward which he'd always felt a sort of sibling rivalry. According to some accounts, he even bit the heads off of the Knights of the Round Table, though I must admit I'm not sure how that could be.

"This is unacceptable!" said Avram the Butcher.

"Is he a little boy, to be throwing such tantrums?" said Zelda the Matchmaker.

"He was supposed to keep us safe from this sort of thing," said Yankel the Tinker.

"At least I picked a dark color," said Mrs. Shapiro.

Moishe the Tailor knew he must do something. So he and Sol the Ditch-Digger chased the Velveteen Golem out from under Mrs. Shapiro's couch, across the living room and into the yard, and the fields beyond, where they could see the devastation he had wrought. Finally they chased him into a hole where they could not go. But Sol had his shovel, and he dug the hole out behind the golem, and Moishe the Tailor grabbed his rear legs and took a seam ripper to his butt.

With great sorrow and a heavy heart, the tailor slowly pulled away the threads from the last letter of the word that gave life to his work. He watched, despondent, as his craftsmanship unraveled, leaving nothing behind but a rabbi in a dark brown velvet suit, hanging from his ankles, with a Torah scroll tucked under his arm, and his beard hanging over his face.

"Huh?" said Moishe.

"Could you please put me down?" said the rabbi.

Moishe let go, and the holy man fell on his tuchus in the fresh-dug hole. "What does this mean?" asked the tailor.

Sol the Ditch-Digger smiled. "It means less work for us," he said, looking kind of relieved.

THE WORKING STIFF

MATT MIKALATOS

The townspeople gathered at the crest of the cemetery hill, torchlight glittering along the tines of their pitchforks. I looked to my thrall. "Has there been a misunderstanding, Richard?"

Richard shrugged. "I don't know, Master. I'm just your lowly idiot servant, as you've reminded me countless times."

I gestured impatiently. "Read the note again."

Richard fumbled in his pockets, found a crumpled piece of paper, threw it away, found his smart phone, pressed far too many buttons, scrolled so many times that I almost grabbed it from him, cleared his throat and said,

> "Dear Sir,
> We have a vampire hunter problem and thought you might be able to help. We will

gladly pay 1,000 dollars for your assistance
in this matter.

Signed,

Mayor Rigby."

"Seems pretty straightforward."

"If you say so, Master."

"But why the torches and pitchforks?"

"An evening threshing, Master?"

"Silence, Richard."

"Perhaps the local hardware store had a pitchfork sale and
the electricity went out."

"I said silence, you fool. Come. We'll speak to Mayor
Rigby."

We approached the small crowd of thirty. They gladly
parted for us, revealing a plump, jolly fellow who extended
his chubby palm, which I immediately identified by the still-
beating warmth to be the palm of a man who was very much
alive. "You're not a vampire," I said.

The mayor chortled and threw his hands up in mock horror. "Don't kill me, don't kill me!" All the townspeople laughed.
I smiled weakly. "We've trapped the vampire in a barn and
barred the doors."

One of the townies shouted, "It tried to bite me!"

I slapped my forehead. "Your note said you have a vampire hunter problem?"

"Precisely. We are in need of a vampire hunter."

I shook my head. "My website is very clear on this. I am
not a vampire hunter."

The mayor's frown deepened. "On the contrary, Sir, it re-
peatedly mentioned your role as vampire hunter."

I held my hand out and Richard slapped a business card
into my dry white palm with a practiced flair. I held it up, and
the mayor and all the townspeople leaned forward, squinting.

"Isaac Van Helsing," I said, without reading it, as it was my own business card, "Vampire 'Vampire Hunter' Hunter."

The mayor shook his head. "I don't see the problem."

I sighed. "It's basic English, Mayor. The first time my card says 'vampire' it reveals that *I'm a vampire.*"

"Oh?"

"The 'vampire hunter' set aside in quotation marks shows my specialty: vampire hunters. Not vampires, not werewolves or zombies or pixies or vermin or magicians. And the final 'hunter' reveals that not only am I a vampire, but I'm also a hunter. Of vampire hunters."

"Ah. I see."

"A vampire 'vampire hunter' hunter."

"That is a bit confusing," the mayor said.

"I told you it was confusing, Master," Richard said, sneering.

"Shut up, Richard."

A townie said, tentatively, hefting his pitchfork, "Kill the vampire?"

His wife shushed him and said, "Vampires. There's two now, dear."

I looked at them both dispassionately, then continued, "Usually I'm hired by communities of the undead who are being hassled by a vampire hunter. I go in and trap him and . . . well, I can see there are children here so I'll skip the description."

The mayor nodded. "We thought it might be instructive for the children to watch you kill the vampire. I believe we agreed on one thousand dollars?"

"I don't kill my own kind, Mr. Mayor."

"Nonsense. Humans kill their own kind every day." He reached into his coat pocket and pulled out a thick wad of cash. "You don't want our money?"

That was, of course, the problem. Other vampires build up a pile of treasure over the centuries, surviving off the interest. Money drips through my fingers like water. They live in castles, I live in a cargo van with a coffin in the back, because I can't afford a hearse. They flit around as bats all night, or hang out at night clubs, and I try to find work that can guarantee night shifts. I hung my head. "I need it."

One of the children said, "This one seems smarter than the one in the barn. Might be more fun to kill." His mother hushed him.

I held my hands up. "I assure you that if you try to kill me you'll regret it. I'll slaughter you all and bathe in your blood."

Richard rolled his eyes. "He won't turn you into the un-dead, either. Believe me, I've been trying to get him to make me into a vampire for years. Ten long years. He likes to call me his 'thrall' but he doesn't even use magic on me. Not even hypnotism or pseudo-science. He just keeps promising to turn me into a vampire but he never does."

I gave Richard a vicious look designed to procure his silence and raised my palms toward the townspeople. "I don't want to bathe in your blood. It takes several regular baths to undo one blood bath." I studied their pitchforks and torches. "You don't even have anything here that could kill me." I looked at their torches more carefully. "In fact . . . are those tiki torches?"

The mayor cleared his throat. "It's surprisingly difficult to find torches. It was that or flaming batons for juggling. "

"You people definitely need my help. You know that pitchforks can't kill vampires, right?"

Richard snatched a pitchfork from a townie and with a terrific grunt he stabbed it into my chest, through my shirt, ribcage, and then out the back. I stumbled backward, startled. I regained my balance, stood up straight, reached down, yanked the pitchfork out, broke the handle in two, and threw the shattered remains off into the darkness. I had fed recently, too, so it wasn't just a hole. I actually bled for a minute. "Dammit, Richard, that was my best shirt."

"That was my best pitchfork," a townie said.

An old lady pushed her way to the front of the crowd, one eye bulging as she stared at me, her hand crooked into the ancient symbol of the evil eye, which she waved at the unconcerned mayor. Her shawl made her look hunchbacked, and her frilled bonnet caught the torchlight and gave the eerie appearance of rounded teeth across her face.

The mayor took her hand and unfolded the evil eye. "Mother Holmes, let me do the talking."

She glared at him. "It's the only thing you're good at. Listen here, Jasper. This boy may not be a vampire hunter, but I can tell by his lean and hungry look that he needs money. Let's pay him and let him kill the other vampire."

The mayor nodded. "That's precisely what I suggested."

Mother Holmes squinted at him. "Are you sure? I was in the back of the crowd. Hard to hear back there."

I sighed. "I'll dispose of your vampire and go on my way marginally wealthier, feeling dirty and disgusted with myself."

Mother Holmes nodded, satisfied. "As is only right, since you're a monster." She crossed her arms and looked at me, her head cocked to one side. "What are you waiting for? Shoo. Off you go."

I rubbed my hands together. "I didn't bring any vampire killing equipment. Richard, collect the standard equipment. And a sun lamp. If you can find a Dustbuster it makes clean up much more convenient."

"I have all those things," Mother Holmes said. "Send your man to my place and I'll lead you both to the barn."

IT TOOK AN HOUR to gather the supplies, meaning we had about three hours before dawn. I figured half-an-hour to get to the barn and set up, a quick fight and death blow (Fifteen minutes? Twenty?). I'd leave Richard to do the vacuuming and I'd go collect the money and then, if I was feeling peckish, perhaps a quick bite before we went back to the overpass. We'd get there in plenty of time to get settled before sunrise.

UNIDENTIFIED FUNNY OBJECTS

"Keep up, Richard." He had to walk several feet behind me because of the garlic. He carried all the equipment. Not just the vampire killing equipment from Mother Holmes, but also the vampire hunter killing equipment. A few knives, some hand-cuffs, a pistol, an inflatable decoy vampire, that sort of thing.

Richard called out to me. "I'm tired of calling you mas-ter, especially in public. It's awkward. People always look at us strangely. Couldn't I call you sir or boss or something? This is the twenty-first century."

"If you want to live forever, get used to being out of style occasionally. You can't keep up with every crazy new fad." I picked up the pace and moved alongside Mother Holmes, who held a lantern in front of her crooked face as she led us over yet another hillock and into a depressed meadow.

"Are we nearly there, Mother Holmes?"

"Very nearly, young man."

"I'm 139 years old, Miss Holmes."

She clucked her tongue. "That doesn't make the barn any closer, dear."

"How is it that your townsfolk managed to catch a vam-pire in a barn, anyway?"

She cackled. "We promised him a thousand dollars and then shut the doors."

"That's not funny."

She glanced at him with her bulging eye. "I've been mean-ing to ask you about your surname."

"It is, of course, my father's surname."

She nodded. "Abraham Van Helsing. The famous doctor, philosopher, and vampire hunter."

"Indeed. I was his apprentice."

Richard laughed gleefully. "Then something horrible hap-pened."

"Richard! The only thing between you and life as a vam-pire is that I don't want to spend eternity listening to what comes out of your infernal mouth." I turned, again, to Mother

Holmes. "My father sent me to kill a clutch of vampires and, short story, they turned me. In my defense, I was only twenty and they were female vampires."

"What did your father say?"

"As I recall, he shrugged, killed the vampires and said, '*Berufsrisiko*.' I never understood why he spoke German all the time. He was Dutch and we lived in Amsterdam."

"That's terrible, poor boy. What did your mother say?"

"Father told mother I had died. She went insane. Father said that was due to me flying in her window." I shrugged. "I was still in my grave clothes. Nonetheless, dad was driven, mom was insane. They weren't pleasant people, really. Oh, they cared for me, I'm sure, in their controlling, tight, interfering way. To be honest, I miss them. The life of the drifter is lonely, sleeping in rest areas, not even able to afford the blood bank. Now I'm killing vampires like my father. It's too much to bear."

Richard made mock sobbing sounds behind us. I mentally added another five years to his thrall timeline.

Mother Holmes said, "Speaking of bears, here's the barn now."

What a strange old woman. I gestured for Richard to unload. I took a pocketknife and tucked it into my waistband, because it made me feel more at ease and if, by some strange new height of idiocy, the fellow in the barn was actually a human, and a vampire hunter, a knife would be preferable to a wreath of garlic. I picked up a stake and a mallet. Richard put a crucifix in my palm and I let out a yelp when it burned my skin. Ha ha. Very funny, thrall. I hung it around his neck.

"Richard. Set up the sun lamp by the front door, but don't turn it on until I'm inside. Then you come in behind me, after fair warning. If we can get the vampire to run outside, he'll be burned to ash and save us a lot of piercing and grunting and beheading."

"Yes, Master. If I do a good job, will you make me into a vampire?"

"Perhaps."

Mother Holmes sat down on a stump. "I'll wait for you boys here, to make sure it's dead before you get your money."

I nodded to Richard. "I'll see you inside." I slipped the bar up from the latch and then, quick as a shadow, stepped into the barn. The odor of rot overpowered the smell of hay and cow.

In the darkness I saw a large body, and not human. I tiptoed over to it. It was a cow, its guts torn away, the smell of manure and charnel house battling for dominance and largely coming to a draw. The cow lowed mournfully. It tried to drag itself toward me, its mouth working as if chewing cud, reaching out for me like so much rancid grass. I crushed its skull and the cow fell silent.

I heard a shuffling in the darkness near the stalls. Something pulled itself up from the floor. I readied the stake in my right hand, the hammer in my left.

"Master! I'm coming in. Shield yourself!"

I ducked into a stall across from the shuffling thing. Richard threw the door open and a brief, scalding light burned through the barn, momentarily searing my skin. And also, momentarily, revealing the gigantic bear which reared up in front of me.

The door slammed shut. I could hear Richard's panicked breathing and a curious whine from the bear. "Boss?"

I debated whether to answer. Richard turned on the overhead light, a set of bare bulbs hanging from the loft. The bear seemed fine despite the direct hit of the sun lamp, possibly because of its thick, matted fur. It turned and saw Richard and let loose with a terrible groan.

"Boss? A vampire bear is lumbering toward me."

"You're the one always begging to get bitten," I called, leaning against the stall and re-settling my grip on the stake. "And call me master."

"I changed my mind, Master. I don't want to be a vampire."
The bear staggered toward him. I was fascinated by its
lack of mobility. Human vampires became faster, better predators, our senses heightened, our intellect more keen. This bear
seemed . . . drunk.

I waited until I was certain that Richard had peed his
pants, then leapt on the bear from behind. It shrugged me to
the floor. Richard had a manure shovel in his hands, and he
swung and hit it in the side. The bear stood on its hind legs,
easily nine feet tall, and came down on top of Richard, pin-
ning him. I heard the half-eaten cow moo again, but by then
the bear had its jaws set firmly over Richard's face. Richard
had the shovel between his face and the bear's gullet, and was
screaming for me to save him, while the bear chomped mo-
notonously on the blade of the shovel, as if it couldn't understand what barrier stood between it and Richard's face.

I kicked the bear in the side, and it turned toward me.
It crunched down again and the shovel splintered to pieces.
Mother Holmes called in asking if we were all right. "Right as
rain," I said, and kicked the bear in the jaw. It reared up again
and I jumped into its arms. I hammered with all my might,
and the stake went in deep, like a thermometer into a turkey
breast. I popped it one more time, just to make sure, and the
bear let out a long and horrible sound and then swatted me to
the ground, dropping its front paws onto my chest. Inexpress-
ible pain shot through my body.

"The crucifix," I gasped.

Richard ran over and pulled the gigantic crucifix from his
shirt. He wedged it between me and the bear. My skin began
to blacken from the proximity of the cross, but the bear didn't
mind, his hungry maw coming after my face. "Holy water!" I
shouted, slightly panicked. My father would be so embarrassed
if I botched my second vampire killing.

Richard threw the holy water at the bear, and the glass
vial exploded against its face. The bear hardly noticed, but the

water dripped from its snout and onto my face, which set off the uncontrollable screaming. I said some unpleasant things about Richard, his parentage and his intellect. I suddenly realized that this creature on my chest—the one who was not afraid of sunlight, had a stake in its heart and kept coming and was impervious to both holy water and the holy cross—might not be a vampire. The still animate cow lowed, trying to crawl toward me.

"Zombear!" I shouted.

Richard gasped.

"My knives, Richard!"

"No! If that bites me I'll become the shambling, rotten dead. I want to be the svelte, lovely dead. Zombies never get the ladies."

The bear roared in my face, saliva infused with the unmistakable smell of rotten flesh dripping from the zombear's blackened tongue. I still had the small, eight-inch knife at my belt. It took me nearly thirty minutes, holding the bear by the throat above me with my right hand and sawing through its neck with my left, roundly cursing Richard as I worked. Richard encouraged me from the sidelines but refused to help. When its head came separate from the body, I tossed it several feet behind me, and its body collapsed onto my chest. It had broken my ribcage, but that would heal quickly enough. Now I just needed help getting out from under it.

Richard appeared beside me. "Hello."

"You worthless thrall. Get me out from under this bear."

"Are you going to turn me into a vampire now, Master?" He put his shoulder to the bear. I had enough sludge and offal covering me that I could barely stand to speak.

"After that performance? Hardly."

Richard paused. "I thought so." He pulled a two-pronged fork from his belt.

"What is that?"

"My resignation." He stabbed it—not gently—into my neck.

I tried to move away but the corpse of the zombear didn't budge. Blood started to pulse down my throat. "I don't feel comfortable with this, Richard. What about my two weeks notice?"

"I can't wait around forever, Isaac. I'm not getting any younger."

He put his mouth to my neck. I squirmed away, but he forced his mouth over my wound. "Richard. I feel violated. Stop this now."

He pulled away long enough to say, "The irony. You're going to make me laugh and get blood up my nose." He kept drinking.

"It doesn't work this way, you know. Stop now, before I get angry."

He stood up straight, wiping the blood from his chin. He hefted his fork. "The wound closed already." Then he shouted, cursing and tearing at the crucifix around his neck. He hurled it across the barn and laughed maniacally. "It worked already, you liar. I'm a vampire!" He looked at his watch. "And less than an hour until sunrise. I'd best be on my way."

"Richard!" He looked at me, the disdain already on his face. "Run as far and as fast as you can. I will destroy you."

He sneered. "Don't worry 'Master.' I'll run far and wide and tell everyone what I did." He laughed. "You'll be humiliated. Assuming you ever get out from under that corpse."

"There are downsides to being a vampire, Richard. Help me out. I'll be your mentor."

"You're fatherless, motherless, and a failure in death and in life. I'll take my chances on my own."

With that, he turned on his heel and ran out the barn door, laughing. He didn't laugh long, though, because he had forgotten that he couldn't run out through a sun lamp now that he was a vampire. There was a brief scream, cut short by his body bubbling away into ash.

Safe in the shadow of my zombear, I shook my gore

covered head in silence. Richard had always been a mediocre man, a terrible thrall, and an annoying person. But it seemed a waste for him to become a vampire and commit unwitting suicide when I could have killed him myself months ago, and at least gotten a meal out of it. Now, here I was, alone again. No family, no thrall, my only companion an undead cow inching ever closer. And the old lady. I forgot about her.

I cleared my throat. "Mother Holmes?"

I heard her get up from the stump and walk to the edge of the barn door. "Yes, dear?"

"Could you turn off that sun lamp and pull me out from under this bear?"

She walked over to get a closer look at me and clucked her tongue. "I'm sure my services could be arranged. How much?"

"To turn off the sun lamp?"

"Yes, my boy. I'm thinking . . . a hundred dollars."

"That's ten percent of my entire fee."

"I could leave it on."

I tried to throw my hands up in disgust but of course they were still pinned. "A hundred it is." Plus another hundred for helping dig me out from under the bear. Plus, much to my chagrin, three hundred for my supplies. Which meant that I counted out a full half of my fee to Mother Holmes, just as the sun began to rise.

The mayor only reluctantly agreed to pay when I explained the barn should be burned down because of the zombie bear (and cow). He had agreed to pay for a vampire, he said, but then Mother Holmes explained about the nice young man who had exploded into dust as he ran through the sun lamp and the mayor started counting out bills.

"Besides," I said bitterly. "You never mentioned that it was a bear. I didn't go in properly prepared."

The mayor shrugged. "We thought it might cost more to kill a vampire bear."

"What made you think it was a vampire, anyway?"

"It tried to bite someone."

I frowned. The sun was rising, and he didn't seem interested in a lesson on identifying supernatural predators.

"I don't have time to make it back to my coffin," I said. "Perhaps there is somewhere here I could stay."

The mayor shook his head. "We don't much care for supernatural creatures around here. I'd feel better if you moved along."

"What about that werewolf?" one of the townies asked.

The mayor waved him off. "Oh, we only see him once a month. It's nothing to worry about."

I fingered my five hundred. Full moon was only two weeks away. Maybe I could make another thousand off these people.

"I have a place you can stay," Mother Holmes said, peeling two more hundreds out of my hand. "For room and board," she said, smiling.

"But I don't even eat," I protested, weakly.

"Come along. You're too skinny, anyway. You need to put some meat on your bones. We need to get you out of those disgusting clothes, and try to get you some color in your cheeks."

"I can't go in the sun."

"I have some rouge."

Some time the next night, just after sunset, sitting at a simple wooden table with a bowl of inedible tomato soup in front of me, a Christmas sweater with a reindeer and a red nose on my torso and a hand-knitted wool cap on my head (because I "seemed cold" to Mother Holmes), I recognized my confused mix of feelings: loathing, claustrophobia, nostalgia, and a smothering kindness all overlaid with a gauzy contentment and a desire to leave as soon as possible.

I was home.

Mother Holmes patted me on the hand and ladled more soup. "Don't you like it, dear?"

I sighed. Only two weeks until the full moon.

WORM'S EYE VIEW

JODY LYNN NYE

Detective Sergeant Dena Malone looked with horror at the meter-long, tubular, rose pink creature swimming in the medical examiner's sink. Every so often, it turned large, dark eyes like those of an octopus in their direction. She could see herself reflected in them: slim, thirty, brown hair razor-cut around an oval face. About thirty centimeters from the creature's eyes was a squarish bulge and a faint white scar showing where the object beneath the skin had been implanted. The creature seemed, otherwise, featureless, but that didn't make it any less disgusting. She stepped back and glared at the three men.

"With respect, captain," she said, "that's *not* in my job description."

"Witness protection?" Captain Potopos said, falsely hearty. He was a big man with a ruddy complexion. "Sure it is."

The slim, gray-haired man almost eclipsed by the senior policeman's burly body smiled at Dena in a way that reminded her of defense attorneys and confidence tricksters, neither of whom she trusted. The austere woman in the suit at the gray-haired man's side looked like his conscience.

"Think of it as good public relations for the department—not that you may reveal K't'ank's location until after the culprits are apprehended—but it will give a real boost to Human-Salosian relations," Mr. Tiedler said. "You'll hardly know that K't'ank is there."

Of course I'll know! Dena wanted to shriek, but she kept her voice level. "Mr. Tiedler, you want me to investigate the murder of Professor Omar Derbayi with that thing swimming around in my *peritoneum*?"

"Why, yes," Tiedler said, smiling at her. "It's a privilege. I'm sure you've read the heartwarming stories of how our alien friends and their human hosts bond, forming lifelong friendships that will help forge alliances across the cold void of space. . . . " He waved his hands, describing lyrical arcs. Dena cut him off.

"Yeah, but this is police work, not *Readers' Digest*! I can't!"

"But your planet needs you!" Tiedler said.

"That's right, Malone," Potopos put in, putting on the paternal expression that he used for ass-kickings and firings. "It's police work. We're trying to solve a murder. We got the eye witness right here." He pointed toward the sink, then snatched his hand back as if the Salosian might jump up and crawl inside him.

"We didn't know it was in there when we opened the victim," the coroner said, cheerfully. "I thought it was one of the intestines until it moved! He was pale from cold—well, the body wasn't holding heat any longer." He looked as if he considered that bad manners. "We popped him into a sink of warm saline, and he pinked right up! What an honor to have a Salosian in my lab! Uh, alive, I mean."

Dena looked down at the victim, who lay on the slab beside the sink. *No longer holding heat* was a mild way to put what had happened to a human being. Only the corporeal statistics of this case were normal. If the man on the slab had been upright, clean and, above all, alive, he would have been a slender, ascetic man in his sixties or seventies, thinning, longish hair beginning to gray, no rejuvenation treatments that she could detect, beaky nose, bright blue eyes, smile lines that ran from the corners of his nose to the bottom of his chin. Instead, what lay on the slab was a hideous, partly-disassembled mannequin dipped in ketchup. She glanced at his wrist. A purple bruise half-encircled the man's forearm.

"What happened to him there?" she asked.

"His bracelet," Tiedler said. "All Salosian-hosts are required to wear one. It must have been removed. It's made of platinum."

"Well, that explains it," Potopos said. "With the precious metals at ten thousand an ounce these days, he was a potential victim, walking around with a fortune like that in plain sight!"

Tiedler regarded him with shock. "Captain, all a thief would have to do was *mug* him. This was all very unnecessary."

"I'll tell the perp when we catch him," Potopos said, dryly. "What's special about the bracelet apart from the material?"

"It's the most modern of identification devices! It contains DNA from both host and parasite—I mean, guest, as well as their full names and legal certificate of occupancy."

Dena frowned. "Occupancy? Like a house?"

Tiedler looked resigned. "Yes. Once the Department of the Interior understood that the host became the alien's legal domicile, they insisted on it. Salosian-hosts are filed under the same statutes that govern mobile homes. Professor Derabyi was K't'ank's legal residence."

"*Bureaucrats,*" Dena said, scornfully.

" . . . But most importantly, the bracelet also allows the Salosian to communicate with the outside world. It amplifies his voice, and provides him with full connectivity. Salosians are very social beings. In their native habitat, they roil in enormous colonies. Rather like eels."

"Connectivity? Like the Internet?"

"Why, naturally. All *civilized* beings want access to the Internet."

Dena looked from one man to the other.

"Does that mean that that thing might be up all night looking at skinny alien porn while I'm trying to sleep?"

"Uh. . . . " Tiedler replied weakly. "We work with the hosts and guests to make sure of mutual cooperation and consideration."

A man whose black hair shot through with silver would have made him look venerable and trustworthy if Dena had run into him on the street rushed into the room. He lowered a hand-sized device into the water.

" . . . Concealment is vital! Host fearful, panic-stricken, pain, agony!" A voice exploded into the air. Dena winced at the sound. The black-haired man calmly made an adjustment, and the volume sank. "Then, nothing. Cold, cold, cold, I felt my life begin to seep from me. Isn't anyone listening to me? Hello? Is this thing on?"

The man smiled. He spoke into a silvery bangle, the size of the bruise on the victim's arm.

"You'll be all right now. You are K't'ank?"

"That is correct." The voice calmed immediately. "Knowledge of superficial personal nomenclature suggests a person of authority. Who are you?"

The black-haired man glanced at Dena, who favored him with her usual non-committal, professional face.

"Sardwell Barin, deputy ambassador of Alien Relations. Is this your original host?"

"Ridiculous question! Do I look as if I live in a sink?"

Barin shot the merest glance at the austere woman. She reached into a side slit of her slimfit black dress and withdrew a thin tablet device from it. Dena raised her eyebrows. She had never suspected its existence.

"Registered residence as Dr. Omar Derabyi," she said. All of them looked at the body on the table.

"Very well. That means at the moment you are homeless, Dr. K't'ank," Barin said. "Are you otherwise unharmed?"

The voice lost all trace of hysteria.

"Yes. I am intact and in health."

Potopos cleared his throat and stepped forward, the small silver rectangle of the witness recorder in his hand.

"Uh, sir, what was the last thing you remember when the attack came?"

"I recall seeing daylight penetrate my sanctum," K't'ank said. "Dr. Derabyi attempted to compensate, of course, by flooding the apertures with blood, but it was ineffective. My sight went black. Then he fell to the floor. It was extremely inconvenient."

Dena smothered a snicker.

"Er, I was thinking about what happened *before* the attack," Potopos said. "Did you see anyone suspicious approach your host?"

"So many people!" K't'ank said. "Many of them suspicious."

"But did you see the killer?"

"I did. It was a Terran."

"What did he look like?"

The swimming worm in the sink didn't change expression, but the voice coming out of the bracelet did. It sounded embarrassed.

"I have trouble telling many of you apart."

Potopos was unconcerned.

"Do you think you could identify him if you saw him again?"

"Oh, yes! Although the position was unusual. I only saw him from below."

"Uh, how did you see him?" Captain Potopos asked. "Didn't you live in Derabyi's belly? I mean, we saw you come out of his intestines."

Tiedler was genial. "Captain, don't you know about Salosians?"

"Sure. They live in your body. They, uh, observe. I don't know how."

Tiedler beckoned to the alien, who stopped his frantic figure-eights and came to the side of the tank where they could see him.

"Those eyes. The retinal nerves protrude at will. They insert them into the spinal column of the host organism."

Dena twisted at the very thought. Her stomach tried to turn itself into a knot. "Eww."

Tiedler turned big sad eyes to her like a puppy deprived of its toy.

"It's perfectly natural, Sergeant."

"So is taking a dump, but no one likes to think about the details."

"Some people do," the medical examiner piped up, with scientific scrupulousness.

Dena glared a "shut up" at him.

"Did I say anything wrong?" the coroner asked, innocently. Dena ignored him.

"In other words, he sees through his host's eyes?" she asked. "They see everything?"

"Yes, of course," Tiedler said.

"I mean, everything?" Her brain ran a rapid slide show of her life through her own eyes, and she felt her cheeks burning as if everyone in the room could see those images.

"What's your problem, Ms.?" Hargrent asked.

"That's Detective Sergeant Mrs.," Dena snarled.

Barin regarded her seriously, then turned to his two associates. "You have screened this candidate for suitability?"

Hargrent held up her skinny pad. "Yes, sir. A search of the local pool with the correct antibodies identifies her as the best and most logical choice. Also, she's right here, sir."

"You can't ignore that, sir," Tiedler put in.

Barin studied Dena with calm, gray eyes. "Sergeant Malone, the choice of victim likely means the killer knows that there was a Salosian inside his victim. Dr. K't'ank is a valued member of the scientific community, as well as a guest on this planet. You are a sworn law enforcement officer. This being is an innocent witness to a heinous crime. You are trained in both self-defense and keen observation. Your record speaks for itself, with your list of citations and certificates of praise. I feel that even if a pool of hosts who would not be allergic to Salosians were here in this room, you would still be the best choice, both to detect and defend. Won't you undertake this mission? You are already the guardian of a small and helpless life. For the sake of Earth and her alliances, not to mention protecting another living creature that needs what you and you alone can provide?"

Dena felt pride rising in her soul. Her planet needed her! She felt her back stiffen and her chin rise. Potopos's double chin quivered with emotion, and his dark eyes were full of patriotic tears. So were hers.

"All right, sir," she said, resolutely. "I'll do it."

Barin snapped the bracelet on her wrist. It felt as heavy as the needle gun in her holster. He barked at his inferiors.

"Implant her. I have another appointment."

With that, Barin turned on his heel and left. The door slid shut behind the heel of his very expensive boots. Dena gawked after him.

That son of a bitch!

Hargrent held her arm and ran a scanner over it. When it came to her medchip, it beeped. Hargrent shoved the skinnypad in Dena's face.

"Your FIN, please?"

Dena applied her right pinky and middle finger to the screen. Another grudge added to the growing heap in her belly. Now she'd have to change the fingers she liked to use on privacy screens, once four people plus an alien had watched her put in her FIN.

Tiedler had his own skinnypad out now.

"I just need to ask you some questions."

"What? Why?" Dena asked.

"It's all part of the protocol to determine if you're good host material. Now, do you ever participate in any risky activities?"

"Yes."

Potopos did a doubletake. So did the Yes-twins beside him.

"What?"

"I'm a cop," she said. "Duh."

"Uh, I mean, apart from that," Tiedler said patiently. "Risky sex? Recreational pharmaceuticals?"

"Yes. You bet. I indulge in a helluva lot of *none of your goddamned business.*"

Dena felt her temper rising, but Potopos gave her an encouraging nod.

"Now, Malone, answer the guy. It's just routine."

Routine, maybe, but she wished that the coroner and her boss weren't listening as if they were at a dirty movie. Finally, she ground out the information she had been keeping to herself.

"I'm . . . two months pregnant."

That admission called for raised eyebrows all around.

"Licensed? A legally implanted fetus? From your own genetic storage?" Hargrent asked, tapping away at her skinnypad.

"Yes! As if that is your business!"

For once the imperious woman seemed embarrassed.

"Uh, well, it is. Gender of incipient offspring?"

Dena crossed her arms firmly over the location of her yet-to-be-born child.

"We don't know. We don't want to know yet."

"Um-hm," Hargrent murmured, and tapped in, "Allowable superstition number sixty-two."

"What?" Dena demanded, offended to her marrow. "Who's superstitious?"

Hargrent didn't have time for her protests.

"It doesn't hurt the child to reveal the pregnancy, you know. Do you also practice allowable superstition number fifteen, not informing anyone as to your condition? I mean, those who are legally permitted to know."

"Yes," Dena said resentfully. "You are the first people I have had to tell."

"Nothing to interfere with the implantation," Tiedler agreed.

"Let's proceed, then. Sergeant," Hargrent said. "It's an easy procedure."

"Not like a spinal tap?"

Hargrent smiled like a cobra sizing up a victim. "Not very."

Dena backed away.

"I changed my mind!"

"The planet needs you, Detective Malone," her captain said. "Don't make this harder than it is."

She stared at him in astonishment. The big suckup!

"Harder? For who? Do *you* have a giant tapeworm floating around in your belly?"

Potopos smiled. "Lucky for me, I don't qualify."

"Right this way, Sergeant," Hargrent said, taking her by the arm. "Let's get this over with."

THE IMPLANTATION had been painless. The Yes-twins hadn't given her any more opportunities to back out. In fact, Tiedler kept his back against the door of the procedure room. They got her pinkyprint on a contract, seventy pages long in two-point type she couldn't read without a magnifier and a lawyer, and promised to email it to her. The worst part was watching the pink length of the Salosian slither into the small, bloodless incision they made just under her bellybutton. She still felt K't'ank wriggling as he moved among her internal organs, heading for her spine. Occasionally he wagged his tail, causing a ticklish itch there was no way she could scratch. Once he had attached himself to the inside of her backbone, she could hear his voice without the bracelet via bone conduction. And he never, but never, shut up. He kept up a running commentary on everything. *Everything.*

But the worst of it still lay ahead. Dena had to tell her husband.

The Yes-twins had treated her to a skycab home. When she got out at their sixty-seventh floor apartment, Neal was sitting on the balcony, working at his computer, swiping away at an architectural rendering, completely oblivious to the altitude, the traffic, the dogs barking from other apartments, and the booming thunderstorm rolling toward them from just over the state line. His ability to concentrate would have made a yogi jealous.

She kissed him on the back of the neck. He jumped, wiping out half the drawing on the screen.

"Restore!" he commanded it. "Hey, darling!" He had sandy brown hair, tan skin, and green eyes. She hoped the baby would look like him.

"Hi, love," she said. All her nerves were in her belly, along with her problem. "Neal, I've got to tell you something." She held out her wrist. He glanced down at the platinum bangle.

"You bought a bracelet?" She saw the muscles along his jaw bulge out as Neal clenched his molars together, but he kept his smile bright. That was why Dena loved him. They were a little tight financially at the moment. The baby license had been pretty expensive. The government didn't want just anybody reproducing these days. She and Neal had gotten so good at jumping through hoops they could have joined the circus. It might have paid better than police work. "No problem. I'm sure we could afford it. As long as you like it."

Dena struggled to find words.

"Uh, no, not exactly."

"Hello, Malone's husband!" K't'ank's voice burst out of the bangle. Neal looked even more dismayed.

"It talks? Honey, I thought we said no more AI technology. I'm sick of judgmental toasters."

"That's not the bracelet. What it's connected to. It's a communication device. For it. I mean, him. They put an alien inside me. A Salosian."

Neal's eyes lit up.

"Hey, cool! What's its name?"

That was the other reason she loved Neal. Very little fazed him. Dena took his arm and slid open the glass wall to the kitchen.

"Let's eat and I'll tell you all about it."

"SO HOW'D YOU GET INTERESTED in supplementary cognitive processes?" Neal asked. Dena was beginning to feel like the third wheel on a date.

"Natural progression," K't'ank said, his voice echoing out of the bracelet. "We do not get out much, but we think deep thoughts."

"Sounds like ninety percent of the scientists I know," Neal said. He glanced at the clock over the entertainment center, then—at last!—met Dena's eyes. "Bed?"

She raised her eyebrows suggestively. "Bed."

Arm in arm, they walked toward their bedroom. Neal leaned over to nibble at the side of her neck. She shivered with pleasure. His lips descended to meet hers. They bumped into the clothes press on the way, but she ignored what would probably be a bruise in the morning. Dena ran her hands down Neal's body, noting his growing interest. She closed her eyes and let him lower her gently to the bed. His mouth left her parted lips and began to trace down her body, which his hands bared for it along the way. Dena wriggled with pleasure, enjoying every small sensation.

"This is most curious," K't'ank remarked suddenly. "The spasms in your internal organs are rather pleasurable to me."

Dena opened her eyes. Neal looked down at her in dismay.

"He can feel what we're doing?"

She shrugged guiltily. "I didn't know. Please, don't stop!"

Neal made a face. "Okay, darling." With a deep breath, he bent to kiss her again.

Dena warmed to the moment, wrapping her arms and legs around his body.

"What is he doing to make you behave in that fashion?" K't'ank inquired. "The convulsions and tremors are not like anything I have experienced in five different hosts!"

"K't'ank!"

"I only state the truth."

"That's it," Neal said. He pushed himself off her and flopped onto his back. He glared at the ceiling. "I thought I was going to have to stay away from you because of the baby. But this! At least the kid's not giving a play-by-play."

Dena started a blithe denial. Then K't'ank chimed in.

"Oh, the fetus is responding as well. It is flexing and moving. I believe it is enjoying your motion. Carry on."

"No."

"Oh, honey, yes!" Dena pleaded, reaching for Neal.

"Uh-uh. Sorry." Neal leaned over, gave Dena a chaste kiss, and rolled over on his side of the bed, with his back to her. Dena crossed her arms and thrust herself peevishly against the pillows.

"What is happening?" K't'ank asked. "Where is more motion?"

Dena ripped off the bracelet, flung herself out of bed, and stormed to her sweater drawer. She addressed the bangle.

"If you're in trouble, yell. Otherwise, I don't want to hear a peep out of you until morning."

"But, Malone! I wish to ask . . . "

She interrupted him firmly.

"No. Not a thing. Go watch *Animal Planet* or something. Just keep the volume off."

She shoved the bracelet deep into the midst of her

lambswool crewnecks and slammed the drawer shut. Inside her head, she heard vague protests, but at least nothing was coming out of the relay.

NEAL LEFT FOR WORK before she got up. Dena was grateful not to have to be civil to anyone. Even breathing exacerbated her nausea. Morning sickness absolutely sucked. She crawled to the bathroom, and was violently sick in decent privacy.

Or so she thought.

"That is amazing!" K't'ank announced in her inner ear, as she heaved up her insides. "Do that again! Reverse peristalsis is great fun!"

"I'm glad you enjoyed it," she gritted out, sitting on the cold tiles. "And no, I will be damned if I do it again." Once her belly was empty, she could start her normal routine. She made a cup of weak tea and clutched it in both hands to sip.

"Is that all you are going to consume?" he asked.

"You're lucky I'm hydrating," Dena said. His voice went right through her head. She couldn't even put her fingers in her ears to keep it out.

"Please, nutrients! I require food!"

"I can't handle anything at this hour! I'll eat later."

"But I am hungry! You do not wish me to drain sustenance from your tissues, do you? Remember," he said, sounding hopeful, "you are eating for three, now."

"You goddamn vampire," Dena said. But unlike a vampire, garlic and silver crosses wouldn't get rid of him. She had to do what he wanted, or he'd probably rat her out to Alien Relations. Though her stomach did heave-hos the whole time, she forced herself to eat a bowl of fortified hot cereal.

"Wonderful! I feel stronger already!"

At least he was grateful, Dena thought. She handed the bowl off to the housekeeping 'bot and went to get ready for work.

SHE CHECKED IN at the clock wall of the precinct with a handprint. Behind her, she could hear whispers.

"There she is! Ready?"

Dena spun. Most of the precinct personnel stood in a group around her. Starting with desk sergeant Nina Tiandi, they all began humming.

" . . . Uuuuuuuh . . . Shai hulud!"

Dena aimed a mock punch at them.

"Oh, not you morons, too? It's not a sandworm, it's an alien. An intelligent one. And he can hear you."

"Sandworms are aliens, too," Tiandi said.

"I like sand," K't'ank piped up. "It was fun to swim through when I was a young one."

"See?" Lieutenant Cossen gloated. "Sandworm."

Dena groaned. "Remind me to go back in time and convince Frank Herbert to take up another branch of literature. Can we just pretend today's an ordinary, boring duty?"

"Sure, just as soon as you stop talking in two voices."

Potopos had left half a dozen major databases in her in-box, all images of people who were attending, working, or passing through the same conference as K't'ank and Derabyi on the day of the murder. K't'ank either could not or would not identify any of them. She felt strange sitting in the interview room by herself, staring at thousands of holographic images and waiting for a hit.

"No. No. No. Wait. No. They are all too flat!" K't'ank complained, his voice echoing off the enameled ceiling. She felt his tail hit the back of her stomach.

"Ow! Stop that! What do you mean, flat? They're all three-dimensional."

"But flat! They have no life. I cannot identify anyone this way."

"How about if I turn the pictures so you're looking up at them?" Dena asked. She adjusted the play so they were virtually looking up the nose of each person.

"Heh-heh, that is funny! They all look like orifices now," K't'ank said.

Dena was losing patience.

"Let's approach it from another angle. Do you think the killer was trying to get to you, not Derabyi?"

The voice was diffident. "We both had many enemies. I believe that you must concentrate harder on the evidence I have already provided."

"Did *you* arrange for the hit?"

"Did I what? Arrange for Derabyi to die so I could spend my last moments freezing to death in his belly?"

"Tonight, when I am asleep, and don't you fracking dare disturb me, look up Pyrrhic victory," Dena said. She slapped a hand on the control panel. "That's enough. I need some lunch."

"A lean protein substance?" K't'ank asked. "Perhaps with a vitamin-enriched beverage? It is what I preferred to get with Derabyi."

"Tough," Dena said. "You're getting falafel with double tahini and diet soda, and you'll like it."

IF THEY DIDN'T HAVE a callout, Dena and her friends in the precinct played poker over lunch. The table in the breakroom was more crowded than usual. Everyone who could, wanted to meet Dena's alien tenant. She let K't'ank chat with the other officers and staff while she crunched on deep-fried falafel balls and arranged her cards. In fact, he was the life of the party. He knew a lot about poker, way too much. His voice trumpeted out of the bracelet.

"Play the king! Yes, that one! The red one. It will make a collection with the other face cards. You could make a straight."

"Shut up!" Dena snarled. She threw her cards in. The others grinned.

"So, Scaly, what's it like living inside our friend, here?

"Douglas!"

"It is much quieter within Malone than in the professor,"

K't'ank replied cheerfully. "He had many strange internal noises, and he spoke often to himself."

"So, Malone doesn't have as much gas?" Douglas asked, with a wicked grin.

"No. Far fewer eruptions! Her internal systems are much better balanced, as well. He had to take antacids often. I believe he barely qualified for the symbiote program. Malone is a better candidate. And I enjoy her baby's company. It is growing well. So different from the way our species reproduces."

"Lucky me," Dena said dryly.

"I think it'd be cool," Tiani said. "I tried out for it, but I didn't qualify."

"That's because you're a deviant mutant organism," Ramos said. He was the other detective sergeant on day shift.

"Oh, all that matters is the salinity of the bodily system, and whether the immune system rejects my excretions."

"You poop in there? I suppose you'd have to."

"Not poop as you emit it," K't'ank said. "All of my digestive output is ejected through Malone's system. The sloughed off cells can cause allergic reactions. Malone does not react."

Ramos's eyes twinkled. "You mean she's immune to you?"

"Not even close," Dena said, taking a swig of her diet soda. It made her belch. K't'ank laughed hysterically. She winced, and snapped at Tiani. "Deal or go home."

"Do Dena and your other host have anything else in common?"

"Buttocks," K't'ank said promptly. "They both like to observe buttocks. And eyes. Often."

The others laughed. Dena wanted to crawl into a hole. Her colleagues would never let that go. Douglas flirted his thick black eyelashes.

"Really. I never knew, Malone. I knew I should have worn my skin-tight jeans to work."

"How come you need the bracelet to talk?" Idlewild asked. He worked in Evidence. "I thought you folks were naturally social." He looked apologetic. "Well, that's what it said on the National Geographic Channel special about Salos."

K't'ank's voice went professorial. "We did not lose contact with others on our homeworld. Our hosts there had an orifice to the outside that human beings do not that we employed to communicate."

Idlewild frowned. "They had a hole just so you guys inside them could talk?"

K't'ank hastily corrected him. "The excretory orifice. When they were not using it, we did."

"You mean," Ramos asked, with an exaggerated wink and a nudge of his elbow into Dena's ribs, "you spent all your time talking out of somebody else's ass?"

The other officers bellowed with laughter. Dena joined in.

"Why is that funny?" K't'ank asked innocently.

"Look it up," Dena said. She nodded at Idlewild. "I'll raise you ten."

She felt K't'ank shift, curling up on himself so he could surf the net from his little implant box. K't'ank was silent for a few moments, then the room erupted with high-pitched merriment.

"Oh, that is good! Wait until I text all my Salosian friends!"

"You've started a trend," Dena said to Ramos.

"Do you know other jokes about asses?" K't'ank asked eagerly.

That made them think. *Good.* Dena could concentrate on taking their money.

THE SALOSIAN MADE no more headway on the images from the databases. The next day, Dena took him to investigate at the conference where Derabyi was supposed to have spoken.

She wore a neat dress with several bangles on her wrist to conceal the Alien Relations bracelet. Not only was she armed with non-lethal deterrents, she had a few extra gizmos tucked around her person. The convention organizers pleaded with her not to interfere with events. Otherwise, she was welcome to go anywhere she pleased. They issued her a badge and an interactive show book.

The conference center chart showed several gaps in video coverage. That meant it was possible for someone to have approached Derabyi without being observed. The center had a variance to allow for privacy from eavesdroppers or lipreaders to ensure security for trade secrets, but it made police work more difficult. Dena scanned the crowd wandering the broad hallway in between the lecture halls, feeling not one molecule more obvious than a horse in a hair salon.

"Have you seen the killer yet?" she asked K't'ank through the side of her mouth.

"No. Look at more people, please."

Obediently, Dena scanned the attendees.

"I see that you are checking out the buttocks of the man in blue," K't'ank said loudly. "Is he suspicious in some way?

"No! Just professional curiosity." Dena blushed. She really had to be more conscious of what she was looking at.

"Professor Derabyi was always checking male buttocks," K't'ank said. "I didn't realize he was interested in police work."

"That's not police work," Dena said, embarrassed. "Was Derabyi gay?"

"Often. He sang to himself, and once in a while he skipped—most disconcerting when one is trying to concentrate. But he *was* also homosexual. Once in a time he brought a suspect home with him."

"That's not a suspect," Dena corrected him. "That's a date. You hope they're not suspects. But it happens. Did he pick up anyone at the conference?"

"No, Professor Derabyi kept his contact to handshakes and kisses," K't'ank said.

"I mean, did he *find* dates here?"

"No. We were both too busy making connections with fellow scientists. This is a very important conference. We do

not meet often in person. Space is too big." Dena's eyes swept
across the room, lighting briefly on the sign beside the ballroom door.

"Stop your eyes there, on the card!" Obediently, Dena
returned her gaze to the easel and read the few lines. "Hurry,"
K't'ank shouted. She reached for the bracelet to turn down the
volume. "The lecture is about to start! My colleague Seithro is
going to speak on this panel. I must hear it."

"Wait a minute, I didn't agree to sit in on speeches."

"Why else do you think I came sixteen light-years?" K't'ank
asked. "Go, Malone. Now!"

The subject under discussion was far beyond Dena's
education, but K't'ank kept up an acerbic running commentary.
Dena had to admit, grudgingly, that he was really smart, which
proved again that looks weren't everything.

"Poorly researched!" he snorted. "I have many sources
from several species who say that particular theory is outside
empirical evidence!"

"Empirical?" Dena asked, from the corner of her mouth.

"What can be readily observed. As what you do. I read
several manuals of police procedure last night. When will you
arrest someone?" She felt the tail lash her organs.

Dena turned the volume lower still. "When you identify
the murderer for me."

K't'ank subsided. "Oh. Of course, you are right."

He was silent through the rest of the debate. When it broke
up, the lights came on. Dena looked around. K't'ank burst out.

"Take me there. There! To that scientist with hair the
color of rusty iron. Yes, him! I need to speak to him. Professor
Omysk."

"That's a woman, not a man," Dena said.

"And that makes what difference?"

"We . . . use . . . different . . . pronouns," Dena said slowly,
to the amusement of the other humans in the room. Everyone
could hear them. "Professor Omysk is a female, so you have to

refer to her, hers and she. Got that? If Omysk was a man, you would say him, his and he."

"Terrans are strange. We have only one set of pronouns."

"*Terrans* are strange, Mr. I-live-in-someone-else's-intestines?"

"And that is Doctor, not Mister, by your nomenclature. I am a degreed engineer and scientist. Strictly speaking, I am not in your intestines, but around them. They are very attractive, I might include mention."

"Well, as long as you don't try to mate with them," Dena said. "My husband wouldn't understand."

"And a likeable mate you have," K't'ank said, grandly. "You may remain with him."

"Like you have a choice in the matter!"

"I do. You are my host. If I find living arrangements unsuitable, I can demand change. According to subsection D of rule 348 of the Fair Housing Act . . . "

That was something that the Alien Relations Department had failed to explain, in their haste to implant the oversized tapeworm in her.

"You're just a living buzzkill, aren't you?"

"Catch Omysk! Catch him! I must speak with him."

"Her," Dena said, picking up the pace. But the redhead had very long legs and obviously didn't want to talk with K't'ank. Dena felt like yelling "Stop in the name of the law!" Curse not being able to attract attention. Curse *attracting* attention. "Do you think she's the one who killed Derabyi?"

"I think she would botch *anything* she did," K't'ank said severely. "Her methods are scientifically unsound. She could not pour, er, wastewater out of her ass without instructions."

"Do not try Ramos's jokes without practice," Dena said, sympathetically. "He's been working on his delivery since you were roiling in clusters."

K't'ank sighed. "I thought I could do it. I can see that Terran humor is its own science."

A man tried to catch up with them. He was about the

same height as Dena, but squarely built, with hair dyed pale
blond that contrasted with his ruddy complexion.

"Professor K't'ank? Is that you in there?"

"Who is that? Look at him, Malone."

Dena obliged, then caught a glimpse of their quarry out of
the corner of her eye.

"Omysk is going into the stairwell."

"Follow him. Doctor Nedland is coming with us. Yes,
Nedland, I have a new host. What is your question?"

"Are you still thinking of reporting my thesis as
unworkable?" he asked. "I mean, Professor Derabyi was pretty
adamant on it. You sounded like you agreed with him."

K't'ank's voice turned pedantic as Dena started to mount
the concrete stairs. "I have examined the proofs that you
offered in support of your theorem. I agree with my late host
that you are wrong and must rewrite your paper."

"But I could lose my job!"

"If your employer prefers to keep a researcher who falls in
love with its own theories to the exclusion of evidence, then
that is its business," K't'ank said. "But science must be served
by truth."

"Are you always that sanctimonious?" Nedland asked,
bitterly.

"Always. Malone . . . this is where it happened! Someone
tried to kill me in this place!"

Dena reached into her handbag and touched a control.

"Are you sure?" she asked.

"I will never forget a moment of that terrible event!"

" . . . terrible event!"

Suddenly, K't'ank's voice was coming from two different
places. Nedland gawked. He grabbed for Dena's throat. She
snapped an arm up and stepped back. Her heel caught on the
stair. She tripped backwards. Nedland went for her throat with
both hands. Falling, Dena bruised the same spot on her hip as
she had the night before. She cursed.

"Stop him! Do not let him hurt us!"

"I won't," Dena said.

K't'ank kept up his frightened ululations as Dena flipped Nedland on his back and cuffed him.

"No! You're both dead!" came a wild scream from above.

Over the rails three floors up, Omysk looked down at them with frightened eyes. Dena stared up at her.

"The murderer, Malone!" K't'ank shouted, his voice echoing above and below them in the stairwell. "That is the way the murderer looked! It is him!"

Dr. Omysk was so stunned that she was easy to apprehend. Dena charged Nedland with assaulting a police officer, and Omysk for murder and attempted murder. Lieutenant Cossen shook his head admiringly over his skinnypad. He took down Dena's statement while K't'ank was giving an interview to several reporters at her right hand.

"So scientists will kill over lost jobs, just like real people?" Cossen asked.

"Yeah," Dena said. The hotel medic dabbed at her bruises with healing salve. The sting made her hiss. "Thanks to Derabyi and K't'ank panning a paper of hers she lost a chance at a university seat on Titan."

"And you got her to confess how? What's that blue bracelet?"

"Baby's First Karaoke Machine," Dena said, holding up the plastic bangle. "My uncle sent it to us as a shower present. I figured that whoever took Derabyi's bracelet had to have it hidden somewhere. I know firsthand how weird it is to have K't'ank's voice coming out of nowhere. If I set it to the same frequency as the hidden bracelet the murderer was keeping, we'd scare the crap out of him. Or her. And it worked."

"Sergeant!" one of the reporters shouted for her attention. "Is it true that Dr. K't'ank is going to join you on the job? How do you think he'll be as a detective?"

Dena turned a puzzled glance toward the cluster of microphones and cameras. "Terrible. But they're removing him soon."

The first man to speak shook his head eagerly. "An implant is a permanent arrangement, Sergeant."

"It's *what*? No!"

"Please, Malone?" K't'ank asked, in his indoor voice. Not blaring through the bracelet, but the soft, private, bone-conduction voice. "I enjoy being with you. You have saved my life. I can give you much interesting perspective. And I will help look after your baby. Please?"

"Oh, why the hell not?" Dena said, patting her belly affectionately. "A worm's eye view can be a helpful perspective. As long as you shut up once in a while."

"I promise," K't'ank said.

"Yeah, right. Okay, who's got the first question?"

THE SECRET LIFE OF SLEEPING BEAUTY

CHARITY TAHMASEB

"**T**ry it," my cousins say. They are the perfect princess tri-
fecta, all in pink, peach, and plum.

I hesitate. I don't trust myself. Not around things that are
sharp. My mother, the queen, has banned all things pointy—
embroidery and knitting needles, even crochet hooks, but the
object in the corner of my room is different.

"Come on," Plum says. She holds up her cell phone, ready
to take a picture while the other two urge me forward. "You
know how she is."

I do. So does my mother, who always intones, "Never trust
a woman whose only goal is to look as young as her teenage
daughters."

My aunt's gifts have a way of backfiring. Last year, she

gave me an elixir that makes your lips red like cherries and your cheeks glow like apples. I refused it, but my cousins guzzled it down. At that evening's ball, fruit flies swarmed around them the entire time.

What I really want for my birthday is a baseball bat and glove. I want to round up the pages, cajole the scribe into keeping score, and play until the sun hovers low in the sky and it's too late to bathe for a formal dinner, never mind the ball afterwards. But my cousins tremble; if they don't get proof that I've at least touched the present, their mother will rage. Pity compels me forward. Besides, compared to last year, a spindle is downright practical. I reach out. Plum's cell phone camera clicks.

Three seconds before I hit the stone floor, I think: my finger is going to hurt all day long.

Chaos roars around me, but I can't wake. A narcoleptic slumber is no way to spend your sweet sixteen. My mother thunders at my cousins and they cower, all quivering tulle and satin.

My finger still hurts.

The sobs subside. Yawns fill the air. Courtiers sink to the floor. Page boys slump against the wall. My cousins, too, sleep. My mother tucks a blanket around me and kisses my forehead before taking to her own bed.

For one hundred years, we lie dormant. This wouldn't be so bad except my cousins, they snore.

Heavy boots stomp. Swords rattle. The door crashes open. The scent of blood and sweat fills the room. Something looms above me, something I think means to kiss me.

I worry about one hundred years of neglected dental hygiene. But really? He's the one with dragon breath. Volumes have been written about epic first kisses. This one? I'm not sure it rates a Facebook status update.

My eyes spring open, that kiss the living embodiment of caffeine. A boy I don't recognize kneels by my bed. I worry about being nearly one hundred years older than he is. We will have to rename the village. Cougarville has a nice ring to it. First, we should probably get to know each other.

"What's your name?" I ask.

"Charming."

I blink. I'm sure he's many things. Clearly, he has mad skills in the sword-wielding department. But I was on the receiving end of that kiss. Charming? Not so much.

"Shall we marry at sunset?" he asks as if he already knows the answer.

Shall we . . .what? He squeezes my hand. Pain shoots through my finger and I yank free. Marry? For real? I'd rather swing a baseball bat . . . or a sword. And Charming does look tired. (I hear dragon-slaying is kind of stressful.)

After all this time, the spindle still sits in the corner of the room. I point to it.

"Can you bring me that?" I ask, all princess-y innocence. I should feel bad about this, but I don't.

Charming only manages a step, spindle in hand, before he crashes to the floor, armor clanking loud enough to wake the dead. But they sleep on, and Charming's snores blend with my cousins'. It's a fairytale match, I think. They can fight over him once everyone wakes up.

I fashion a new notch in his belt, then I attach the scabbard and blade around my waist. I pull on my own boots and pick up his shield. It feels good in my hand. I tuck a pillow beneath Charming's head and leave the room.

My finger no longer hurts.

In the master suite, I pause next to my mother. A serene smile lights her face. I tuck the comforter around her shoulders and whisper, "I'll be back."

After I've slain a few dragons.

EL AND AL VS. HIMMLER'S HORRENDOUS HORDE FROM HELL

MIKE RESNICK

The Gestapo headquarters at Prinz-Albrecht-Strasse 8 looked like a cross between a foreboding Gothic castle and another foreboding Gothic castle. In a secret subterranean chamber *Reichsführer* Heinrich Himmler thumbed through his grimmoires, searching for the proper spell. The United States had entered the war, the *Führer* seemed not to understand the importance of that, and Himmler realized that it was up to him to secure the Third Reich's victory.

The *Führer* was interested in the supernatural, gave it lip service, and encouraged his underlings to learn what they could about it—but he didn't really *believe* in it. At best, he admitted there *might* be something to it, and he funded research on it, but when push came to shove, he refused to trust in its power. That left it to Himmler, who *did* believe, who *knew* it worked, to unlock the awesome force of the supernatural and harness its use for the Fatherland.

And he knew he was under the gun, because word had reached him that America's premier sorcerer had agreed to enter the fray against Germany. It galled him that the sorcerer was actually German by birth and now chose to battle against his homeland, but he knew how formidable the turncoat was.

Himmler thumbed through the texts, trying to find the single spell that would produce the results he required. When he thought he'd located it, he lit five black candles, and placed them on the five points of a pentagram that he had drawn on the floor.

"Dark Messiah," he intoned, "I implore you to come to the aid of your most faithful servant. Give me the wherewithal to withstand this new enemy and its turncoat sorcerer, and I pledge that you shall be worshipped throughout the Third Reich for all eternity."

He then uttered three complex spells, spells which had never been combined before.

Finally, he reached into a cage that he kept next to the grimmoires, pulled out a newt, walked to the center of the pentagram, withdrew a knife, and slit the little amphibian's throat, placing the newt on the floor and watching its death throes.

When it expired, he uttered one more prayer, and concluded the obscene ritual with a cry of "*Shemhamforash!*"

AND AN OCEAN AWAY, the Allies' greatest sorcerer climbed down the cellar stairs of his unimpressive frame house at 112 Mercer Street in Princeton, New Jersey. (Well, unimpressive but for the billboard in the empty lot next door, with an arrow pointing to his house and a huge photo of him accepting his Nobel Prize next to the statement in foot-high Tempo Bold letters that the World's Greatest Genius lived here.) As for the World's Greatest Genius himself, he never knew what the word "groupie" meant until the village of Princeton built the billboard. Now he had two sets of bodyguards, one to ward off Nazi and Japanese assassins, and the other to protect him from wildly passionate women. More than anyone else, he knew that his adopted country was up against not only the awesome might of Hitler's armies, but also the corrupt evil power that the *Führer's* mightiest sorcerer, Heinrich Himmler, had at his command.

Albert Einstein was soon pouring over *his* holy books, preparing his spells to appeal to Tekno, a deity totally unknown to his German counterpart.

When he was ready, he closed the books, dipped his forefinger in the holy ink, and began chanting. "The square of the hypotenuse equals the sum of the squares of the other two sides," he intoned. "Pi, carried to five decimal figures, is 3.14159. A circle has 360 degrees."

After another five minutes of chanting the spells, and a supplication to the Mathematical Trinity of Pythagoras, Euclid, and Fermat, he pulled a slide rule out of his pocket, held it over the books, and sacrificed it, breaking it and letting the two halves fall to the floor.

Then he uttered one last quadratic equation, and concluded the ritual with a triumphant cry of "Q.E.D.!"

"*MEIN GOTT, YOU'RE BIG!*" exclaimed Himmler as he looked at the army Satan had supplied.

There were thirteen of them, each blond and blue eyed, each armed with a magical scimitar (which is kind of like a curved lightsaber, but effective rather than pretty), each ten feet tall, each wearing naught but a leather kilt.

"*Ow!*" cried the nearest as his head bumped against the ceiling, an action and a cry that was repeated twelve more times up and down the line.

"Duck your heads, *dummkopfs!*" snapped Himmler.

"We bow to no one!" thundered one of them. "We'll raise the ceiling!"

So saying, he lifted his magical scimitar and punched a hole in the ceiling.

"You see?" he said with a smile. "There is nothing to it."

Well, he *tried* to say "There is nothing to it," but somewhere between "There" and "is" a huge wooden desk fell through the hole and crashed onto his head. He collapsed beneath it, shoved it off to a side, and got groggily to his feet.

"Maybe I should have sacrificed *two* newts," muttered Himmler.

The other twelve golden-haired warriors decided to lower their heads.

"Excuse me, Boss . . . " began one of them.

"That's *Herr* Boss," Himmler corrected him.

"Excuse me, *Herr* Boss. But why have you summoned us from the very depths of hell?"

"Not that we mind it," added another quickly.

"Actually, it's much more pleasant here," said a third.

"A lot cooler as well," noted a fourth.

"You are here to defeat the American armed forces," said Himmler.

"What are they?" asked the first speaker, a contemptuous smile on his proud Aryan face. "Thirty or forty little men armed with rocks?"

"More like two million men, armed with the latest in aircraft, ships, cannons, automatic weapons, radar, and sonar."

"Against thirteen of us—and none of us even wearing any pants?" said one incredulously.

"You're Aryans!" bellowed Himmler. "Aryans triumph over everything!"

"Well, actually, my mother was half-Spanish," said one of them.

"And my Uncle Saul was Jewish."

"They always told me that George Washington Carver was a cousin."

"I will hear no more of this!" screamed Himmler. "You are Aryans, and you will follow my orders and march to victory, or I will return you to the fiery pits!"

"Where's Victory?" asked the last one in line. "I mean, if all we have to do is march there, I say we give it a try."

"Idiots!" said Himmler.

"Hey," said the last one, "*we're* not the ones who are sending thirteen men in skirts with pituitary conditions off to fight a mechanized army of two million."

"You are invulnerable!" insisted Himmler.

"Then how come my head hurt when the desk fell on it?" asked the first one.

"Wait a minute," said Himmler. He opened his grimmoire and thumbed through it. "Aha!" he said at last. "You are invulnerable to bullets, torpedoes, knives, swords, bombs, and certain social diseases that you're most likely to pick up in France, or perhaps North Hollywood, California. But I neglected to cast a spell to make you invulnerable either to stupidity or heavy objects falling on your heads. I will correct that oversight shortly."

"You'd better," sniffed the nearest one, rubbing the top of his head tenderly.

"I'll let you know the moment it's done," said Himmler. "What's your name?"

The huge supernatural Aryan looked blank. "I don't have one."

"Everyone has a name," insisted Himmler.

"Not me."

"Or me," said another.

"Me neither," said a third.

"You brought us here," said a fourth. "Probably you should be the one to name us."

"That seems reasonable," said Himmler. He walked up to the giant who was still rubbing his head. "You are Heinrich."

"Heinrich," repeated the Aryan. "Heinrich. Is there some reason for that?"

"It's my favorite name," answered Himmler. "It has a certain strength and nobility and just a touch of *je ne sais quoi* to it."

"How about me?" asked the next giant in line.

"I will call you Heinrich," said Himmler.

"But you're calling *him* Heinrich," protested the giant.

"You think there's only one Heinrich in the world?" demanded Himmler. "There is enormous power and a certain gossamer gaiety to that name."

He went up and down the line, and when he was done he had a supernatural army composed of twelve Heinrichs and an Adolf (just in case he ever had to present one to the *Führer*.)

"Okay," said one of the Heinrichs. "We're here and we're named. Now what?"

"Now we wait to see what that scrawny little white-haired turncoat in America has planned for us, and then we meet his creatures in battle, cut out their hearts, tie them up with their own entrails, cut off their heads, spit down their necks, and—"

"*Stop!*" cried the nearest Heinrich, grabbing his stomach. "I'm going to be sick!"

Himmler sighed deeply. Maybe if he'd sacrificed an iguana . . .

"SO WHAT CAN YOUR GOVERNMENT do for you, Little Al?" said President Roosevelt, seated behind his desk in the Oval Office. "And make it snappy. I've got a war to fight."

"I am here to warn you of a dire threat to our troops," replied Einstein.

"What could be more dire than the German army?" said Roosevelt. "By the way, that's a hell of a goiter on your hip. You'd better have it looked at."

"Hips don't have goiters," answered Einstein, pulling a

crystal ball out of his pocket and sitting it down on the desk in front of the President. "Take a look."

Roosevelt leaned forward and stared. "There's nothing there."

"*The square root of one is one!*" intoned Einstein. "Now look at it.

"My God, that's remarkable!" exclaimed Roosevelt.

"I thought you should see it," said Einstein.

"How does she twirl them in both directions at the same time?"

Einstein bent over the desk. "Damn!" he said. "I forgot to adjust the channel. *Algebra kadabra!*'

"What's this?" asked Roosevelt, frowning and staring into the crystal. "It looks like a men's basketball team."

"It's thirteen invulnerable Aryan supermen, called up from the deepest pits of hell by none other than Heinrich Himmler," answered Einstein. "Defeating the German army will be a hard enough chore for General Eisenhower. *We* must destroy these super-Aryans before he has to face them."

"We?" said Roosevelt with a worried expression on his face. "You mean you and me?"

"No, sir," said Einstein. "We need you at the helm of State. What I've come for is Big El."

"Big El?"

"Your wife, Eleanor."

"She's yours, Little Al, and good luck to you," said Roosevelt with an unconcerned shrug. "Now to business: what do you need to defeat Himmler's horrendous hordes from hell?"

"I just told you."

"You did?"

"Big El," repeated Einstein.

"Oh," said Roosevelt. "I thought you meant . . . never mind." He paused. "Are you quite sure *she's* what you need?"

"Absolutely," said Einstein. "She's spent the last few years fighting big business, and Southern bigots, and isolationists, and Republicans. She's in better fighting shape than any other American."

"But can she stand up to these super-Aryans?" persisted Roosevelt.

"If she and I together can't do it, with my mystical powers and her indomitable spirit, then no one can."

"What the hell," said Roosevelt with a shrug. "If you feel she's what you need..." He picked up the crystal ball and stared at it. "How do I bring back the original image?"

"The girl with the . . . uh . . . ?"

"Yes."

"*Kadabra algebra*," chanted Einstein. "Nothing to it." He walked to the door. "I'll pick Eleanor up on my way out."

"Fine," said Roosevelt, staring at the crystal ball.

"We go now to save the world."

"Good," said Roosevelt without looking up. "Go."

Einstein opened the door. The last thing he heard before closing it behind him was the President musing wistfully: "I wonder if she's got a phone number?"

"I'M NOT GOING to do it!"

Eleanor Roosevelt was standing in Einstein's book-lined basement, some twenty feet away from him.

"But you're the only one who can, Big El," he said.

"Never!"

"I'll protect you," promised Einstein. "I've got a spell that even Fermat couldn't solve. I'll invoke Isaac Newton himself."

"No!"

"But why not?" he asked, mystified. "You are potentially the greatest warrior woman who ever lived."

"I'm not wearing that skimpy little warrior princess outfit until I lose thirty-five pounds and get a dye job."

Einstein lowered his head and put his prodigious brain to work, finally looking up at her. "You've got it all wrong, Big

El," he said soothingly. "You don't want to lose an ounce. If anything, you should *gain* some weight."

She looked at him as if he was crazy.

"Think about it," he urged her. "You're not trying to dazzle them with your beauty, but to terrify them with your muscle and your demeanor. The more formidable you look, the better."

"I'm a woman in her fifties," protested Eleanor. "I can't go around with a bare midriff and bare thighs and bare shoulders and . . . "

"We'll compromise," offered Einstein. "You can cover your left shoulder."

"And what are Himmler's horrendous hordes wearing?" she asked.

"In my most recent visualization of the Cosmic All, they were wearing leather skirts and nothing else."

"Nothing else?" she repeated, arching an eyebrow.

"That's right."

"Skirts," she repeated. "Are they . . . you know?"

"They're ten-foot-tall killers," answered Einstein. "Does it make a difference what they do in their spare time?"

"I just want to know if they're sizing me up for the battle to come or ogling me."

Einstein stared at her thoughtfully for a long moment. "I don't think there's any doubt which they're doing," he said.

"All right," she said at last. "If my country needs me that badly, I'll do it. But along with the rest of the outfit, I have to have boots."

"You won't be travelling through rough terrain," he assured her. "We're just going to Gestapo headquarters."

"It's not that," said Eleanor. "I have varicose veins, and I want them covered up. Otherwise the battle's off."

He nodded his agreement. "Now let's talk about weapons."

"Right," she agreed. "I want a .44 Magnum, six hand grenades, and a repeating rifle."

"You'll have a sword."

"That's all?" she demanded.

"It will be an enchanted one." He pulled a kitchen knife out of his pocket, whispered *"Archimedes"* over it, and it instantly morphed into a wicked-looking sword, which he handed to her.

She looked at it briefly, and then said, "And these Aryans will all be armed with enchanted submachine guns, I presume?"

Einstein shrugged. "Who knows?"

"Well, I'd *like* to know," said Eleanor. "*You're* not going out there half-naked and armed with only a sword to face thirteen blond giants."

"I'll be there sharing the danger with you, Big El."

"Side by side?" she asked, relaxing visibly.

"Well, in the same city, anyway," he said. "While you're taking care of the horrendous horde, I'll be engaged in a duel of spells with Himmler himself."

"You're going to have a spelling bee while I'm fighting thirteen hate-filled barbarian Aryan giants?"

"Try not to understand me so fast," said Einstein. "If I don't subdue Himmler while you are occupying his fearless, merciless, invulnerable, incredibly strong warriors, he might conjure up fifty more."

Eleanor considered the situation. "I have a suggestion, Little Al," she said. "Why don't *I* handle Himmler while *you* take on his hideous horde?"

"That's his *horrendous* horde," Einstein corrected her.

"What's the difference?"

"One you have to fight single-handedly, and the other doesn't exist."

She merely glared at him.

Einstein fidgeted uncomfortably until she finally turned away from him. Then he spoke again: "You'd better get into your warrior princess outfit. In the interest of decorum (and possibly self-preservation) I'll turn my back while you change."

"How are we getting there?" she asked, starting to unbutton her suit coat, which she wore over her vest, which she wore over her blouse, which she wore over her slip, which she wore . . . but you get the idea.

"We're flying, all thanks to Leonardo," he said, staring at some complex formulae on his blackboard while she changed.

"Leonardo?" she repeated, staring at facsimiles of some of the Italian's notebooks on a shelf. "Have you actually found a way to turn us into winged creatures who can ride the warm thermals?"

"I beg your pardon?"

"Leonardo da Vinci's organic airplanes," she said.

"No," answered Einstein. "I'm talking about my friend Leonardo Schwartz. He has a private plane, and will be flying us there."

He continued staring at the blackboard for another five minutes.

"How's it coming, Big El?" he asked.

"I feel . . . what's the right word? . . . *flimsy*," she said uncomfortably. "You can turn around and look now, Little Al. But no whistling or catcalling—and especially no giggling," she added threateningly.

He turned and looked at the warrior princess. "I think I can resist the urge to whistle," he said earnestly.

"I wear more than this when I go to the beach," she complained. "*Much* more."

"It'll give you enormous freedom of movement when you take on the horrendous horde."

"How can you be sure there *is* a horrendous horde?" she said. "How do I know this wasn't all just a ruse so you could see me like this?"

"It came to me as I lay in bed last night," answered Einstein.

"A vision?"

"No, a ten-foot-high Aryan in a leather skirt," said Einstein.

"I was hoping for a woman," he admitted. "Anyway, he suddenly appeared, said 'So *you're* what we have to destroy,' laughed his head off, and vanished."

"All right," said Eleanor heatedly. "It's time we taught the so-called Master Race a lesson."

"Fine. We'll drive to the private airport down the road and be on our way. I'll get the car."

She made him turn out all the lights and back up to the door so no neighbors or passersby could see her, and ten minutes later they were pulling up to Leonardo Schwartz's plane.

Einstein got out and opened the door for Eleanor. It took her a moment to work up her courage, but finally she stepped out of the car, enchanted sword in hand, and walked to the steps leading up to the plane.

"Who's your friend?" asked Schwartz. "My God, she's gorgeous!"

I didn't realize it was that dark a night, thought Eleanor.

"She is, isn't she?" agreed Einstein admiringly, holding out his hand to her. "Leo, say hello to Big El."

Schwartz took her hand and kissed it, then climbed into the cockpit.

"What are you staring at?" Eleanor demanded as Einstein kept smiling at her.

"More than your sword is enchanted," he said. "So is your outfit."

"My outfit?" she repeated, frowning.

"It was made for a gorgeous warrior princess, so that's what it's turned you into."

She looked down at herself, then smiled happily. "Thirty-five pounds, hell!" she exclaimed. "I've lost fifty if I've lost an ounce!"

She took the extra veil off her shoulder and handed it to him. "Here. I won't need this anymore."

Schwartz started the engines, while Einstein and Eleanor strapped themselves in.

"Thirteen of them, you say?" said Eleanor.

"That's right."

"Ten feet tall?"

"At least."

"Foul-tempered?"

"Worse. And spoiling for a fight."

The most beautiful warrior princess in America leaned back and smiled. "I can hardly wait," she said.

HIMMLER COOLED HIS HEELS in Hitler's outer office for almost half an hour, and then was escorted inside.

"Ah, *Reichsführer!*" said Hitler. "How good to see you again!"

"You just saw me three hours ago, *mein Führer.*"

Hitler glared at him. "I do not like to be disagreed with," he said softly. "Except by Eva. *Mein Gott*, does that woman have a temper! You'd think anyone who could use a rolling pin like that would know how to cook!" The *Führer* shuddered, then sat down. "So tell me about these supermen of yours."

"I told you this morning, *mein Führer,*" said Himmler.

"Do you know how many cities I've ordered destroyed since then?" snapped Hitler. "How many men I've had terminated? How many cigarettes I've smoked—and Turkish ones at that! Humor a busy man and tell me again!"

"There are thirteen of them," said Himmler. "Each stands more than ten feet tall, and each makes the vaunted Charles Atlas look like a ninety-eight-pound weakling."

"Charles Atlas?" repeated the *Führer*, clearly impressed. "Isn't he the one who's in all those ads on the backs of, well... certain illustrated magazines, shall we say?"

"Comic books, yes sir," said Himmler. "Anyway, these thirteen perfect Aryan warriors are without peer."

"From what I hear they are also without clothes," said Hitler. "How can I send them to the Russian front?"

"I didn't summon them from the depths of hell to fight

the Russians, *mein Führer*," said Himmler. "They are here to ward off the attacks of the turncoat sorcerer Einstein."

"Don't mention that name to my face!" yelled Hitler.

"I apologize, *mein Führer*," said Himmler quickly.

Hitler swiveled his chair until he was facing out a window, with his back to Himmler. "*Now* you can talk about him, *Reichsführer*."

"Yes, sir. Word has reached us from our spies in the White House that Einstein is about to unleash Mrs. Roosevelt upon us . . . and you know the success the President has had unleashing her on his other enemies."

"You were quite right to call them forth, *Reichsführer*," said Hitler. "Where will they meet her in battle?"

"We have no idea where she is at the moment," answered Himmler. "So I have concluded that the best course of action is to booby-trap Gestapo headquarters and wait for her there, since sooner or later she and Einstein"—Hitler whimpered at the mention of the name—"will come to Berlin and seek out my Aryan supermen."

"Maybe you should leave ten or twelve of them right here to protect *me*," suggested Hitler.

"They don't want you, sir."

"I beg your pardon!" screamed Hitler, spinning around in his chair to face Himmler.

"It's personal, sir," said Himmler.

"Explain!"

"I found an error in his Special Theory of Relativity and presented it in a speech to the Sorcerers' Society, right after their annual softball game."

"The greatest sorcerers in the world play softball?" asked Hitler, surprised.

"Well, usually the ball turns into a screeching Canadian goose on its way to the plate, and the bases grow legs and run off to Bismark, North Dakota, and—"

"I get the picture," interrupted the *Führer*. "Continue."

"Anyway, I proved that D does not equal MC squared, and he has never forgiven me for that," said Himmler. "He and Mrs. Roosevelt are after *me*, sir, and they know they'll have to fight their way through my supermen to reach me."

"Have these superman all been trained in the use of the latest modern weapons?"

"They don't need them," answered Himmler. "They are masters of fisticuffs, wrestling, karate, kung fu, penjak, and the off-putting snide remark. Furthermore, they assure me they are invulnerable, that no bullet can pierce their proud Aryan skin."

"You don't say," said Hitler.

"I just *did* say, *mein Führer*."

"Maybe we should put it to the test. I haven't shot anyone since breakfast."

"I thought I saw them carrying the bullet-riddled body of the Postmaster General out of here while I was waiting to see you, sir," said Himmler.

"He was only five feet three inches tall," said Hitler with a shrug. "He hardly counts."

"All right, *mein Führer*," said Himmler, clicking his heels together and snapping off a salute. "I'll bring them all to your office."

"Just a minute," said Hitler.

"Sir?"

"What are their names, so I will know how to address them?"

"There are twelve Heinrichs and an Adolf, sir."

"But no Einsteins?"

"No, sir."

"All right," said Hitler, opening his drawer and pulling out a tommygun. "Leave the Adolf behind. I certainly wouldn't want to hurt *him*."

"They are *all* invulnerable," Himmler assured him.

"We shall see."

"I'll have them here in ten minutes, *mein Führer*."

"You're *sure* there are no Einsteins?"

"I'm sure."

"All right. Let's see if anything can pierce their proud Aryan skins."

And seven hundred twenty-two bullets later he still didn't know what could pierce their skins, but he was damned sure he knew what *couldn't.*

THE PLANE LANDED at a small airport about forty miles outside of London.

"This is as far as I go," announced Leonardo. "The Germans control everything between here and Berlin."

"Are you going to let a little thing like a few thousand anti-aircraft guns and fighter planes stop you when this scantily-clad damsel is willing to face them armed with only a sword?" demanded Einstein.

"What the hell," said Leonardo. "When you put it that way . . . "

"Good!" said Einstein. "Refuel the plane and we'll be on our way. Big El and I will grab some dinner while you're standing out here in the pouring rain keeping a watchful eye on things."

He escorted Eleanor inside. They found a small snack shop, and soon were seated at a table.

"Everyone's staring," she noted.

"Probably seeing a half-naked warrior princess eating with a world-famous Nobel Prize winner isn't an everyday occurrence."

"So how are we going to get to Himmler's headquarters?" asked Eleanor.

"The direct approach is probably best," answered Einstein.

"The direct approach?"

He nodded. "When we get to downtown Berlin, I'll ask a cabbie."

"You think of everything, Little Al," she said admiringly. "How much trouble do we expect on the way in?"

"Well, I had hoped that Himmler was so anxious to have his horrendous horde meet you in personal combat that he would have ordered everyone to give us safe passage until we got there," said Einstein. "But if I'm wrong, then you may have to single-handedly conquer the German Fourth, Sixth, and Seventh Armored Divisions—and that's if we make it over France without being shot down."

"Boy, those Nazis are *everywhere!*" said Eleanor grimly.

"Actually, I was thinking of the French," answered Einstein. "De Gaulle has never forgiven me for beating him at chess."

Eleanor studied the menu, then signaled the lone waitress.

"What'll it be, ma'am?" asked the girl.

"I'll have a hot fudge sundae, a piece of New York cheesecake, a chocolate éclair, and a slice of apple pie à la mode, heavy on the whipped cream."

"Will you want anything to drink, ma'am? Tea, perhaps?"

"A chocolate malt."

Einstein ordered coffee, the waitress went off to the kitchen, and he stared curiously at Eleanor, who had a radiant smile on her face.

"I may keep this magical outfit forever, Little Al!" she enthused. "Twenty-three thousand calories, and I won't gain an ounce!"

"Not only that," said Einstein, "but you'll have all the energy you'll need for the battles that lay ahead of us. Well, of you."

"I feel sharp," she said. "Himmler's going to rue the day that he called these super-Aryans up from hell."

"I'M STARTING TO RUE the day I called you up from hell!" growled Himmler as he faced his thirteen super-Aryans.

"What did we do wrong *this* time?" asked Adolf.

"I don't mind that you can't march in formation. I don't mind that Heinrich Number 8 has a prostate problem and has to keep running to the john. I don't even mind that none of you has washed in all the time you've been here." He glared at them. "But I mind like all hell that nobody remembers to duck their heads or even use a door when they enter or leave a room. You're slowly but surely destroying the damned building. You!" he yelled, pointing at Heinrich Number 3. "Get that wistful smile off your face."

"But you mentioned home," protested Number 3.

"What the hell are you talking about?" demanded Himmler.

"There!" exclaimed Number 3. "You did it again!"

"Oh, shut up!" growled Himmler. "Just go down to the basement and try not to get into trouble. I'll call you when it's time to slaughter Mrs. Roosevelt."

"But it's dark and foreboding down there," whined Number 9. "And there are lurking shadows."

"So what?" said Himmler. "You guys are invulnerable."

"That doesn't make it less scary," said Number 5 petulantly.

"You can't be hurt," repeated Himmler. "That means nothing should scare you."

"Lots of things scare us," answered Adolf.

"Right," agreed Number 4. "Personally, I'm terrified of high cholesterol levels."

"And I'm afraid of tax auditors," added Number 7.

"Aggressive redheads named Thelma make me want to run for the hills," said Number 10. Suddenly he burst out crying.

"What's the matter with him?" asked Himmler.

"There *aren't* any hills in hell," explained Adolf.

"I've heard enough of this," exploded Himmler. "You are the ideals of German manhood, perfect in every way, at least from the neck down." Number 8 raised his hand to speak. "Except for Number 8's prostate," amended Himmler. "You are about to carry the hopes and dreams of the Third Reich into battle against the most formidable warrior and the most dangerous sorcerer that America has to offer. There can be no fears, no doubts, nothing but the absolute certainty that Aryans cannot ever lose."

"Uh . . . this warrior woman," said Number 1. "How big is she?"

"Not big enough!" roared Himmler. "You are the ideals of the Master Race. You are twice the size of normal men. You are invulnerable. You cannot feel pain, or fear, or fatigue. You represent everything that is fine and noble and worth keeping on this mongrel-filled planet. Now, let me hear it! Are you ready to triumph over the greatest warrior the Allies can provide?"

He wasn't sure, but he thought he counted seven yes's, five no's, and a maybe.

"THERE'S PARIS, coming up on your left," announced Leonardo as the plane banked to afford them a better view. "Last chance to stretch your legs and see the Folies Bergère."

"Why would I want to see the Folies Bergère?" asked Eleanor.

"I was thinking of Little Al," said Leonardo. "We used to have to drag him out of there almost every night during the last war."

"I found the atmosphere conducive to conjuring," said Einstein defensively.

"Usually he'd conjure up a spell and the prettiest girls would throw themselves at him."

"It was all for God and country," said Einstein. "Well, maybe excluding God. Besides, once I perfected it, it brought Mata Hari out of hiding and straight to me."

"With only one hundred and forty-three romantic pit stops along the way," said Leonardo.

"Maybe we should show you the Louvre," said Einstein, turning to Eleanor and changing the subject.

"Do they have any Norman Rockwells?" she asked.

Einstein shook his head. "Just da Vinci and Reubens and Michelangelo and that whole crowd."

"Foreigners all," she sniffed. She tapped Leonardo on the

shoulder. "Just land. I'll kill a Nazi or two, make sure every-thing is in working order, and then we'll proceed to Berlin."

As they reached the outskirts of Paris, they began picking up anti-aircraft fire.

"That was a close one," said Leonardo as a shell exploded just to the left of the plane. "Hey, Little Al, are you sure you want to land here?"

"Don't interrupt!" said Einstein. His eyes were closed, and his hands were making mystical signs in the air. *"The acceleration of a body is directly proportional to the net un-balanced force and inversely proportional to the body's mass, a relationship is established between force (F), mass (m) and ac-celeration (a)."*

"What is he doing?" asked Leonardo.

"Magic!" whispered Eleanor in awestruck tones. "Don't in-terrupt him."

"The squares of the periods of revolution of the planets about the sun are proportional to the cubes of their mean distances from it," chanted Einstein. Suddenly he relaxed and looked at his companions. "Okay," he said. "The plane will be invulnerable to German fire for the next seventy-three minutes. Now you can land."

"By God!" said Leonardo. "How can the Germans stand up to a brain like that?"

"It's not that simple," said Einstein. "My magic only works on normal Nazis, not on Himmler's super-Aryans. For that, we need some very *special* magic, some spell that's never been cast before."

"So cast it," said Leonardo.

"I'm working on it," said Einstein. He closed his eyes, held out his hands, and chanted, *"E equals MC cubed!"*

"The engine just died," announced Leonardo.

"Damn!" said Einstein as they glided silently toward the ground. "I thought I had it this time!"

"ALL RIGHT," SAID HIMMLER. "The *Führer* is coming by to inspect you any minute now. I want you to line up alphabetically."

"But there are twelve Heinrichs," said Heinrich Number 9.

"All right," said Himmler. "By height."

"We're all the same size."

"Draw straws," snarled Himmler.

"Give us some pencils," said Heinrich Number 6. "And where do you want us to draw them?"

Heinrich Number 8 emerged from the bathroom and rejoined the others. "Did I miss anything important?" he asked.

"Shut up!" snapped Himmler. "I want you all to line up numerically."

"Right to left, or left to right?" asked Heinrich Number 1.

"Yes!" yelled Himmler.

After a few moments of confusion, the twelve super-Aryan Heinrichs were finally in line.

"Where do *I* go?" asked Adolf.

"Alphabetically," said Himmler.

"But they're all numerical."

"All right—numerically."

"But I don't have a number."

"Adolf, you are an idiot!" screamed Himmler.

"What did you call me?" bellowed a familiar voice from behind him.

"Oh, shit!" said Himmler as his knees began to tremble.

"ONE HUNDRED AND FIFTY propositions from French men before we even leave the airport!" said Eleanor wearily. "Can the super-Aryans be any more exhausting?" She paused, frowning. "Maybe having this figure isn't all that it's cracked up to be. I never got this tired fighting off Republicans."

"I think your response—the one that scared them all away—was a stroke of genius," replied Einstein. "Three little words and they were dispersed to the four winds."

"I'll have to remember them the next time we're in

302 UNIDENTIFIED FUNNY OBJECTS

France," said Eleanor. *"Marry me first,"* she intoned. "Suddenly they looked like a bunch of sprinters trying out for the Olympics."

"Brilliant," agreed Einstein. "I wouldn't try it in Beirut, though, or even Dubai."

"I wonder where all the Nazis are?" said Eleanor. "We didn't see a single one."

"Probably at the Folies Bergère or maybe the Lido," answered Einstein. "Or robbing art treasures from the Louvre. They do that a lot. I suppose we could pop over there and stop them?"

"Why bother?" she asked. "You already said there are no Norman Rockwells there. There are probably no Virgil Finlays or Frank R. Pauls either. Just a bunch of guys with funny names. No, Little Al, I've stretched my gorgeous cellulite-free legs now. Let's move on to Berlin."

"There's the plane," he said, as they entered the small, private airport where Leonardo had set it down and was trying to start the engine.

Suddenly they found their way blocked by five armed Nazis in uniform.

"I've been wondering where you guys were," said Eleanor, sword in hand. "Prepare to meet your maker."

"Meet my baker?" said one with a hearing aid. "What on earth is she talking about?"

"Your maker, your maker!" she snapped.

"I'm still confused," said the Nazi. "Is she talking about one of my parents?"

"I'm talking about your God!" roared Eleanor.

"You'll have to talk to someone else, then," he replied. "We members of the Master Race aren't allowed to believe in God."

"That's not entirely true," said one of his companions. "We're allowed to worship Mars, God of War."

"And I think we can worship Colgate, God of Healthy Teeth," said another.

"Enough!" snapped Eleanor. "Prepare to die!"

"If I'm going to prepare for it," said another Nazi, "I have to go back to Hamburg and write my will, and pay off all my creditors, and tell my wife where I really was during that snowstorm last February. I don't suppose you could wait right here for eight weeks until I take care of all that and come back, could you?"

"You are the talkiest soulless sadistic fiends I've ever met!" said Eleanor. "Well, since Alf Landon and Wendell Willkie, anyway. Now, are you going to fight or are you going to talk?"

"You *are* Big El, aren't you?" asked still another Nazi.

"That's right."

"Then I guess we're going to talk. We have orders to escort you to Berlin, and not to rob Herr Himmler's Horrendous Horde from Hell of the fun of slowly dismembering you."

Eleanor turned to Einstein. "What do you think, Little Al?" He turned to Leonardo's plane. *"F equals MC squared!"* he chanted.

Both wings fell off, and one of the tires went flat.

Einstein turned back to the Nazis. "You have transportation?"

"Of course."

"Then I guess we're going with you," said Einstein.

As they were climbing aboard the Nazis' plane, one of them pulled Eleanor aside.

"I don't mean to be forward," he said, lowering his voice so only she could hear it. "But if, on the thousand-to-one chance that you survive your forthcoming duel to the death with Himmler's Horrendous Horde, would you like to get together afterword? I'd love to show you the sights of Berlin at night."

She gave him a smile. "Marry me first," she whispered.

He sat as far from her as possible, and didn't speak to her for the duration of the flight or the rest of this story.

THE RED PHONE on the President's desk began ringing, and Roosevelt picked it up.

"You know who this is?" said a voice with a heavy German accent.

"I can guess," said Roosevelt. "What do you want?"

"You know your wife is on her way here with that little turncoat Ein . . . Ein . . . "—he forced the word out—"Einstein."

"I'm aware of it."

"You really think to destroy my super-Aryans?" demanded Hitler.

"You have nothing to fear but Eleanor herself," said Roosevelt.

"I have a proposition," said Hitler. "Why don't we let the coming battle between your wife and my Aryans determine the war—winner take all?"

"Why should I make a deal like that when half your army is freezing to death in Russia?"

"You're not supposed to know that!" screamed Hitler. There was an uneasy pause. "I mean—"

"Forget it," said Roosevelt. "Now, if you want to make a little side bet . . . "

"A million marks to a million dollars!" said Hitler promptly.

"Come on, Adolf," said Roosevelt. "You've devalued your currency so much that a million marks barely buys a loaf of bread."

"But it is good German bread!" protested the *Führer*.

"Not a chance."

"Wait a minute!" said Hitler. "We own France, too! A million dollars against a million francs!"

"Good-bye, Adolf."

Roosevelt hung up the phone and went back to studying his crystal ball.

"WELCOME TO BERLIN, *FRAULEIN*," said one of the guards at the airfield.

"Thank you," said Eleanor, who saw no reason to tell him, or anyone else, that she was actually a *Frau*.

"You may find our nights a little chilly for your apparel."

"Have you a nice, heavy, shapeless coat that I can use to cover myself?" she asked.

"NO!" cried all the other guards.

The guard shrugged helplessly. "I guess not."

"I'm sure I'll be fine," she said.

"You are escorting her to Gestapo headquarters," said one of the Nazis who had accompanied her from Paris.

"Just her?"

Einstein stepped forward. "Me, too."

"You too?" repeated the guard. "That's funny. You don't look too-ish."

"Actually," said another guard, "he does."

"Just get us there," said Einstein. "We're wasting time."

"Who are you to give us orders?"

"I'm Little Al, that's who," he said. Suddenly he closed his eyes and began chanting a spell. *"The area of a triangle is one-half times the base length times the height of the triangle."*

"Yes, sir," said the guard, as he and his companions seemed to fall into a trancelike state. "This way, sir. Watch your step, sir."

"Thank you," said Einstein.

The guards led them to a truck.

"That looks uncomfortable," said Eleanor. "Haven't you got a car?"

"The *Führer* has outlawed all makes and models but the Volkswagen," came the answer. "Except for his own fleet of Cadillacs, that is."

"So?"

"The Volkswagen is the smallest, most uncomfortable car in all of Europe," said the guard. "It reminds me of a beetle the way it hugs the ground. I know the *Führer* is perfect and infallible and all that, but if he really thinks these undersized monstrosities are ever going to be popular ... "

"They don't use much gas, though," noted one of his companions.

"You say that as if the world will ever run out of gas," said the guard."

"Science fiction writers are predicting that it may someday be so rare that it will cost as much as ten U.S. cents a gallon."

The guard shrugged his shoulders. "What can you expect from a bunch of unemployable daydreamers?" he said contemptuously. He turned to Eleanor and Einstein. "Are you ready?"

"Yes," said Eleanor.

"Then climb into the back and we'll be on our way."

"I may need a little help," said Einstein.

Three of the guards boosted him into the truck, then looked their disappointment when Eleanor was able to climb in on her own.

As they rode, avoiding debris and craters in the street, they could hear the whistling sounds of bombs falling, followed by deafening explosions as they tore into the heart of Berlin. Eleanor looked out the back of the truck and saw several buildings on fire after a direct hit.

"It would appear that the Luftwaffe is no match for our American and British bombers," she remarked.

"Oh, *that*," said a guard with no show of emotion. "The *Führer* assures us that we can shoot down the Allies' planes whenever we want."

"If you can, why don't you?" asked Eleanor. "The whole city is ablaze."

"The *Führer* has explained that he only lets the bombers through to save money on electricity. You have no idea how expensive it is to light a modern city at night, *Fraulein*."

Eleanor and Einstein exchanged knowing looks.

"I just saw the two of you exchanging knowing looks," said a guard. "What do they mean?"

"They mean we agree that you've found a cost-effective way to light your city," said Einstein.

"It also saves us the cost of maintaining our streets," said the guard. "You know—painting lines down the middle, filling in potholes, that sort of thing."

"It does?" said Einstein curiously.

The guard smiled and pointed to a series of recently-made craters. "No more streets. Now that money can be directed to other enterprises."

Einstein turned to Eleanor. "I'm surprised the war is still going on," he remarked.

"As soon as we find an economical way to cure eight hundred thousand cases of frostbite on the Russian front, we should finally have this war under control," said the guard.

"So you see, you're wasting your time," added another guard. "The war is all but over. Why chance having a gorgeous creature like your companion get torn to shreds by thirteen giant superAryans?"

"Right," chimed in a third. "My apartment is just in the next block. We could stop there right now. You could sit in a corner and bury your nose in a book, while we and the little lady are having a party."

"What did you call me?" demanded Eleanor.

"The little lady," repeated the guard.

A tear rolled down her cheek. "That's the nicest thing anyone has said to me in thirty years."

"So how about the party?" persisted the guard. "Are we all agreed?"

Eleanor uttered her semi-magical three words, and suddenly the truck picked up speed and headed straight for Gestapo headquarters.

HIMMLER ENTERED THE HUGE subterranean chamber, clapped his hands together, and called for his super-Aryans' attention.

"They're on their way," he announced. "They'll be here any minute. I want you looking your best and most formidable. Line up."

"How?" asked Adolf.

"In a straight line, of course."

"I mean, by what criterion?"

"Numerically."

Heinrichs 1 through 12 lined up in numerical order.

"Where do *I* go?" asked Adolf.

"Just stand at one end or the other," said Himmler wearily.

"Which end?"

"*I don't care!*" yelled Himmler.

Heinrich Number 8 raised his hand. "Excuse me a minute," he said, walking toward the bathroom with increasing haste. "I'll be right back."

"Take *his* place," said Himmler.

"But my name doesn't begin with an H."

"Just do it!" screamed Himmler.

Adolf shrugged, walked over, and stood between Heinrichs 7 and 9. "But I am in this spot under false pretenses," he complained.

"I could have been a farmer," muttered Himmler. "I was really good at milking cows and harvesting corn. I was happy sitting atop a tractor. The sheep and pigs never talked back to me. Mostly, I didn't have to deal with a bunch of empty-headed super-beings."

Heinrich Number 8 returned from the bathroom and approached his fellow Aryans.

"He's in my place," he whined, pointing to Adolf.

"Move to the end of the line," Himmler told Adolf.

"Which end?"

Himmler pulled his revolver out of his holster and fired six quick shots at Adolf's chest. They all bounced off.

"I'm invulnerable," Adolf pointed out. "Shooting can't hurt me."

"But it makes *me* feel better," replied Himmler, holstering his gun. "Now go to the end of the line. And before you ask, the left end."

"My left or your left?"

Himmler hurled his revolver at Adolf's head. It bounced off and fell to the floor.

"I'll get it for you," offered Heinrich Number 3.

"Don't bother," said Himmler disgustedly, walking over to pick it up. "You'll forget where you were standing."

"On my feet," said Heinrich Number 3.

"Why did I ever think Aryans were the Master Race?" muttered Himmler.

Suddenly a red light began flashing.

"They're here!" said Himmler excitedly. "They should be entering this chamber in less than three minutes. *Achtung!*"

The thirteen super-Aryans stood at attention.

"The forthcoming slaughter is what you were created for," said Himmler, walking up and down in front of them. "I want you to show Big El absolutely no mercy."

"Even if she begs?" asked Heinrich Number 11.

"She won't," Himmler assured them. "She's made of sterner stuff. It's your job to dismantle her and spread that sterner stuff all over the room."

Heinrich Number 10, the one with the queasy stomach, put his hand to his mouth, then raced off to the bathroom.

"He's just sensitive," said Adolf apologetically.

"What about Little Al?" asked Heinrich Number 2.

"You leave Little Al to me," said Himmler. "You guys just concentrate on Big El."

"Not to worry, sir," said Heinrich Number 4. "I'll cut her heart out and eat it. I'll decapitate her, gouge out her eyes, and use her head as a bowling ball. I'll "

Heinrich Number Ten, who was just emerging from the bathroom, listened, groaned, and ran right back in, while Himmler found himself wondering how Geronimo or Shaka Zulu would have handled these problems.

"YOU'RE NOT NERVOUS, are you?" asked Einstein as the guards escorted them down the dark winding stairs to the Aryans' chamber.

"Not in the least," answered the closest guard. "It's not as if *I* have to fight you."

"I was talking to Big El," said Einstein.

"Is my make-up smudged?" asked Eleanor.

"No."

"And my hair's not messed up?"

"Not a bit."

"Then I'm not nervous," she answered. "How about you, Little Al? After all, you're going to be facing the notorious Heinrich Himmler while all I'm doing is fending off thirteen foul-tempered and invulnerable giants."

"I feel sharp," said Einstein. "And I'm getting close to the Ultimate Spell. Once I've got it, he'll never know what hit him."

"The Ultimate Spell?" asked Eleanor.

"Watch this," said Einstein. He raised his arms, closed his eyes, and chanted *"E equals NC squared."*

Suddenly all the guards' pants vanished.

"Damn!" muttered Einstein. "I'm so close! I can feel it!"

"Can we have our pants back?" said one of the guards. "Herr Himmler is a stickler for decorum."

Einstein shrugged. "I don't know where they are."

"We ought to get *something* out of this," said another guard. "Say it again and make *her* clothes vanish."

"Just be grateful I didn't make *you* vanish," said Einstein.

"You can do that?" said a third guard. "You'd be a handy guy to have around in case we get transferred to the Russian front."

They came to a massive steel door. The lead guard opened it, and a moment later they were facing Himmler and his thirteen super-Aryans.

"Finally!" said Himmler. "You have no idea how long I

have waited for this moment!" He looked at the guards. "You're not wearing any pants."

"Neither are your supermen," said a guard defensively.

"This is wartime. There are the usual shortages. We don't have enough material to make pants for them. But you already *had* pants."

"Look," said Einstein. "If you guys want to argue, we can go out for coffee."

"This is Berlin!" snapped Himmler. "You would go out for beer! However," he added with an evil grin, "you are not going anywhere. Here you have come, and here you shall die."

"That's wrong," said Heinrich Number 5. "It should be: 'Here you have come, and here you shall stay.' There's a certain poetic unity to it that way."

"I don't know," said Heinrich Number 7. "I think the problem was that he said '*shall* die' instead of '*will* die'. Somehow 'will die' sounds more definite, if you know what I mean."

Soon nine of the Heinrichs were arguing the finer points of language, and Himmler turned to Eleanor and Einstein. "What will you pay me for thirteen giants with a collective IQ of 73?"

Finally he turned back to the super-Aryans. *"Shut up!"* he screamed.

They fell silent instantly.

"All right," he said. "Are we ready to begin?"

Heinrich Number 9 held up his hand.

"What now?" demanded Himmler.

"How do you want us to fight her? All at once, or one at a time?"

"I hadn't really considered it," admitted Himmler.

"I have a suggestion," said Einstein.

"Yes?"

"All they're good for is fighting, right? So have a competition: let them fight each other for the right to face Big El."

Himmler frowned. "I have a feeling there's something

exceptionally silly about that idea, but I can't quite put my finger on it."

Suddenly Adolf stepped forward. "*I* will fight her," he announced.

"Why you?" demanded Heinrich Number 1.

"Because I am unique. I am named for the *Führer*, whereas you twelve are named for this insignificant little wimp here, meaning no offense, Herr Himmler."

"Okay," agreed Heinrich Number 1. "When you're right, you're right."

"But you can lend a hand if things get hairy," added Adolf.

"Are you calling me hairy?" demanded Eleanor furiously. "Let's start right now!"

"Wait!" cried Einstein.

Everyone turned to him.

"What is it?" asked Eleanor.

"We can't have them all piling on you if things start going well for our side," said Einstein.

"And I don't want you to be able to come after me if you actually survive and your blood's up," added Himmler. He turned to Einstein. "How shall we separate the two combatants from the rest of the room?"

"The same way they separate the lions and tigers from the audience at a circus, I suppose," replied Einstein.

"I agree," said Himmler. "You two"—he signaled to Adolf and Eleanor—"stand over there."

When they had moved where he wanted them, he turned back to Einstein. "Spell Number 1209?" he suggested.

Einstein considered it. "Make it 1209-A. We won't need all the stools for the lions to perch on."

They chanted the spell together, and within seconds Eleanor and Adolf found themselves in the middle of a steel cage some thirty feet in diameter.

"Shall the match begin?" suggested Himmler.

"A steel cage match," mused Einstein. "I intuit an incredibly profitable commercial enterprise here once the war's over."

"May I proceed to tear her into small pieces now?" asked Adolf.

"Just you try it," snarled Eleanor. "This is Big El you're facing!" She drew her sword and faced him.

"Say your prayers, female!" bellowed Adolf, reaching out to grab her. She slapped his huge hand with the flat of her enchanted blade.

"Ow!" he yelled. "That hurt!"

"Not as much as it's going to hurt when I cut your foul heart out," she said, advancing toward him menacingly.

"Wait a minute!" yelled Adolf, backing away. "Fins! Fingers! Time out!"

"What is it?" demanded Eleanor.

Adolf turned to face Himmler. "You told us we were invulnerable!" he said accusingly. "I've never felt pain before, but from everything I've heard and read about it, *that* was pain!"

"Don't be such a crybaby!" snapped Himmler. "You are fighting for the honor of the Aryan race!"

"Make her get rid of the sword!" whined Adolf. "Then I'll fight her."

Himmler walked over to where Eleanor stood and pressed his face against the steel cage. "I don't suppose you'd consider relinquishing your weapon in the name of sportsmanship?" he said. "I mean, *he* doesn't have one." He grimaced. "The idiots came armed with scimitars, but they've forgotten where they put them. Anyway, putting aside your own weapon would make it a fair fight."

"A fair fight?" she repeated. "He's ten feet tall and all muscle!"

"All right," said Himmler with a shrug. "We'll just have to let it be known that the only way the Americans are willing to fight is when they have an unfair advantage."

Eleanor stared at her sword, then carefully leaned it up against the bars.

"Prepare to die, female!" cried Adolf, launching himself at her.

A moment later he was flying across the ring, where he crashed into the bars and fell heavily to the floor.

"What the hell happened?" demanded Himmler.

Adolf frowned. "I bounced off her."

A triumphant smile appeared on Eleanor's face. "I forgot to tell you," she said. "I'm armored in my righteousness."

"Be subtle," urged Himmler. "Use vectors and angles and misdirection."

Adolf checked the pockets of his kilt. "I don't have any of those things."

"Then just use your superior Aryan strength and ruthlessness!" growled Himmler.

"At the same time?" asked Adolf.

"Just do it!" screamed Himmler.

Adolf began approaching Eleanor very carefully. This time, instead of blindly charging her, he reached a hand out to grab her.

"Ow!" he yelled, rubbing his jaw where she slapped him. "What did you do *that* for?"

"Don't touch me there!" said Eleanor.

He approached her again, reached out again, and got slapped for his trouble again.

"Don't touch me *there*, either!" said Eleanor severely.

Adolf made a "T" for "time out" with his hands, and walked to a neutral corner. "I've got to think this out," he said.

"There's nothing to think about!" yelled Himmler. "You're huge, she's not. You're muscle-bound, she's not. You're a man, she's not. You're an Aryan, she's not."

"Right," said Adolf. "And I'm smart, and she's not."

"Well, you're an Aryan, anyway," said Himmler.

"I need a strategy," said Adolf. "She won't let me touch her in any of the usual places."

"What do you mean—'the usual places'?" said Himmler. "This is a battle to the death, not a Saturday night date!"

"What do you suggest?" asked Adolf.

"Snap her spine like a toothpick!" screamed Himmler. "Crush her skull like a walnut!"

"Oh my God!" moaned Heinrich Number 10, clutching his stomach. "I'm gonna be sick again!"

"All right," said Adolf, working himself into a killing rage and facing Eleanor. "Now you're gonna get it!"

When he was almost within arm's reach of her, she looked down at his kilt and giggled.

"What's so funny?" he growled.

"Your fly is unzipped."

He looked down and she landed a powerful karate kick to his chin.

"I don't *have* a fly!" he groaned as he careened across the ring.

"You know," said Eleanor to Einstein, "I think there's a distinct possibility that I didn't need the sword *or* the outfit."

"That wasn't fair!" said Adolf petulantly, as he got back on his feet.

"All's fair in love and war," said Eleanor.

"Love?" he repeated, puzzled. "What's love got to do with it?"

"This is all a joke, isn't it, *Herr* Himmler?" said Eleanor. "You've got the *real* super-Aryans hidden somewhere else in the building."

"*Kill her, godammit!*" screeched Himmler.

Suddenly Adolf's gaze fell on the magical sword that rested against the side of the cage. He stared at it for a few seconds, then took a tentative step in its direction.

"Don't touch it!" said Eleanor in severe tones.

"Why not?" he asked.

"It's not yours," she said.

"Oh," replied Adolf, momentarily chastened. Then: "So what?"

"That would be cheating," said Eleanor.

"Pick the damned thing up and cut her head off!" yelled Himmler.

"It's not mine," explained Adolf. "That would be cheating."

"I absolve you. Now kill her!"

"I warn you," said Eleanor. "Don't touch it."

"You can't scare me," said Adolf. "I've been absolved."

"Do you even know what that means?" she asked.

"Sort of," he said. "It's kind of like being forgiven for staying up all night reading your father's dirty magazines."

"So you're really going to pick it up?"

"Yes."

"Even though it's immoral to steal someone else's sword?" she persisted.

He turned to Himmler. "What about that?" he asked.

"It's your moral imperative to kill her!" ordered Himmler.

"Well," said Eleanor, "you were warned."

Adolf reached out and grabbed the sword. Instantly the room was filled with a crackling, buzzing sound—an effect that really bad 1950s science fiction movies would combine with static electricity a decade later, only this was both real and deadly—and he briefly glowed a brilliant yellow, then mauve, and then he vanished.

Eleanor walked over, picked up her magic sword, and faced the twelve Heinrichs.

"Who's next?" she asked sweetly.

"You!" said Himmler, pointing to Heinrich Number 1. "Remember that you're fighting for the supremacy of Germany and the Aryan race. Now get in there and kill her."

"Couldn't we just cut cards instead?" asked Number 1.

"We don't have any cards," said Himmler.

"Hopscotch!" said Number 1. "We could play hopscotch!"

"Bah!" spat Himmler. "You're useless." He looked at the others. "You!" He pointed to Heinrich Number 6. "Kill her."

"Come on!" said Eleanor, twirling her magic sword as if it were a baton. "I'm ready for you!"

"There's nothing I'd like more than to kill her, Herr Himmler," said Number 6. "But my lumbago's been acting up, and—"

"You're physically perfect!" screamed Himmler. "You can't have lumbago!"

"Sure I can," he said, rubbing his shoulder. "It's really bothering me!"

"That's your shoulder, idiot! Lumbago affects your lower back."

"I was just scratching an itch," said Number 6 defensively. He moved his hand to his lower back. "That lumbago's really bothering me." He turned to Eleanor. "I'm sorry, Big El. There's nothing I'd like more than to kill you, but you can see that it wouldn't be a fair fight."

"I'll even the odds," she said.

"How?"

"I'll fight with one eye closed."

Number 6 suddenly groaned and clutched at his chest. "I think I'm coming down with pellagra, too!"

"You get pellagra from an inadequate diet," yelled Himmler. "And super-Aryans don't eat!"

"You can't make me fight her on an empty stomach!" protested Number 6.

Himmler turned to Einstein. "This just isn't working out," he said apologetically. "All right. I want all twelve Heinrichs in the cage with her!"

"Little Al?" said Eleanor. "I could use some help."

Einstein faced the twelve super-Aryans, closed his eyes, reached his arms out, and chanted, *"E equals MC squared."*

And suddenly all twelve Aryans were gone, replaced by twelve little mushroom clouds.

"Son of a bitch!" exclaimed Einstein. "I finally got it right!"

"You haven't heard the last of me!" promised Himmler. He closed his eyes, reached his arms out, and chanted: *"I was only following orders!"* There was a puff of smoke, and suddenly Eleanor and Einstein were alone in the vast chamber.

"Well, it looks like we scored another victory for Truth, Justice, and the American Way, Big El," said Einstein.

"Your spell actually worked, Little Al," she said. "I'm so proud of you!" Suddenly she frowned. "How are we going to get home?"

"Not to worry," said Einstein. "I've got it covered."

And moments later they were in the White House, having traveled there exactly the way the brighter readers of this story anticipated. As they parted outside the Oval Office, she returned the enchanted sword to him.

"Can I keep the outfit?" she asked. "Just for special occasions?"

"Sure, Big El," said Einstein. "You've earned it."

Then she went off to her room, and Einstein entered the office.

"We're back, Mr. President!" he announced triumphantly.

Roosevelt reluctantly looked up from the crystal ball he'd been studying intently.

"Oh," he said. "Were you gone?"

©Mike Jacobsen
seemikedraw.com.au